The Art of Survival
a crime mystery set in Scarborough
by Kate Evans

AVENUEPRESS
SCARBOROUGH

First published in Great Britain in 2015 by Avenue Press
Scarborough
Copyright © 2015 Kate Evans

The right of Kate Evans to be identified as the author of this work has been asserted by her in accordance with the Copyright, Designs and Patents Act 1988.

This is a work of fiction. Names, characters, organizations, places, events, and incidents are either products of the author's imagination or are used fictitiously.

All rights reserved. No part of this book may be reproduced, stored in a retrieval system, or transmitted in any form or by any means, electronic, electrostatic, magnetic tape, mechanical, photocopying, recording or otherwise, without the written permission of the publishers.

Photo copyright © 2014 Mark Vesey.

Printing & cover design by McRay Press
Unit 3, 66 Londesborough Road, Scarborough, YO12 5AF

AvenuePress
Scarborough
AvenuePressScarb@talktalk.net www.writingourselveswell.co.uk

What Saves Us

You can't summon an angel
but sometimes,
when you least expect it,
an angel appears.

You can't call upon the celestial,
but sometimes,
when you least expect it,
the moon comes into view
above the rooves,
full and melting.

You can't order-in hope,
but sometimes,
when you least expect it,
hope is there.

You can't compel love,
but sometimes,
when you least expect it
it arrives,
in a text,
in an email,
in a word
that saves you.

"What Saves Us" by Kate Evans, 2013
The first line of this poem is taken from
Michele Robert's poem "On Midwinter Night"

Chapter 1

The sea sucks in through its incisors – hesitates – then spits out the bitter brine. Hannah Poole hunkers deeper into her padded anorak, pulls her woollen hat further down over her ears and then digs her gloved hands into her pockets. The wind smells of snow. Hannah drinks it in like it's a numbing alcohol, clearing her airways of the odours she's carried from home: shit; bleach; unwashed bodies. Both of her parents appear to have given up on washing over the last several weeks. Her father drags himself from bed to commode, refusing to surrender pyjamas or dressing gown. While her mother layers on perfume and increasingly brassy make-up. Her numerous friends have turned out to be mere acquaintances and have stopped calling.

The graphite waves stealthily begin to retake the pathway that encircles the old South Bay lido (filled in years ago) where Hannah stands braced against the metal railings. The concrete turns to froth, which flicks tongues of ice up the pool's crumbling wall and over the tips of Hannah's wellies. She imagines herself easing into those dark mountains and being enveloped by a watery blanket, her oxygen cut off, a Viking princess gently launched into her grave. *Drowning happens quickly,* she tells herself. *Over before you know it. Just let go. Fall. It would be easier not to exist.* Still the railings hold her back and she knows she does not have the strength to resist them. She turns abruptly and starts to walk. *I will find another way.*

As she comes down from the grassed and tarmacked lido to the path which leads along the bottom of the cliffs to the Gothic-style Victorian Spa buildings, she notices an over-sized sprite standing on a concrete promontory the other side of the sea wall. She pauses, watching the hunched form advance towards the titanic waves, its podgy bare arms forming an inadequate umbrella over its head. *Another person contemplating oblivion. Good luck to them. They have grasped the truth: life isn't worth the effort.*

Hannah moves on. Then she stops. Something is nagging at her brain, something along the lines of, *I'm a (not-quite-qualified) counsellor, I don't walk past someone in distress and do nothing.* The conversation in her head continues: '*So? People make choices and that person has made their choice. Who am I to interfere?*' '*You're a counsellor, you have some ethical responsibilities.*' '*To interfere with a person's freely taken choice?*' '*How do you know it's a freely taken choice? Go back, at least find out what's going on.*' Slowly she turns and walks towards the rotund apparition in black who is now performing some kind of dance, two steps forwards, the waves crash over and she stumbles back. *Jump, you coward.* The words clatter into Hannah's brain. *Do it for me. Because I can't.*

By the time she reaches the would-be suicide a couple have arrived there first. The woman, with her carefully coifed blonde bob and smart camel-coloured coat and matching knee-length boots, is seated on the wall. Her arm is stretched out towards the person, who Hannah can now identify as a young woman, possibly in her twenties, possibly younger, not lost her puppy fat under all her black. Blonde-bob is coaxing her in, calmly but assertively. She never takes her eyes off the shivering urchin who is still tangoing with the waves. The male companion of blonde-bob is speaking into his flash phone. *They are doing what I should have done, should be doing.*

She feels awkward. She notes that she used to have as good dress sense as blonde-bob. *Didn't I?* Her hair was once that well kempt. *Wasn't it?* All before she left London, some twelve months ago, to come to her parents' chosen place of retirement, this last-stop-on-the-line town by the sea. She thinks of her years lodging on the top floor of her friend Lawrence's Highgate house, working as copyeditor and proofreader to him and others at his publishers. She remembers it as being cosy, untroubled. *Wasn't it? Why did I leave? To finish my training as a counsellor,* she reminds herself. *To complete something for once in my life.* Then she tells herself off for wasting precious minutes. She should be in there, helping blonde-bob, using her skills, taking charge. She sees the intimacy being built up between the woman on the wall and the youngster now being tempted from her fascination with the water. Hannah hangs back. She realises she should not intrude at this critical moment. She berates herself for not having gone forward in the first instance.

'That's it, that's it, come on over, now, that's better. You sit beside me. I like the sea too, but it's cold this time of year, isn't it?' Wet and shiny as a freshly caught seal, the young woman crouches on the sheltered side of the wall. Blonde-bob is still talking as if they had bumped into each other on a sunny summer afternoon, 'My name's Pam. What's yours?' No response. 'I'm up here for the weekend, from London. Where are you from?' No response. 'It's cold today for a swim, isn't it? How about we go for a coffee, warm up?' No response. Up close, Hannah sees the scars that ring the fleshy arms and even the neck. She balls her hands up in her pockets. *Jealous? Could I possibly be jealous? This woman's scars are on show.*

The youngster's name finally escapes from between her clattering teeth.

'Loretta Lynn? Like the country singer? That's a pretty name,' responds Pam. 'You put your jumper and coat on and we'll go for a coffee.' As she dresses in her abandoned outer clothing, which is almost as soaked as she is, Loretta Lynn does not notice what both Hannah and Pam do: Pam's male companion has finished his phone conversation and is jerking his head towards the town. Following his gaze, Hannah sees a police car turn off the main foreshore road and carefully pick its way along the narrow thoroughfare past the Spa towards them.

They make a strange cameo. Loretta Lynn, her drenched jumper and coat hanging about her, ragged mourning weeds, stumbling between Pam, who is keeping up her cheerful chatter, and her bloke, dressed for a day at the races. And Hannah bringing up the rear, a disgraced terrier all too aware of its failings. They are met in front of the rows of closed-up beach huts by the police vehicle. Hannah hesitates, *Maybe I could be of use even now?*

A large PC gets out and goes towards Pam and her charges. Hannah recognises the officer from another episode earlier in the year, which she would rather forget. Though finding a dead body, especially if it belongs to an eminent psychotherapist you've only encountered in books before, is not so easily filed away. She searches for the PC's name; *I did know it once.* And beside him is Theo, *Detective Sergeant Theo Akande*, she corrects herself. She has come to know him as Theo since he and Lawrence became an item. Theo's spare frame is resolutely wrapped in his duffle coat and red scarf, his mahogany skin all the more startling in this wintry world of greys and whites. It is he who speaks to Loretta Lynn, while the PC splits off the other two to get their story. Theo bends forward to catch the young woman's words, which she lets fall to the concrete. It's moments before he is able to persuade her to the car, where there is a woman PC who guides her into the back.

Hannah turns towards the winding route which ascends between the beach huts, through the cliff gardens and onto the Esplanade. *I've done nothing, nothing.* She doesn't want Theo to express his disappointment to her. But she is too late, his call reaches her and she halts. He bounds up the rickety steps and gives her a quick hug, she can smell his warmth, could sink into it, if she could let herself. He draws back, his hands on her shoulders. His brown eyes gaze quizzically from behind their glasses. Red frames today, to go with the red scarf, which Hannah identifies as cashmere, and, therefore, almost definitely a gift from Lawrence. He asks her if she's OK, but she knows what he really wants to find out is her connection to the incident he is currently dealing with. She tells him what she witnessed, making her role sound supportive, essential, almost. 'Why'd they send a detective out on something as routine as this?'

He mutters quickly about a missing girl and Hannah remembers the news reports. *A different girl. A little girl. A girl with bunches of brown hair and a blue bike with stabilisers. A girl without scars on her arms and neck. An altogether more lovable girl.* He says, 'Do you know her?'

He means through her work at the Scarborough Centre for Therapy Excellence, nicknamed SC4Tea. She shakes her head. 'Today's the first time I've seen her. By the looks of her, though, I'd say you'll find records about her in some mental health service or other.'

He nods, he glances towards the waiting police car, still he does not go. Finally he says, 'You're sure you're OK? You look ... I mean with your dad and everything ... are you OK?'

'I'm fine, yes, absolutely.' She presses her lips together to stop anything further tumbling out.

'If you're sure?' His hands have fallen to his sides, his feet have turned imperceptibly away from her.

She nods. And he hurries back down to where his job awaits him. She continues on her way, beginning to clump up the rest of the steps and onto the path, the words, *My father will be dead very soon*, falling in with the rhythm of her feet.

Chapter 2

It had been the previous afternoon when the call had come in. Theo had been the most senior officer in the section. An eight-year-old girl is missing.

Two PCs have already been over to check the veracity of the situation and it is they who are summoning CID. In the eight months since his sideways move from Manchester to Scarborough, Theo has discovered how little support he can expect from his direct superior, DI John Hoyle. Partly due to his return-to-work programme after his by-pass operation and partly due to his own inclination not to get too bogged down in any case this close to his almost certain – and eagerly awaited – early retirement, Hoyle is always on his way home by 3.30 p.m. Nevertheless, following procedure, Theo now gives him a ring. There is hesitation at the end of the line. *This is a missing child, after all.* Then Hoyle says, as if reassuring himself, 'She won't be far away. She'll turn up when she's hungry. I know I can leave this in your capable hands DS Akande.' As usual he's taking extra care with his pronunciation, *he doesn't fancy getting bogged down in a racism row either.* It gives the impression he has something unpalatable in his mouth. He signs off, 'I want a full report once you've assessed the situation.'

DC Harriet (Harry) Shilling drives Theo the ten minutes from the police station in the centre of town to Beech Tree Drive. It is one of several drives, avenues, crescents and closes built in the 1930s between the Beck and the golf course on the north edge of Scarborough, at right angles to the sea. The wide pavements are protected from the roadway by mature trees: beech, birch, rowan and one very large horse chestnut on a corner announcing a close named after it. The white or cream rendered semis are protected from the pavements by privet hedges and leylandii. A few discreet coloured bulbs adorn downstairs windows and pruned bushes. 'No one's going to have seen anything,' Harry says, as if reading his thoughts. She smoothly pulls up behind the marked car already at the kerb and turns off the engine. A strand of her pale hair, escaped from her ponytail, has fallen across her feverishly blushered cheek.

Outside, the few street lamps glimmer dully orange across the tarmac. Looking up beyond them, Theo can see the scatter of white pinheads in the dark fabric of the sky. Every now and again grey clouds skid by blotting them out before hurrying on. It's barely 5 p.m., yet night has tumbled in quickly across the waves as it does in winter on the north-east coast, booting the wan sun along the horizon until it takes refuge in the west. There's a wind blowing down from the Arctic. Theo is glad of his duffle coat and cashmere scarf, and notices Harry is finding her brown suede jacket inadequate. He can see the movement of the leafless branches, sometimes inky shadows, then tipping into the unearthly glow of the sodium bulbs. 'Winter draws on, Mrs Akande,' one of his Cardiff uncles would unfailingly say to his elder sister, Theo's mother, at some point during this month before Christmas. And Theo would join with his parents, his sisters and the other adults who were around in the laughter and the shaking of heads. Though he didn't understand the pun for many years, he would feel cradled by that laughter, carried along and protected by the many elders who were a part of his childhood.

By comparison, the Everidge's house appears empty. It isn't just the bodies which are missing, but the emotional energy. It's PC Trevor Trench who lets them in. They follow his bulk, thankfully divested of his even bulkier jacket, through the small hall into the sitting room-diner which occupies one side of the ground floor, a small bay at the front and a large picture window looking into the garden at the back. The pelmets have been decorated with dark green and red swags of fake spruce needles, hung with small, silver-painted charms: stars, reindeer, sledges and elves. These swags also trim the tops of the glass-fronted cabinet and of the doors, and the bases of the polished candleholders. Theo can see the two square rooms of the original 1930s house have been knocked through to make this one. There's a sofa, two armchairs and TV at the front. A well-used family-sized table with four upright chairs, plus a display case with little china animals and numerous framed photos, are in the back. The artificial tree sits in the bay, adorned with glass baubles, wooden figures and white lights. The display makes Theo think of one in a shop window. *This house hasn't witnessed any outpourings of emotion, good cheer or otherwise. Not during the five years it's been home to the Everidges.* Then he cautions himself, aware of how fear and grief can flatten even the most lively of atmospheres.

Yvonne Everidge is sitting on the sofa with another woman who turns out to be a neighbour called Janine Coates. Ian Everidge, a man in his forties with rather obviously dyed black hair combed over his scalp and wearing what looks like a work suit and a pale blue open-necked shirt, is sitting in one of the armchairs. The two PCs have been occupying a couple of the upright chairs. Everyone has been served tea, though only the officers have managed to drink theirs, along with at least a couple of biscuits if the evidence of the crumbs on the table is anything to go by.

The tea maker is a boy in his late teens, wide and compact like his father and with the mass of dark curls Mr Everidge might once have had. The boy says his name is Paul and offers refreshments, both Theo and Harry accept a coffee each. If the familial similarities to Mr Everidge are obvious, there is little which ties Paul to Mrs Everidge, who is thin, on the tall side, with a bony flat chest, her skin a bleached calico. Her brown hair is simply cut to just above the shoulders, discreetly highlighted. She is also maybe in her late twenties, young to have a teenage son. First impressions are borne out by Janine who says to Mr Everidge, 'He's a treasure your lad.' Before mouthing more to Harry than to Theo, 'Her stepson,' while jerking her head towards the woman beside her.

The introductions, the departure of the two PCs to call in reinforcements and start the house to house, plus the arrival of the coffee, all bring some movement to the room. However, once everyone is seated again, Theo in the other armchair, Harry and Paul on dining chairs, the atmosphere resumes gathering dust. Theo asks to be told what's happened and Janine launches into a story. Theo gently interrupts, 'It was Mrs Everidge who realised her daughter was missing?' Janine nods. 'Then I'd like to hear from her please. Mrs Everidge would you mind telling me what occurred?'

    Mrs Everidge requires some cajoling from her husband and Janine, then she says in a rather high petulant voice, 'It's Ray what's done it.' Theo recognises the heavy vowel sounds of the local Scarborough accent.

    Mr Everidge sighs and says softly, 'Now Yvonne, this isn't helping, love.'

    She snaps her head round and says sharply, 'It's him, I know it is.'

    Theo lifts his hand slightly to suggest to Mr Everidge he says no more and the other man slumps back into his seat. Theo again asks Mrs Everidge to tell him what took place, this time with more firmness in his voice. Her gaze turns to him. There's a stubbornness around her mouth and, for a fleeting moment, Theo thinks she is going to insist on speaking to an officer who is white. The instant passes and he thinks maybe he was mistaken. She begins to talk to her hands, gripped together in her lap, her voice monotone, her accent less obvious. He recognises the impulse having consciously toned down his (albeit posh Moseley) West Midlands intonation.

    Victoria, eight years old last August, had spent the weekend with her father, the accused Ray, and had returned subdued and unhappy. This morning, Wednesday, she had felt unwell and Yvonne had taken the day off her work as a part-time dental receptionist. 'They're good like that, understanding. When my baby's sickening, all she wants is her mother.' Yvonne pauses, sniffs dryly. As it turned out, Victoria wasn't sickening for long, by two she wanted to go out on her bike. 'She loves that bike, Ian and

I gave it her for her birthday,' she looks briefly at her husband who gives an encouraging smile. Yvonne allowed her daughter to go to the end of the street and back as long as she stuck to the pavement.

'When she weren't back by two-thirty I went looking for her. All I found were her bike, at the corner.' Again the dramatic pause where tears might have been though they weren't. 'I thought she must have gone off somewhere, to look at the sea, though she'd have had to cross some roads for that and she knows not to. I walked round and round, up and down, calling Victoria, Victoria, I never call her Vicky, she doesn't like it. Then it was getting dark and I thought maybe she'd gone back home, found me out, she knows where we keep a key, but still, so I dashed home. But she wasn't, there, I mean.' Yvonne falls into silence, head bent over so her face is hidden, her hair forwards, a protective curtain.

Don't look away. Theo wants to see her features, her eyes, wants to seek out any dissonance between them and her words. She doesn't move. Instead Janine, who has been bursting to speak, does so, 'She came straight to see me and I said, "Honey, Vicky—".' She corrects herself quickly, '"Victoria's a good lass, she won't be long coming home." But then I thought about everything you hear on the news and I said maybe she'd better call Ian and the police, just to be sure. She did phone Ian and he came straight away, bless him, and, of course, Paul was in from school by then. But I had to call the police, poor Yvonne, she couldn't manage it, so I had to do it.' She finishes with a grin, then realises how inappropriate this is and hides it.

Theo asks softly, 'Mrs Everidge, did Victoria have any reason to leave home, had she talked about it?'

'She's eight.' The words come with an angry energy and a forceful darted look which surprises Theo. He recovers to ask about friends and Ian says they've called round to everyone Victoria knows at school.

'And her father?'

There's a pause before Yvonne responds abruptly, 'I rang him, said he'd better bring her back or there'd be trouble. He says he hasn't seen her since Sunday. But you can't believe anything he says, inspector.' She looks up, her eyes are blue flint.

'Sergeant, and we'll, of course, check him out. We'll need his contact details.'

Mr Everidge sits forwards, 'He wanted to come over, to help look, but Yvonne ... well we thought it best he stay away for now.'

'I'm guessing,' Harry says slowly from her perch, 'Victoria didn't have a mobile?'

Mr and Mrs Everidge shake their heads. Then Paul says tentatively, 'I set her up a Facebook page.'

'What?' his dad splutters and Yvonne and Janine look at him in horror.

'She saw mine and wanted to have a go.' Paul looks glum. 'I didn't see any harm, I made sure all the privacy settings were on and she could only go on when I was there, she doesn't know the password to my computer.'

Ian and Yvonne begin to protest, Harry cuts through them saying they will have to look at both Paul's computer and any others there are in the house.

Theo would prefer to continue to talk, to learn more. *None of them seem to be clarting about.* He lets his gaze travel over them one more time. Paul, Ian and Janine are looking at him expectantly. It is Yvonne who is resolutely staring downwards. *But the answer to what has happened will come from these people here, the family. It always does.* However, there are some practical things which need to be got under way. A search of the house and garden for one, PC Trench had done a preliminary one, just to check this wasn't some kind of elaborate hide and seek the little girl was playing. A more detailed one is needed, despite the obstinate set of Yvonne's jaw which looks like it might turn into a refusal. She has stood up and Ian comes to put his arm around her rigid shoulders, 'Come on love, of course they have to do it,

Victoria might have got herself stuck in somewhere, not be able to get out.'

'What? In this house?' She turns to Theo, 'It's out there you need to be looking, out there, in Ray's car and his flat, that's where you'll find her.' Her voice rises to a shout and she thrusts her pointed finger towards the window.

'And we will, Mrs Everidge,' Theo says reassuringly. 'We will.'

Chapter 3

The room is cold, carpet-less, the floorboards painted a merciless orange. There are other people in the house, she has heard them moving about, a toilet flushed, a shouted, 'I'm off!' Hannah doesn't know who they are. She doesn't know where she is, not exactly. In one of the terraced houses which fan out from behind the station, built for railway workers at the end of the nineteenth century, in streets named after the then Queen or her myriad offspring or connections to minor royals around Europe. This is Princess Alice Road or maybe Prince Leopold Way, once providing homes with all mod cons to the deserving working classes. *Doesn't Theo rent in one of these streets?*

The brick walls are still sturdy, despite the lack of care lavished on the building in recent years, the inadequate storage heaters and the damp. Hannah feels safe lying on the mattress on the floor under mounds of musty blankets. She was in no state to inspect it last night, however, the sheet resting against her cheek smells none too fresh. Still, she feels secure. It won't be long before she will have to brave the frost-laden air and the state of the communal bathroom; but for the moment she can lie blissfully still, weighted down by the aged woven wool which might formerly have been coloured warm maroon.

Beside her Maya is purring gently, her mussed hair a black cobweb in which is cradled her pale elfin face. She could be in her early twenties though she's actually twenty-eight, only five years younger than Hannah. Maya hadn't bothered to take her make-up off before sleeping, so there are smudges of pale pink around her petite mouth and claggy black and glittering blue around her eyes, which remind Hannah of a sleeping bat. The creamy foundation has been rubbed off parts of Maya's cheeks revealing a few faded freckles underneath, as if a mask has been half pushed away. Hannah can almost feel affection for her, could kiss the slightly parted lips through which warm breath escapes to become mist.

Only then Maya would awake. And Maya awake is quite a different proposition.

She'd turned up last night, unannounced as always, without any explanation for her absence, and dressed for a night out. Her red over-sized shirt and black leggings along with glossy, spike-heeled boots and the red lacy panties and bra are now strewn across the livid floor. Hannah had been on the point of going to bed, going out to a club was the last thing she wanted to do, but Maya would not be denied. *Maya can never be denied.* She wheedled and criticised and bullied until she got her way.

Hannah wonders, as she often does the morning after, *Why does Maya keep coming back? She always says I'm such a bore, a liability. Maybe it is merely because she cannot bear to be seen to be out on her own, needs adoring company, male or female. I know I'm the last scrape of the barrel. She has to be desperate to come back to me.* But there is something else, something about power, a cat playing with a field mouse when she's not even hungry. And beneath all that, Hannah senses at times a fear. *Maya has to keep tabs on me for fear I will ... what? What harm could I possibly do Maya?* Ben comes to mind. Ben who Maya claims as her own. Could Maya be jealous of Hannah's one night out with Ben? She'd have no reason to be, it had ended in an embarrassing misunderstanding. *As usual,* Hannah's stomach grumbles unpleasantly. *The oh-so-perfect Benedick Cartwright, psychotherapist extraordinaire, doesn't know his own mind,* she repeats to herself caustically, to make herself feel better.

Her gaze moves up to the discoloured patch on the ceiling and then sweeps the room. There is a battered wardrobe and the few books on a shelf look abandoned rather than stored. Maya hasn't brought her here before, it's very probably not even Maya's room, each time she knows somewhere convenient to 'crash'. She stubbornly refuses to go back to the house where Hannah is currently living. She cannot quite call it home herself; it is the home belonging to her parents who, Maya was quick to remark, stink to hell.

The need to get up and use the facilities is getting urgent, yet Hannah wants just a moment's more peace. She hopes she can get away without disturbing Maya, who will either dismiss her with a wounding remark or insist on being bought breakfast for giving her a good time last night. *And we did have a good time. In a way.* Getting bladdered in a dark room where pounding music made conversation impossible was certainly preferable to a fractured night, waking to listen to her father's endless perambulations, his weak wails of pain, unheard by her mother already knocked out by gin and pills. And the sex was good, it is always good with Maya.

As she moves her head, the incipient ache at her temple asserts itself and her stomach roils. *I'm getting too old for this. Lawrence would say it serves me right, I shouldn't be out carousing and drinking. I won't tell him*, she promises herself, knowing she will, she tells Lawrence everything. *Anyway his telling-offs are his way of caring. Besides he's got softer since Theo. No more Young Turks breaking his heart. I am happy for him. Even if it will change our friendship, it will have to, it ought to. Come on Hannah, get going.* She is sure she has somewhere she ought to be this morning. She searches the folders in her brain. *Of course, the woman from the hospice is coming, I have to be there to make sure Dad gets taken away. Preferably to the hospice, though anywhere will do.* Another phone call from her brother Stephen the previous night had been a further reason to accept Maya's 'invitation' and the numbing effect of the shots she consumed. He'd spent twenty minutes telling her how much he disapproved of her plan. *It's alright for him, him and Veronica never visit. It's alright for him, issuing orders from his swanky office and swanky house in York. He doesn't have to live it every day.* But he's also told Dad he doesn't have to go, and if I'm not there, him and Mum will persuade the hospice woman they're coping fine.

Then there are Hannah's clients. Yes, she remembers, she has two booked in this afternoon. She begins to move slowly and her stomach lurches up towards her mouth. God, even she can smell the alcohol coming off her. *What an idiot I am. What a complete fool. Fool, fool, fool, bitch,* the self-recriminations beat the same tempo as the pain within her head. Finally she manages to extract herself from the bed. Maya whimpers quietly, before turning over. Hannah grabs her underwear, jeans, silky top, coat and bag and makes a dash for the bathroom which she has calculated is just along the landing. Luckily she meets no one and it is empty. It is surprisingly grime-less and she considers a brief shower, only the concern that Maya might wake soon makes her dismiss this thought.

She readies herself quickly. Her hair's coppery tendrils have frizzed themselves into a nest which she can hardly get a comb through. Her hazel irises are embedded in blood-coloured crazy paving. Her face is bleached, reddened pores causing a faint rash across her cheek. She splashes some water on. Then she reaches to draw back the bolt on the door. She hesitates. There's every possibility that Maya could be waiting furtively on the other side. Hannah takes a firm grip on the worn metal stub, yanks it to the left. The bolt makes an unnecessarily loud whack as it shoots back. For a moment her instinct is to lock the room again and stay cowering inside. *Until when?* she asks herself severely. *Come on Hannah, don't make a greater fool of yourself. Get going.* And she does, reaching the sharp morning air of the street unimpeded. Without looking back, she flees.

Chapter 4

In response to his wife's increasingly caustic requests for his assistance in making their son's first Christmas special, Max Harris had begun to festoon the sitting room with decorations before leaving for work. It wasn't what she had asked him to do, exactly, and it meant he departed in more than his usual rush, abandoning tinsel and baubles in a heap on the carpet and leaving the TV turned on. Which is why Aurora Harris catches the local report. She normally avoids the news now as much she can, especially when she has Oliver in her arms; she doesn't want the horribleness of the world to seep into her son, through his delicate caramel skin. Yet she hovers, remote in hand, watching another mother struggle for words. *She doesn't cry easily*, Aurora can tell, this woman on the other side of the screen. Her nose and mouth and forehead are pinched with the effort of not crying, for to weep would be to admit, admit the possibility she doesn't even want to think about. That's how Aurora imagines it to be.

She has met mothers who have lost children when she worked as a family solicitor. *I am still a family solicitor*, she has to remind herself, *I'm on maternity leave*. She's had mothers – those who cried, those who didn't – across her desk from her and she had managed to remain dispassionate, assessing, asking herself whether she really believed what she was being told. Now, she doesn't doubt this other mother. There's a physical contraction inside her chest, a leaping out of her heart's cavity towards this woman who she has never met, as if they are kin. For they are, in motherhood. Aurora knows now how she would feel if her child had gone missing, she knows the fear, the panic, the bewilderment. She has felt it in the early hours of the morning, when she has had to get up to go and check on the cot in the next door room. She knows because of Oliver. Everything changed because of Oliver.

Aurora sits on the settee ignoring her desire to straighten the explosion of tinsel and coloured lights which are the result of Max's early-morning activity. She cradles her child between her knees and arms. She traces the line from his thick dark eyebrows, across his chubby cheek, to his full mouth. He is smiling. She smiles back. He says, 'Dada, Mama.' She repeats it back, then hums a tune which could be some half-remembered nursery rhyme or the backing to an advert. His thick fingers are tugging at her sweatshirt and she lifts it so that he can begin to suckle. Max has started muttering that she must wean Oliver properly. He is worried she is going to use breastfeeding as an excuse not to return to work in a few weeks' time, in the New Year. She tells herself she is allowing herself the pleasure of this intimacy for just a little longer. Though it had not always been this easy, this delightful. In the first few months she hadn't wanted to touch her son. She had been a different Aurora, there had been a different Max, a different Oliver, and the bits hadn't fitted together; they had sharp, incomprehensible edges. She still can't fit them together, nor can she put them next to now, so she brushes them away.

Her eyes return to the mother blinking in a barrage of flashing cameras. *How old is she? Late twenties? Maybe eight years younger than me?* Only her face has the appearance of having suddenly aged. Her hair is awkwardly tugged back, dry and brittle. Her name scrolls onto the screen: 'Everidge.' *I know it.* She recognises it from her other life, the life before Oliver, though she can't recall how.

'I know you're out there, sweetheart. Mummy will see you soon,' the bereft mother finishes, her voice wobbling into falsetto. The camera cuts to the journalist walking down a tree-lined road in front of tall neat hedges. A decent part of Scarborough where this kind of thing, children disappearing, doesn't – shouldn't – happen. There are photos of the eight-year-old, frozen in time: smiling toothily at the camera; patting tentatively at a donkey's neck on the beach; riding away on a blue bike with stabilisers. She had been playing on this when she vanished, along the wide pavement under the skeletal trees. When her mother had gone to call her in, the bike was there, the little girl not.

The pictures move on, onto a line of bodies covered in sheets laid out along a dusty street, US and British soldiers in desert uniforms standing uncomfortably by, their hands gripping sub-machine guns. A chill settles into Aurora's stomach. She snaps the TV off using the remote, leans deeper into the generous cushions behind her and turns her focus onto Oliver. He is still happily feasting and she knows she should stop him. The midwife had been unable to hide her horror at his weight gain at the last check-up and Aurora suspects the tendency to be plump has been passed down through his genes. She knows upstairs there are charcoal and navy suits with matching court shoes that will no longer fit her, and she has to find a solution to this as they can't afford for her to buy new.

She starts to hum. *There will be time enough for you to know deprivation, my love, to know what it is like to not have your mum at your beck and call. It won't harm you to have it for a little longer.* And it won't harm her either. She strokes the thick dark curls on Oliver's crown. His colouring mirrors hers, the inheritance of his Indian grandfather, her father. She cut her long, straight black hair short as a teenager, now it is in a straggly knot tied by a bright scarf on top of her head. She wonders about letting it grow again, having it luxuriantly swing down her back as it used to, or caught into the intricate plaits and whorls she'd learnt from her Indian cousins. She holds the gaze of her baby's bronze eyes and smiles. He lets go of her nipple and holds out his hand for her finger, soft flesh on soft flesh, they both giggle quietly to each other.

The doorbell crashes through their reverie. Aurora considers ignoring it but it continues to chime unrelenting, and Oliver twists his head round away from her, he likes visitors. 'OK,' she tells him, 'we'll go and see who it is, but if it's the Jehovahs again don't expect me to invite them in, however much you grizzle.' Slowly she manoeuvres herself upright, still holding her child. Her arm is beginning to ache, and a sharp pain as she stands warns her of the greater damage in her elbow which the doctor cautioned her about. So, reluctantly, she places Oliver in the carry seat, tucks a blanket around him and takes him into the hallway. She sets him down, not too close to the door – *It's cold outside* – but near enough for him to see the entertainment of someone being on their top step. He would not be denied this without a great deal of bellowing and fuss.

Their uninvited guest is Val Poole from next door. She is dressed in a smart tweedy jacket thrown over a none-too-clean nylon slip, and has a pair of collapsed carpet slippers on her feet. Her hair looks like a dishevelled wig sat atop her red face, further inflamed by greasy blusher and misapplied lipstick. She reeks sourly. Aurora lifts her chin, taking in the fresher air blowing across Val's grey head. The older woman is talking, screeching almost, barely coherently. Something about Hannah, had Aurora seen Hannah? She'd gone off with Rose's daughter last night and hadn't come back.

Hannah has been out with Maya again? Aurora receives the news unimpressed, even Rose had been dubious about the healthiness of that liaison for Hannah, despite vigorously defending her own child's right to be a free spirit.

Val finally comes to a halt, finishing, 'Stan's dying and Hannah has to sort it out.' Stan Poole has been effectively dying of cancer raging through his organs from bowel upwards for several months. Aurora is unclear whether Val means this ongoing struggle, or whether he is actually on the point of being dead. Oliver burbles behind her, she glances round to see him welcoming his visitor in with a gesture of opening and closing hands. *No way is Val stepping over the threshold.* Aurora is aware that she is squaring herself up to her full height and the other woman, shorter in stature, is shrinking away. *Nor am I going to take Oli next door, it's worse than a morgue. And I'm not going to leave him. But I should help out, not for Val's sake, for Hannah's.* Without Hannah and Rose, she wouldn't have got through those confusing months after Oli's birth, what she's designated (when she has to think about it) her 'bad patch'. She's grateful to them both, feels indebted to them both.

She stalls, saying she hasn't seen Hannah and asking whether Val has tried calling her on her mobile. This doesn't seem to have occurred to Mrs Poole, so Aurora offers to do it. 'Stay there,' she says authoritatively. She hurries to retrieve her phone from the kitchen and back out into the hallway, speed dialling. She relaxes a little when she sees Val still rooted to the front step, being enticed into making faces from there for the amusement of Oliver.

Hannah picks up, she is on her way, will be five, maybe ten minutes. Tell her mother not to worry, whatever's happened, she'll deal with it when she gets there. 'Send Mother home and tell her to put the kettle on, you don't want her cluttering up your place,' she finishes before cutting the connection. Relieved, Aurora relays (most of) the message and ushers Mrs Poole homeward before closing the front door. She briefly wonders, *Should I have done more?* Then she hears Oli's chuntering. *No, I need to be here.* She turns to become at once absorbed in her son.

CHAPTER 5

Into the chaos comes order, the structure of the therapy session: the routine of the greeting and the farewell, the sixty minutes held securely within placid walls. OK, some clients are not able to be as organised as Julia Carter. In the last month since they started working together, she's never been late, despite having to come from York, and she's never re-scheduled, despite having a demanding job.

'Your time together is clearly important to her,' said Orwell Winters, Hannah's supervisor. On the other hand, he did question whether she should be seeing clients at all during her father's illness. 'It could go on for ages yet, years,' she protested, knowing it wouldn't. 'And I can keep it separate. I feel good when I'm working, alive, I know I can be there for my clients.' Orwell looked less than totally convinced, 'You shouldn't use your clients as a crutch, Hannah.' Then he sighed and agreed to support her as long as they keep a close eye on everything.

If Julia is a crutch, Hannah reflects, she's a strong one, made of solid hard timber, an oak maybe, or a lofty elm. She is tall and broad with toned muscles; she has a regime of good food, good wine and five visits to a swanky gym every week. Her short hair is highlighted with bronze, giving the impression of a helmet around a lightly tanned, oval face. She is always carefully made-up and manicured, usually in a couture trouser or skirt suit with a silk blouse and a designer shawl coat. She owns some kind of online gaming company based in York, though her work often takes her to London and abroad. Given the high-powered nature of her work, Hannah is constantly surprised that Julia has carved out their hour together every week. She remembers Orwell's suggestion that this shows the significance of the sessions, *of me,* to Julia. She finds it hard to believe.

Julia was disappointed in the initial phone call, when Hannah said she was not cognitive behavioural therapy trained. 'I understand,' Julia said in a tone which conveyed enforced patience, 'cognitive behavioural therapy is good for phobias.' Hannah agreed it could be and suggested Julia look for a CB therapist if that's what she felt would help her. 'You can't then?' asked Julia.

'I don't know,' Hannah replied uncertainly. 'I work relationally, with what emerges between us when we're together. The intention is something useful would come out of it.' Hannah was aware of the long pause from Julia's side emphasising the inadequacy of this response. She expected Julia to say thanks, but no thanks. Instead she asked whether they would talk about her childhood.

'Probably, yes.'

'There'd be no need, it's of no relevance.'

Hannah heard her own conviction in her reply, 'I believe much of what troubles us today comes through from what we've experienced in the past.'

Another pause, before, 'You've no plan, then, of what to do with me?'

'It doesn't work like that, I'm not doing things to you, we're exploring together, going on a journey together.'

'Sounds a bit hippy-dippy to me.' Julia blew out a breath, 'Oh well, you'll have to do, there's none of those CBT people in Scarborough and you were recommended.'

'I was?' Hannah was startled.

Julia mentioned the name of someone Hannah had seen once through her placement at the GP's surgery, adding quickly that, of course, she hadn't said she was looking for a therapist for herself. There was a gap into which Hannah gave the reassurance about confidentiality she realised Julia wanted. After that Julia told her what day and time she had available, Hannah said it also suited her, and the deal was done.

At their first session, Hannah went through some preliminaries: full name; age (forty-eight, Hannah would have guessed her younger); contact details. Next of kin? 'You'd better have my PA's mobile, if you have to have something.' GP's number, any medical conditions, any medications. Any suicidal thoughts? 'Absolutely not! I'm not crazy!' And then she invited Julia to tell her why she had come.

'I have a phobia.' For the first time Julia looked away from Hannah's face, towards the corner of the room by the window. Her voice was quieter, 'At least, I don't know if it's that. I was ill, very ill – I'm never ill, I don't do ill. And I, I don't know, I've been having these terrible nightmares ever since. It all started when I was ill, or maybe it was before that, I don't know.' Her voice petered out and she glanced up at Hannah, suddenly a little girl, a little girl lost.

What had come out at the first session was that she'd had a nasty virus which had kept her in bed for a week and away from her business for two. Since then, Julia had had difficulties sleeping and was troubled by a generalised anxiety. 'I wake up nervous, I get nervous before a meeting, before giving a presentation. I'm never nervous, I don't do nervous.'

Attempts to find out about the nightmares, about the little girl Hannah had glimpsed, were dismissed as irrelevant, what Julia wanted were strategies. Hannah suggested some breathing exercises. Each time she expects Julia to say she isn't coming back, and yet she does. 'She has something to tell you,' said Orwell. 'She'll say it when she's ready, all you have to do is be there and wait.'

Hannah sees her clients at SC4Tea. The building is a Victorian villa built in the 1860s. It was a time when the south side of town was being developed for the newly rich and the aristocracy down on their luck. The ceilings are high, the proportions generous, the windows expansive.

Hannah goes to collect Julia from the waiting area where intricate plaster mouldings still crown the corners and the walls. This is their fifth session. There is already something different. Anger crackles in the air, though there is nothing disturbing the other woman's poised features while they greet each other and make their way to the room. Hannah uses the time to gather herself. *What have I done to upset Julia?* She instinctively takes the blame for the anger. Izzie, her therapist, and Orwell have encouraged her to consciously talk herself out of this position. *If I have upset Julia, I can't think how I might have. She'll have to tell me.* Watching the tensed back walking in front of her, it occurs to her, *But this anger is about something else, something much older.* They enter the therapy room and sit. Hannah smiles. Julia is sculpted, or rather hewn, from the solid centre of a hardwood. Hannah says, 'So, what's going on?' She waits.

Eventually Julia says briskly, 'I dumped him.'

'Ah.'

'It's over. It doesn't matter anymore.'

'No.'

'Shame, he was fun to be around,' her voice is brittle, as disassociated from her words as it can be. 'Good in bed. Well, of course, he's young, got the energy of the young. But, anyway, it's over.'

'Do you want to tell me more?'

'Not particularly.'

Hannah waits and slowly the tale comes. Yellow. Buttercup yellow. The fine silk scarf pooled in its tissue wrapping was buttercup yellow. Julia doesn't do scarves and she doesn't do yellow, especially not buttercup yellow. Normally she would not hesitate to say so. But this was their first weekend with the kids – his kids – and they had bought her the scarf. So she attempted a smile. 'How lovely,' she said brightly and lifted it up, before letting it run through her fingers back into its nest. 'How lovely,' she managed again, before putting it to one side. 'I'll try it on later. Now,' she looked from face to face, ignoring their shared appalled expressions. 'Shall we get ready to go? The table is booked for one.'

Later, after he had taken them back to their mother's, he was loading the dishwasher with the glasses his kids had used for orange juice; she had not thought to get in the preferred coke or squash. She wrapped an arm around his middle and kissed his bent-over back. 'I think it went rather well, don't you?'

'You could have worn the scarf,' he said, standing up straight, banging the washer's drawer in and its door shut. 'They spent their pocket money on it. You could have worn it.'

'You know I don't like yellow and I don't like scarves,' she said, keeping her tone reasonable. 'You could have briefed them better.' She moved her massage to his neck, but he twitched her hands away.

'And you could have made more of an effort ... for me.'

She picked up her wine glass and the bottle and took them back into her sitting room. She knew it was over. Maybe they'd have one more night together or maybe he'd take his coat and go. Either way it was over. She hoped he wouldn't try to 'get her to see'. Unfortunately, he did, and she had to be firm. This was not the deal, never has been. She has no interest in being a mother, to his kids or anybody else's. 'And he left,' she finishes, her voice the smooth surface over something brewing. She smiles unconvincingly, 'I've taken the scarf in for the new girl, a "welcome to the team" gift.' She continues, her brightness also unconvincing, 'One of these days she'll wear it and he'll see it, and then he'll know.'

'Know what?'

She rouses herself a little, her grin full of sharp teeth, 'I don't do scarves, and I don't do buttercup yellow.' Then the energy seeps away from her.

'You look sad.'

'Do I? Well it's not over him.'

'What is it over?'

She shrugs.

After a moment Hannah realises what has stayed with her most is the phrase, 'I've no interest in being a mother.' She repeats it quietly.

Julia looks up. 'It's true.'

'Except – there sounds like there is an "except" at the end of that sentence.'

She's slow to reply, 'There's Meech's kids, I suppose.'

'Who is Meech?'

She breathes in wearily, 'Someone I once knew. She's got five. The three youngest are not with her anymore. I try and help out, sometimes.'

'Tell me about Meech.'

She looks at her watch and shakes her head, 'Not today, another time. You know, Hannah, I came in all wound up about that stupid scarf and I'm not anymore. I didn't believe it before, but sometimes it is good to talk. I'll see you same time next week.'

'We still have five minutes,' Hannah replies firmly. 'Enough time to hear something about Meech.'

'Meech would take a lot longer than five minutes. Did I tell you that feline-bitch-on-heat I took on against my better judgement has brought a discrimination case against me? What a cheek!' Her usual robust energy is back in the room as she expertly fills the final few minutes with complaints about her former employee, before allowing Hannah to bring the session to a close.

CHAPTER 6

The first twenty-four hours in a misper case are crucial. After that, if the missing person is a child, it almost intangibly begins to turn into a murder investigation. Now it's Friday, and Victoria Everidge has been missing fifty-one hours. DC Harry Shilling is wearing a trouser suit fit for a funeral, Theo notices, her blonde hair caught up in a severe bun.

They're continuing to search the area, dredge the Beck. Teams of locals have joined them, Ian and Paul Everidge and the father, Ray Marchant, at the forefront, walking across fields, along the cliffs, into the nearby woods. Eyes stretched for the smallest clue, a caught piece of cloth, an abandoned shoe.

The sea is, as ever, a trickier proposition, but Theo has enlisted the in-shore lifeboat and the fishermen who set pots for crabs and lobsters to scan the waters and the coves. He has consulted the coastguard to get some idea of where the currents and tides might have carried an eight-year-old's body, should Victoria have reached the beach, on her own or with someone else. This last conversation had left Theo uncommonly glum. 'There's bodies we've seen go in that's never been found, sergeant,' the coastguard had concluded levelly. 'You're not from around here?'

'No, Birmingham originally, Manchester more recently.'

'Ah.' He had probably expected somewhere more exotic. He had scanned the horizon where the grey sky met charcoal sea, 'It's a big place, bodies don't last long in the water, what with the waves, the fish, the birds.' He had stopped short as if aware of Theo's disappointment.

Theo had followed the coastguard's gaze. For him the sea had been for holidays, often the tame Gower Peninsular, with his mother's extended family from the well-established Cape Verde community of Cardiff. His father's brothers, immigrants in the 1950s from Lagos, were more likely to stick to cityscapes, taking their nephew to football or cricket matches. The sea, once a benign re-fueller of rock pools, now has the capacity to devour eight-year-olds.

Since Victoria has not turned up as he prophesised, DI Hoyle is more present than usual. He has appeared a couple of times in the office with the DCI and Detective Superintendent in tow, obviously uncomfortable, eager to assert he's in charge and he's got the best detectives on the job. Seeing him cowed and sweaty, Theo can almost feel sorry for him. Though Hoyle still gustily partakes in the force's social life, makes full use of the police membership of the local golf course, he has long ago lost interest in police work. If the rumours Theo has heard are correct, any enthusiasm for it had dissipated a mere few weeks after Hoyle joined as a PC, only he was from a police family, he had no other game plan. His stall at DI shows that even his superiors recognised his lack of application.

'Someone saw something, lad,' Hoyle offers up frequently as if this is the mysterious key to police work only he possesses. However, that someone is proving hard to find, despite more officers being drafted in, their best efforts and frequent appeals on TV and radio. Theo's natural optimism would be more dented if it were not for his conviction that the solution to a person's disappearance, particularly a child's, often lies in the family. The stepfather and stepbrother both have solid alibis. *Which leaves the mother and the father.*

Theo had talked to Yvonne Everidge again earlier in the day, learning little more than he did at their first meeting except for more detail about what a drunken no-good her first husband was and still is. So Theo has asked Ray Marchant to come into the station this evening to help with enquiries. DC Shilling approves, 'For Victoria to disappear this completely, she must have been taken. Marchant has the most to gain from taking her, Mrs Everidge was less than keen on him spending time with Victoria.'

And the most to lose, thought Theo. *He had only just gained the right to see his daughter, after a long and acrimonious war with his ex-wife. Kidnapping her is the surest way of losing her again.*

Harry has something to report from her day's work: 'According to her teachers, the lass had started writing her name as Vicky Marchant, but not on anything her mother would see.' *A smart kid then, understands the adults around her.* And there is something else, Theo can tell. He encourages his DC to come out with it. 'It may be nothing. Victoria has a set of, um,' she falters. The skin around her neat nose pinkens, her blue eyes quickly glance away from him, then she ploughs on, 'Um, maybe you know, sir, you can get knickers for little girls with the days of the week on?'

'I have sisters and nieces, Harry. Your point?'

'Sunday to Tuesday are there, they're in the wash. Wednesday is gone, she was wearing those Mrs Everidge says, and so are Thursday, Friday and Saturday.'

'What does Mrs Everidge say about them?'

'She appeared a bit nonplussed when I first asked, then she said she'd put them in a dark wash, they'd got a pink rinse and she'd thrown them out.'

'But?'

'She doesn't seem the type, to me, to mess up the laundry. And throw them out because they've turned pink? When Victoria liked pink?'

'It brings in the possibility, I suppose, that this was a planned departure. Are there any other clothes missing?'

Harry shrugs, 'Hard to tell, there's plenty left in the wardrobe and drawers, and we really only have Mrs Everidge's say-so on what was there in the first place.'

'Have a word with Paul, he seems to have had a soft spot for his little stepsister and may be able to say if something has gone. And have a closer look at some of those photos of Victoria, match up what she's wearing with what's left.'

The first and last time Theo had met and talked to Ray Marchant was on the night of his daughter's disappearance. At the moment when Ian Everidge had been telling the police he'd dissuaded Ray from coming over, Mr Marchant had been sitting in his car just around the corner. Theo had met him there after ascertaining this during a call to his mobile. Short, with clipped brown hair around a thickset head, and casually dressed in jeans, a plain terracotta-coloured pullover and a weather-proof jacket, Ray was fidgeting: with his keys, tapping on the steering wheel, fiddling with the heater. It looked like he, at least partly, lived out of his car, a remarkably tatty one given its owner was a specialist car mechanic. It had containers from various takeaway meals, a holdall, a leather jacket, some smart shoes and a work bag strewn across the back seat.

    He was impatient to find out what had happened, 'She can't be missing, I only saw her Sunday, she was fine then, we had a great weekend.' Theo had asked him to run through his recent movements from dropping off Victoria at 5 p.m. on Sunday to this moment, just over seventy-two hours later. He had replied he travelled for his work, he'd been in Preston Monday, Tuesday, one local call-out Wednesday morning, then home from lunchtime. 'What's this got to do with … Oh I see …' he had drummed harder, a faster tempo. 'She's got you thinking I've got Victoria, I've taken her. Bitch,' he had breathed the last word. Then he had turned to Theo, 'It'll be a waste of time, detective, but you can have your lot go over my flat, my car. I haven't got her, I swear. What can I do? I just want to find her.'

    They had gone over his flat and his car and a garage he rented and had found nothing of interest. He has no one to collaborate where he says he was at the time of his daughter's disappearance. On the other hand, there is nothing to put him in Scarborough, and no one had seen Yvonne (or Victoria) either since her husband and stepson left for work and school.

This evening Ray is belligerent, 'You're barking up the wrong tree, detective, it's her, that bitch, you should be investigating.' His face is taut. Though Theo knows he is around the same age as his ex, he looks a lot older. His stout fingers are constantly on the move, clasping and unclasping, smoothing over his hair, landing in his lap and then back onto the table again. He's angry with the police for not having found Vicky. How can it be so hard to find an eight-year-old? She can't have gone far. She wouldn't have got into a stranger's car, he's told her enough times not to do it, though this thought obviously troubles him. He repeats that it's 'the bitch' Theo should be pursuing.

'We are doing everything we can to find your daughter, Mr Marchant, including talking to Mrs Everidge. I'd like to know a little more about Victoria, about you and her.'

'Why?' Ray bursts out. 'How can it possibly help? All the time we're talking in here, she's out there somewhere, that's where you should be looking,' he points towards the door, unconsciously aping his ex-wife. 'She could be hurt, lying in a ditch somewhere, cold, hungry,' suddenly his voice cracks and he covers his eyes with his hand as if shading them from the sun.

Theo waits. He wonders whether Ray knows he can walk out, refuse to talk. He has a criminal record, narrowly avoided a prison sentence: drunk and disorderly, some minor fighting. He's been in police cells, interview rooms like this before, he probably knows he doesn't have to stay. However, he does and he begins to talk, 'I was young, stupid, a bit of a wanker. I didn't even love Yvonne, always thought she was a stuck-up bitch. We grew up on the same street on the Westedge Estate. Her parents were more respectable than mine. They worked, him over at Chandler's coach makers, her cleaning in the school, but they were still a Westedge family. Yvonne's aunt overdosed, an uncle was in and out of prison, petty thieving mostly. Only Yvonne's mother put her daughter on a pedestal, she was going to leave Westedge, maybe go to university, marry someone nice.

'She was devastated when Yvonne took up with me. I don't really know what Yvonne saw in me, maybe it was my rugged good looks.' He allows himself a wry smile, 'Or she wanted a bit of rough. Or the sex. Or she was rebelling against her mum. Who knows? It wouldn't have lasted five minutes if her mum hadn't made a fuss, tried to ground her, I do know that. And then, of course, Yvonne was pregnant within weeks. Neither of us had planned it. At least,' he pauses. 'I hadn't. I wasn't ready to be a dad. As I said, I was a wanker, into my beer, getting leery, thumping people to make myself feel better than them.

'We did get married before the baby came. Yvonne's mum insisted, me dad turned up around then and said I should step up and be a man or I'd regret it. I think it was his apology for not being there for me. Then the baby came and I went to the birth, half-cut if I'm honest, and I freaked, just couldn't cope with all the blood and the screaming and seeing my girl's fanny split open. We were both traumatised by it. I don't think Vicky would have made it if it hadn't been for Yvonne's mother making sure she was fed and clean and warm. I have to thank her for that. Maybe I will one day. Make reparations, that's one of the twelve steps. I must've spent most of those first weeks drunk. Then I tried to get to see Yvonne and Vicky and her mum wouldn't let me and I pushed her. OK, being honest, I hit her, not hard, but I hit her, and I'm not proud of it. I'm really not proud of any of it.'

He stalls, his face strained of colour, his hands still. After a moment his palms open, in supplication. 'I couldn't stay around then, had an injunction against me anyway, almost ended up in prison. Old Reggie Harvey got me off. And I left. Leeds, Manchester, Birmingham, just drifted and bummed around, got work when I could, stole when I couldn't, drank myself stupid. Would probably be dead by now if I hadn't seen this kid in a park, a little girl, toddling she was, wearing a pair of flowery trousers, holding onto a man's hand. And I saw the look that went between them, her intense gaze on him, trusting him to keep her upright and his look of, um, I guess it was love. What can I say detective? It was like a cold slap in the face or a knife of ice through my heart. Seeing her take her first toddling steps set me off fumbling down my own path of redemption.'

He smiles awkwardly. 'They had some creative writing classes at the rehab centre. Anyway, it took me a long time and it was really hard, but I cleaned myself up, I got some decent training, found myself a job and came back to find my daughter. Only, as you can imagine, Yvonne was not happy to see me, not at all. She'd married Ian. He's a nice bloke, steady, I can see why she'd want to be with him. They had a nice house, a nice life, and Vicky was turning five and the only father she knew was Ian. I'd missed the first five years of her life. Maybe I had no right to expect to be welcomed with open arms, so to speak, but I knew I could be there for the rest of her growing up. I was determined to do what I could for her for as long I was on this earth. That's what I told Yvonne. She wasn't impressed, I guess I can't blame her, she said I was too late, Ian was going to adopt Vicky and I was irrelevant to her, she didn't want to see me.

'Of course she didn't, what does a five-year-old know about this kind of stuff? I knew I would have to earn her trust, the right to be her father again. I got myself a solicitor, Aurora Harris, what a wonderful woman, and two years later I got access, and last weekend was mine and Vicky's first full weekend together. She's a beautiful little girl, bright, cheery, thoughtful too, doesn't get that from me, that's for sure. You know what? I think she's getting to like me a bit, see me as someone she can rely on. It's all I want, to be someone she'll turn to if she's in trouble. But she wasn't in trouble, she was fine, so where's she gone detective? Where's she fucking gone? Because whatever Yvonne might make out, I haven't taken her, I wouldn't do that to her.'

For the first time Theo feels a connection with Ray Marchant, he believes every word he's said. So what changes when he asks, as he does again, about Wednesday afternoon? Out comes once more the bland answer about returning home for lunch and spending the afternoon not doing much at all, watching TV, maybe napping a bit. *Why don't I believe you mate?* Then there's the repeated and agitated assertion, 'It's out there you should be looking, detective, not wasting time questioning me. My little girl's out there, somewhere, and you've got to find her.'

Chapter 7

As the first fall of snow threatens, in the approach to midwinter's day, Stan Poole might have caught sight of the glint of the reaper's scythe, if only he were looking. Neither he nor his wife are ready to acknowledge the approach of his death. Stan Poole's move to the hospice, agreed on Friday, will be a little holiday for him, just until he 'gets himself right'. However, since there is no bed available, his palliative sojourn remains an aspiration rather than a reality. This is the situation when Rose arrives Saturday morning to do her weekly clean. Recently Rose has been prevented by Val Poole from cleaning anywhere but Hannah's room and bathroom in the attic. Hannah is arguing with her mother that Rose must be allowed to do her work throughout the house.

'You know how he hates being fussed around,' Val keeps repeating. 'It'll be the death of your father.'

That's not what's going to kill him. Frustration and anger begin to trill through Hannah's voice as she tries to remain reasonable: Rose is a paragon of discretion and the deteriorating condition of the kitchen and her parents' bedroom and bathroom are more likely to cause harm, not to mention being increasingly unsavoury for the other occupants of the house, namely herself. Finally she screeches, 'And how much longer do we have to be tiptoeing around him, I've been doing it all my life, when's the bugger going to finally shuffle off and leave me alone?' She watches her mother's face turn puce.

'How dare you?' Val Poole's voice is as strident as her daughter's. 'How dare you, after everything I've done for you, how dare you speak to me like that?' Then Rose lets herself into the hallway. Val Poole immediately begins to whimper, her face sagging away from its bone structure. 'What would I do if anything happened to Stan?' Her wrinkled claw clutches at Hannah's arm, 'We have to do what's best for Daddy. You have to help me do what's best for him.'

Hannah holds back her urge to slap the collapsed face and searches around for some compassion for the old woman in front of her. She slowly begins to unhook her mother's fingers.

Rose Short, rotundly muscular in her overalls, with her long white hair twisted into a plait down her back, ushers Val Poole into the kitchen for a coffee. Hannah says she'll call the hospice again to impress upon them the urgent need for a bed. 'You get on out Hannah, take a break,' Rose says over her shoulder. 'I'll organise everything here. Your dad'll be in the hospice by this evening.'

Hannah doesn't hesitate. Rose, like Ben, dabbles in the ancient mysteries and Hannah has come to believe her capable of something akin to magic. If Rose decrees it, then Stan Poole will be in a hospice bed before sundown.

Hannah phones Agatha, a colleague on her counselling training course, and suggests meeting for a chat. At the front gate, she glances back. Her parents' house, coupled to Aurora's, had been the project in the 1920s for an architect enamoured by ocean liners. Though modest in size, they both have the white rendering, the curving bays and, over the stairs, long narrow windows, which echo cruising decadence. At the end of the then newly created Sea View Lane, the Poole's was in fact the only one to have a view over the water with its cliff-top position. From the outside it looks untroubling. Inside, Hannah is more aware of malevolent forces, of the legends which tell of witches hung on this spot. No amount of brick, plaster and whitewash can keep their souls from stirring. She hurries away. They would not follow her to the tea shop where she and Agatha will spend the next couple of hours.

Agatha Begood is older than Hannah, having taken early retirement to become a counsellor. She is taller, *but then most people are.* She is neatly dressed in jeans, cream pullover and brown jacket, her grey hair in a finely spun cloud around her face with its rice-paper skin. Reminding Hannah of a shrew determinedly scratching a crab out of its shell, Agatha doesn't accept Hannah's initial vague responses about how she is. *Agatha wants to know, she wants to hear.* The thought warms Hannah as much as the tea, sweetens as much as the first, and final, forkful of cake. She can talk about the misery of living with her parents, of the guilt of not doing enough, *never doing enough, never being good enough, of not loving them enough. Not loving them at all.* She repeats some of her brother's admonishments.

'And where's Stephen?' asks Agatha, her thin pale eyebrow raised.

'Oh, you know, busy, advising people about their finances.' Her insides are as crumbly as the mess of uneaten sponge on her plate.

'If he's not here in the middle of it, he's no right to comment. You know that Hannah.'

She nods.

'Will Lawrence be coming up?'

'Yes, he says so. Soon, I hope.' *He would come for Dad, his mentor in his early days of journalism. He's the child Stan Poole had wished he'd given life to.* Her throat is clogged. *But I want him here for me.* It's becoming difficult to breathe, to speak, impossible to eat. She puts down her fork and takes a tentative sip of tea. It manages to slide down. She asks Agatha what's keeping her busy. Her final pieces of work are handed in and being marked, so she's researching an article she might write based on an aspect of her case study: the existence or not of false memory syndrome.

False memory syndrome, the facility of the brain to invent a narrative which doesn't fit the facts. Or more precisely, doesn't fit with what other people have observed. Most often claimed for memories of abuse, not memories of happy childhoods. My family wasn't always like this, was it? There were times when we got on, when we were happy? Dad would make us laugh and he taught me and Stephen some mean card tricks. And there was a time when Mum could cook something appetising and we'd eat it together without wanting to gouge each other's eyes out. Wasn't there? Or are those the bogus memories?

'Hannah are you OK? You've gone a funny colour.'

She puts down her cup, slopping tepid tea over her sleeve which she now notices is frayed. The noise of the café crashes in on her, she feels dizzy. 'I'm fine. Your article sounds fascinating, I'd like to read it, when you've a draft. Look, sorry Agatha, I think I should be going. Do you mind?'

Agatha gives her a long hug and makes her promise to keep in touch before she lets her go. Hannah walks away, the floor swaying under her feet. *I need air, all I need is some air.* The pedestrianised high street is disorientatingly busy. She shoves herself along as fast as she can. *False memories. You don't know what happened, Hannah, you're making it up.* She reaches the Spa bridge and hangs onto the railings looking down at the rolling sea, the wave crests, barbed wire slung across slate. The pregnant bellies of the grey clouds dip to the freezing water. Chilled air blasts into her lungs, she begins to ease back into the heaviness of her body, the earth stops its shifting. Reluctantly she heads home.

By the time she gets back, the house is clean. The downstairs hall, snug and sitting room, though cluttered with her mother's choice of ornate, dark-wood repro furniture, are at least dusted, vacuumed and polished. The kitchen gleams and the fridge is emptied of the foul-smelling leftovers that Hannah's mother has been refusing to throw away. Hannah pauses by the French windows which open onto the ordered if listless garden. The aspen by the fence, shorn of all green, tilts its spectral arms to the snow-burdened sky.

The house is quiet. Val Poole is showered and watching TV in the snug with a drink by her side. Hannah's father is asleep and the hospice has rung announcing an ambulance will pick up Stan Poole in an hour. Hannah briefly thinks about the person who has vacated the hospice bed. *In which direction did they leave, towards the morgue or towards home?* She hopes the latter and then turns her attention to what needs to be done. On her way out to go and help Aurora next door, Rose had said, 'You'd better get your brother over here, to say goodbye.' She had patted Hannah's shoulder and added she'd be back later.

It is Sunday afternoon before Stephen Poole and his wife Veronica drive from York to see Stan Poole now peaceful in a morphine-induced sleep, stately in a freshly made bed in a spotless room at the hospice. Veronica joins Hannah in the little family room overlooking the hospice garden, vibrant with grasses and holly trees and festive lights, where Hannah had hoped to secrete herself for a moment's quiet. Veronica drapes her willowy self languidly into one of the armchairs and says how exhausted she is by having to make the journey after the day she's had.

Since Veronica doesn't work and both her sons, at present being looked after by their other grandparents, are weekly boarders at school, Hannah wonders what could possibly have exhausted her sister-in-law. She doesn't ask for clarification, she isn't interested. Anyway, Veronica is already on a different tack, about how sad it is to see dear Stan in such a sterile environment, how much better if he could have stayed at home.

Better for whom?

And Veronica is worried about Val, 'She doesn't seem quite herself, is she ...' here Veronica drops her voice, 'washing enough? It's the first sign, Hannah, of dementia.' She mouths the last word.

Hannah considers and discards possible responses: *If you think she's bad today, you should have seen her yesterday.* Or, *Maybe if you had come over a bit more often in the last few months, you wouldn't be so shocked.*

However, Veronica once again moves on, 'A new hairstyle, Hannah? I must say it's different.'

Hannah involuntarily touches the nest of brown curls which she has allowed to grow untinted and untampered with since the summer.

Veronica sighs, 'I suppose you don't want to trust yourself to one of the hairdressers around here. You should come to York and I'll introduce you to mine, does such a lovely job and so cheap, only £80 for the works.'

Hannah can see herself in the small mirror hung by the door, presumably to allow grieving family members to smarten themselves up before facing the dying. She is goblin-like in unflattering jeans and sweatshirt, her eyes murky mossy pools in her pale round face, at this moment blighted by inflamed pores. It had been a while since she had been able to afford a decent hairdresser or a facial, *Maybe I should have put some slap on before coming out.*

The short day makes the evening interminable. Val Poole does not leave her husband's bedside. Stephen and Veronica don't linger, they both say they have something to get back to, though they don't specify what.

Hannah stands in the chill of the family garden and calls Lawrence. He takes a while to pick up. *Is he screening out calls from me? No he wouldn't do that.* It was because of what he felt he owed her father that Lawrence had, firstly, given her a room when she'd dropped out of university and had, secondly, helped her find proofreading and editing work. He still put some her way, thankfully, for her increasing indebtedness. *But we're friends now, Lawrence and me, and I'll go back to my room at his when I'm done here. And I'll pick up with my friends, Rickie and Steff, they'll come round once this is all over.* It had been weeks since she had heard from Rickie Quirk and Steff Courtney, whose success in journalism had been as substantial as her failure. *Death, it drives people away. It'll be different once I'm back down there.*

'Hannah.' Abrupt, it's his style.

'I think you'd better come.' She hears the wobble in her voice. *For me not for Dad.*
'Now?'
'Yes.'
'I'll see what I can do. It might have to be tomorrow.' A hesitation. 'You OK?' There's not really a question mark. 'Looking after yourself? Eating properly?' *His way of caring.*
She controls her tremor, 'I'm fine.'
'Good. I'll get there as soon as I can.' He cuts the connection.
She goes back into the family room and curls herself up on the sofa. The chill won't go away, she hears herself making a sound like an abandoned kitten might emit. *I won't cry.* She doesn't feel like crying, it's more a dryness, a heaving up of something shrunken. *And monstrous.*
She pulls out her writing journal. *Distraction, it's what I need.* She'd begun it at Izzie's behest, at first reluctantly. Now she finds it diverting to scribble in it. She's also picked up some poetry by Plath and Sexton from the library, reading bits at random, noting lines down. She reads over some pages, selecting some words from Sexton and some of her own and writing them over, playing with the order:
> You go from madness to breakfast
> from the howling of the cauldron children within
> from the nightmare choking
> you walk that journey
> from the disordered to the ordinary
> an office worker in a pink floral dress
> in a wall-less Bedlam.

When the door opens, she thinks it might be Lawrence, despite it being humanly impossible for him to have made the journey in the time. It's Ben. *What's he doing here?* His explanation is that he's brought Rose. *Has she forgotten how to drive then?* She makes an effort to hide her annoyance with a smile. She retains at the back of her mind the awkward night over six months ago when they had gone out together and she had misread the signs, thinking he was more interested in her than he turned out to be. He had kept his distance somewhat since then. They had seen each other several times in the interim, for a meal, at the cinema, always in a group instigated by Lawrence and Theo. Lawrence had been an older boy at Ben's school and Theo plays footie with him.

Hannah feels frumpy, uncomfortable. She has only turned on a side light in the family room, so she and Ben are in the semi-gloom. He sits in one of the armchairs. She can see the outline of his compact body garbed, as usual, in black, a pullover and jeans. His shoulder-length chestnut hair feathers around his round fleshy face; his brown eyes disappear into shadows. He leans forwards, his elbows on his knees, to ask her how she is doing.

What does he care? She would normally have gone for a concise and evasive phrase. However, maybe because of the darkness, which brings with it the sense of there being only the two of them in the world, or maybe because it is the truth, she says, 'I wish he'd die now. I've had enough.'

Enough. Enough. Not just of the querulous old man he'd become in the last months, but of the father who was never satisfied, who picked fights, who was always disappointed. And yet, and yet, wouldn't let me go. It was like I had to be bound to him, had to be held close to him. Something clicks into her mind, a whisper of a memory, perhaps, though she can't place it, his fingers digging into her shoulder, something solid behind her so she has nowhere to retreat to, his sour breath in her face. Her body is rigid, any sound of protest strangled in the base of her throat. She hears her name being called from far away, perhaps another part of the house. *Which house is this?* There had been so many in her growing up. Constantly on the move, for Stan Poole's career. *Whose voice is it? A man's. A kind voice. The two do not go together.*

She hears it again, accompanied by a touch on her elbow. This time Ben and his voice solidify out of the darkness and the soothing decor of the family room around him. Her shoulders ache, her stomach twists, her fingernails scrape at the thin skin on her wrists. She makes a sound which is somewhere between an 'Oh' and a sob, though it reverberates much more loudly in her head. Ben moves onto the small couch next to her, puts one arm across her back and his other hand on hers. She continues to make these strange gasping noises which ricochet around her skull causing it to ache. At some point she does sink forwards, her face against the rough texture of his jumper. *You fool, you fool, you idiot Hannah*, words form themselves in her mind. *You bad girl, you bad, bad girl.*

A millennium has passed; though when she finally gets to see the clock she sees it is only several minutes. She manages to take a shaky breath and pull herself upright again. 'I'm sorry,' she mumbles, realising how much dribble and snot she has transferred onto him. She takes the tissues he gives her. She wishes she could be entombed by the floor.

'No worries,' he says.

She glances up at him long enough to see his calm face, 'I guess you've had worse.'

'Hazards of our profession.'

She peeps round again to catch his smile, she feels an ember catch and glow behind her sternum, *Our profession? You'd elevate me to your standing?*

'Tea?'

She shakes her head. 'I'm drowning in it.'

'Water then?'

'Whisky?'

He looks around in a make-believe search. 'I don't think they've got it on offer here.'

'Water it'll have to be then.'

He moves over to the cooler in the corner and draws them both a cup. 'Do you want to tell me about it?' he says, casually resuming his place next to her.

She immediately feels herself shrink away inside her outer skin which becomes toughened leather. Dismissive remarks about lack of sleep and 'your dad dying tends to have this effect on you' roll up to her tongue. She swallows them back down. She knows he is asking her about something else. She fears what he might have seen. 'I don't know how to explain,' she says eventually, it being as near to the truth as she can get. He waits. She knows he is good at waiting. *Could out-wait me no problem. Years of practice.* The clock ticks. Someone strides purposefully past the closed door. The wind keens. The reds, blues and greens of the lantern-lights jig in the bushes beyond the window. Flurries are beginning to descend, casually skittering in circles, giving no intimation of the deluge to come.

She suddenly thinks of a little girl lost, an eight-year-old with brunette bunches, maybe bruised and battered, alone, afraid. 'It's like he's suffocating me, choking me and I can't get away. I can't scream. There is no one to help me, no one will come.' She has articulated this twice before to her therapist and it has left her depleted, exhausted, the words are too heavy, lead plated. She has resisted Izzie's attempts to dig down further. But she wants to know it from Ben, now, in this cave of a room. 'What did you see?'

He responds slowly. 'I saw a very young girl, scared and struggling.'

She is dissatisfied, she wants him to have noticed more, to be able to tell her more. She shrugs, 'It's no secret I've a complicated relationship with my dad. Stan Poole – charming, witty, clever, a sod to his children. Ain't it always the way?' She drinks deeply of the cold water. A dull headache is taking hold, she reaches forward for her bag to find some painkillers. As she does so, Ben puts his hand on her forearm. She is glad it is covered, though he has seen what is underneath before and she suspects he knows what her long sleeves are hiding.

'Hannah, I'm here for you, if you want to talk, I hope you know that.'

She looks up; his eyes are huge and dark, full of kindness, affection even. *If only it were all for me and me only, and not for any passing miserable stray. I could tumble for those eyes.* She smiles falsely and says with deliberate levity that she knows it, of course she does, and she needs to find her tablets.

Stan Poole dies with the first inundation of snow, in the early hours of the ancient festival celebrating the birth of the new sun. Only his wife is present. His daughter stands shivering, her back against the rough brick of the hospice wall at the edge of the garden made strange by drifts, icily gleaming in the subdued lamplight.

Chapter 8

Theo is not a walker, unless it's on streets lined by shops, historic buildings or clubs and restaurants. He gets his exercise at the gym and at a regular friendly five-a-side with Ben and Max. Yet, in Scarborough, he walks. He walks by the sea, his favourite leather boots becoming salt spattered, or, as now, between interviews. He has been to Westedge, a complex of brick-built houses on dead-end roads at the edge of town. It was built in the 1970s: an answer to an increasing population, to families no longer wanting to live with multi-generations under one roof and to the dilapidated housing around the harbour. Council, now social, housing for the poor and disadvantaged of Scarborough. It was once thought quite desirable to be moved there; for a short time, forty years ago.

It is nothing like some of the sink estates Theo has worked around in Manchester, though he still recognises the clues. An abandoned garden strewn with car parts here. A window hung with a sheet instead of a curtain there. A gang of little kids on the corner with an ugly dog, trying their best to look menacing, starting their thieving vocation by lifting packets of sweeties from the corner shop. The majority of people getting on with their lives: thinking education isn't for them; enjoying nights out in town; holding down a job of sorts; having kids; perhaps getting married. While, not entirely uncomplainingly, accommodating the criminal elements amongst them; through fear or because they prefer their sense of community to any association with the police.

Compared to elsewhere around town, it is in Westedge that Theo has seen the most elaborate displays of Christmas lights and decorations strewn across the house fronts and bedecking the cramped living rooms. He has been delving into the intricate web of Ray and Yvonne's relations who still reside on the estate. Yvonne's father died years back and her mother is in a care home with galloping dementia. She has no siblings, but there is an aunt and uncle and a couple of cousins with children to talk to. None of them had seen much of either Yvonne or Victoria for years, they consider Yvonne a stuck-up bitch and are anxious about the 'poor little mite' Vicky. Ray's relations, his sister, mother, a couple of aunts and two male cousins, were more cautious about speaking to him. They didn't say much, except that now Ray had got 'hisself straightened out', he's a devoted father and everyone is 'just devastated' about little Vicky.

Near the end of the unsatisfactory interview, Ray's mother had fluffed herself up, a brooding hen about to peck, and delivered her verdict: the police didn't know what they were about, as usual. 'My boy had nothing to do with our Vicky going missing and what the police ought to be doing is checking out number 41 up the street, the council's moved in a right weirdo.'

Ray's sister agreed, 'He could have seen our Ray bringing Vicky round here the other Sunday and taken a fancy to her.'

Ray's mother crossed her arms under her ample chest and said, 'It ain't right the council moves him in here when there's families with children all along. Used to be a decent street this one, not like some of the others. You go and look up there at number 41, Mr Detective, and see what you see.'

Thus dismissed, Theo did stroll up the road. Number 41 wasn't the tattiest house, nor was it the smartest. *Ray's mother would have got the prize for that one.* Along with its model stream, watermill and ducks in her front garden, it was currently strung with fairy lights. Theo guessed her working children had contributed to creating for her something of a stately home, given she was a woman who had no visible means of support except for benefits. The paint on number 41 had been recently refreshed, the lawn was neat and there were curtains at the window, drawn against the dusk, though they didn't look as if they moved much. There were no lights, Christmas or otherwise, to be seen, though it was possible any occupant was sitting in a room overlooking the rear yard. Theo rang through to the station with a request for information about the resident of number 41 and to say he was going home.

He could have caught the bus if he'd wanted to join the dejected queue at the bus stop. Instead he begins to walk. The snow, which had disappeared from the road and is slushy on the pavements, is pristine on the steep hill the road girds. The air is sharp against Theo's cheeks, a relief after the over-heated houses he has just left. A balm to the raw emotions which have been swirling around him, and inside him, these last days.

Where is Victoria Everidge, or Marchant as she has also been calling herself lately? An ordinary eight-year-old, average in most respects, except one: she's gone missing. And suddenly she is being talked about as if she is extraordinary, an angel, faultless. Theo has noticed this occurs with disappearances, with murders, *Yet it is the ordinary faults of the victim which could be key to finding out what has happened. Where is Vicky?* The question nags more at Theo, snags at him, a sharp hook into his thoughts, *because we are running out of things to do.* As long as he is doing, he can keep the sense of weariness, of hopelessness, helplessness, at bay. But after a week there are no leads. The child has simply vanished, and a world where this can happen is not a safe world, for his own nephews and nieces, maybe even for himself. He has to stop to breathe in the jagged air. The snow hasn't helped. He scans the shadow-absorbing white slope by his side, *If she is out there on her own, she's not going to survive it.*

He puts one foot in front of the other and wishes he had waited for the bus, even more so as it wheezes past smelling of burnt chip oil. *Then there is Lawrence. Or rather, Lawrence, Hannah and the death of Stan Poole.* Lawrence should be waiting for him at the house where Theo is living. He's still renting, rather than looking to buy. 'Are you sure you're staying Sarge?' his colleague Suze frequently teases.

Theo knows Lawrence will have cooked one of his delectable meals and opened a good bottle of red wine, so they can spend the evening together. It is not a good time for Lawrence to be here, in the middle of a case, when Theo might be called out at any time. However, with their schedules, they have to take what opportunities they can. *If we're going to build our relationship. If? Still an 'if' after six months.* Maybe only because Lawrence is different from Theo's previous boyfriends: coming up to his forty-second birthday, only three years older than Theo, even if sometimes it seems more. *On occasion Lawrence can be overly serious, overly pedantic.*

For once, Lawrence hasn't asked why Theo doesn't apply to the Met and move in with him in London. Theo is glad of this, for he cannot bring up an answer, except for the unsatisfactory, 'it's too soon for me to move on'. Though the reason why Lawrence hasn't posed the question perturbs Theo too. *Lawrence is distracted. He is distracted by Hannah.* Theo has to admit to himself, *I don't like it when Lawrence is distracted by Hannah. Can I even be slightly*, he fails to find another word for it, *jealous?* Lawrence and Hannah have known each other so long and there are so many strands running through their friendship. They can do the anticipating thing, when they know what the other is going to say or how they are going to react. Theo is still learning to read Lawrence and feels it might be a lifetime endeavour. And Lawrence takes care of Hannah. Of course, Lawrence takes care of Theo, Lawrence takes care of many people, but there is something poignant about the care Lawrence accords Hannah. *She is one of those people who invites others to take care of her,* Theo thinks to himself, not un-nastily. *The perpetual victim.*

Furthermore, there is all this stuff about the departed Stan Poole. *The great Stan Poole, journalist and editor extraordinaire.* Lawrence had repeated some of the comments already out there on social media and local radio. Theo thought they came down to something like, *You knew where you were with Stan Poole, straight* talking, upfront, some would say a little brusque, a little harsh, not overly 'PC', but someone you could trust, you could rely on. In between making sure Hannah is eating and organising the funeral, Lawrence is writing the eulogy. Theo senses Lawrence's growing disappointment as he fails to muster quite the recognition for Stan Poole's professional acumen that Stan Poole felt he deserved from his erstwhile colleagues, despite their eagerness to attend the funeral. 'They're coming to gossip and drink my excellent wine,' he's said testily more than once.

Lawrence had been brought up in a Kent village without a father; by a mother and aunts intent on guarding against any adverse male influence. This was until, at the age of thirteen, he had been packed off to an all-boys boarding school in York. It was here he had met Ben; 'a scholarship boy', as Ben is apt to quickly add. Lawrence's education had apparently been secured by a bequest of his father's. In recent years, it's become clear Lawrence's father had gone to another woman rather than been fatally departed. *Another reason for him to cling to his substitute father, Stan Poole.*

Theo finds he is pounding the paving faster and faster, his heart beating into his ears. He stops. Once he has brought his circulatory and pulmonary systems under control, he can hear the quiet. There is no traffic for this instant. The air is still. Rising up steeply beside him is a field, its muddy ruts hidden by the frozen mantle. The sky above is dark blue, pink tendrils bleeding down into the white earth. At the top of the hill is a shed, one solitary star gleams above the ramshackle roof. All at once he sees two of the beach donkeys nosing their way out of the doorway to stand captured in the biblical tableau. Theo begins to chuckle to himself and then feels tears in his eyes. There's something frail about the scene, any second its perfection will be broken and irrevocably lost. *Such is the fragility of all moments. It's a sign.* Muriel, his only white-skinned aunt, would have seen it as a sign, and his other aunts and his mother would have joked at her expense. Even so,

Muriel was kind to the young Theo, to the best of her abilities, and he sensed her desperate need to believe in tea leaves swirled in cups and ciphers dropped from heaven. He walks on, determined now to enjoy his evening with Lawrence, whether Hannah and Stan enter into it or not.

CHAPTER 9

Aurora can tell by the way he is fidgeting with his (for once) subdued tie, and by the heightened colour of his fair skin below his white-blonde thatch, Max doesn't want to be here. He'd grumphed morosely all the way through getting ready. Despite it being only four days into the New Year, he wants to be at his design business. *He is worried about money. That's also why he pushed me to shorten my maternity leave.* The notch between his eyebrows is becoming carved into his large boyish face.

I don't want to be here either. She has left Oliver with Max's mother. She didn't want to. *I know he'll be doted on, as Max was, and it is good practice for when I'm back at work next week.* She explains it to herself, *I'm here and I badgered Max into coming, not for Stan Poole, but for Hannah.* Hannah, the unexpected ally who had been there for Aurora when she had fallen into a deep emotional pit after her son was born. Aurora has consigned her 'episode' to a dusty corner of her mind, though memories of it reappear unexpectedly at times, as if they are the recollections of someone else handed onto her. She cannot believe she could have distanced herself so much from Oliver and Max. She feels uncomfortably hot contemplating it. *Max didn't help*, she reminds herself. His capacity to not tell the whole truth to her still rankles.

She turns her attention to the crowded church. *There's been a good turnout, for sure.* She knows many of the locals, she grew up with them. They are school or current friends, or relatives of them. They are mingling with people from the newspaper world from around the country, since Stan had edited many a regional paper. Hannah is at the front between her mother and Lawrence. In his Savile Row suit, Lawrence is a basalt monolith, the smaller block atop beginning to go the shade of faded newsprint.

Aurora had taken Hannah in hand this morning, and her Titian curls are pinned to cascade down the back of her magenta tailored jacket. There was no way Aurora was going to allow her friend to be overshadowed by the elegant Veronica, who has opted for traditional black, even adding a tiny lace mourning veil to her long dark hair. Veronica's boys are either side of her, stiff in sombre suits. The eldest one – *Edmund or is it Harry?* – has done a reading from the Bible. He must be nearly twelve now, his brother a couple of years younger, his self-possession and careful enunciation cultivated by his fee-paying school in York. *Isn't it the same one Lawrence and Ben attended? I wonder what school Oli will go to? Max will want him to attend somewhere posh, if we can afford it, though he never did. I think I'd prefer somewhere ordinary.*

The service is going at a good pace, they are on to the prayers. She would have happily parroted them in the past, yet today she can't be bothered to. Rose has been coaching her in what Rose calls the old ways, connecting with the changing seasons, the darkness and the light, the incandescent power of the moon. This is the first time she's been to a church service since, and the words are woodwormy in her mouth. She watches Theo and Ben, the other side of Max on the pew. Today both are in black, Theo wearing owlish wire-rimmed glasses. They don't join in either, only her husband adds his lusty voice to the congregation. *We've become a bit of a gang. Hannah, me, Max, Theo, Lawrence and Ben,* she muses cheerfully. *I'm sure there's something possible between Hannah and Ben, he's here today because of her. What's she wasting her time with Maya for? Rose can defend her daughter all she likes – and what I wouldn't defend Oli against, I get that – but Maya's no good for Hannah, no good at all. Plus she's not bothered to even turn up for this, that's how little she cares.*

The service comes to an end and the coffin leads those from the front seats down the nave. Apparently Stan had wanted a burial with due pomp, or so Val had claimed, but somehow she had been overruled by Lawrence and Hannah with some backing from Stephen. There is to be a swift cremation, followed by a gathering at the Poole's house which Aurora is to help Rose prepare for. She therefore hurries out, leaving Max to come on after with his footie buddies.

Most of those who attended the church have decided they need a stiff drink or cup of tea following the service, so there is much to keep Rose and Aurora busy. Amongst the people congregating in the sitting room, hallway and kitchen, the conversations are boisterous: some about old Stan, but mostly about the Tony Blair revelations concerning his attitude to going into Iraq and how much he really knew. Hannah, unnervingly quiet and looking stunned, arrives to help take round the food. She obviously doesn't know many of the attendees of her father's funeral and some of them mistake her for some kind of help. Aurora gives her a hurried hug, finding her as ready to snap as a winter twig.

After consuming more beer than is beneficial for him and laughing a good deal with Theo and Ben, Max makes his excuses. Theo quickly follows saying he has work to do. *Still no news on the missing girl. Her poor mother.* He and Lawrence have hardly spoken. Aurora watches their short conference before Theo leaves, Lawrence having to lean down, his greying flop of hair next to his lover's shorn dark one. She sees that Lawrence's eyes suddenly become two blue pools on either side of his stout nose, and Theo passes over his own lawn handkerchief to catch the brief overflow. Then he is gone, and Lawrence rejoins Ben, quickly appearing relaxed and convivial, circulating easily, making sure glasses are topped up.

The crowd thins by mid-afternoon and Aurora is clock watching for when she can get back to Oliver. Rose and Hannah tell her to go. Hannah, effusively grateful, more talkative than she's been all day. *Possibly the result of the wine she's consumed.* As Aurora is about to leave, Veronica comes into the kitchen, also saying they must be going, since the boys are getting overtired. Though Aurora can see they are still exuberantly playing a version of Grand Theft Auto on Lawrence's laptop in the snug.

Lawrence and Ben follow in behind Veronica. It is only later that Aurora realises it is an impressive pincer movement which leaves Veronica with nowhere to hide. She has to hear Lawrence out and in front of the audience of Rose, Hannah, Aurora and Ben. She is going to find it hard to say no to him when he suggests she and Stephen take Val home with them. Then he and Hannah can get the house straight, while Stephen could sort out the will which is lodged with a York solicitor.

'Lawrence, you know I would say yes in a heartbeat if it wasn't for the boys,' says Veronica. 'Edmund has his exams coming up, he can't have any disruption ...'

'They're not for weeks, Mum,' Edmund has come in and is roaming the platters for something to eat. 'Gran can come and stay if she wants to, can't she?'

'I'm sure it's not a good idea for her right now,' says Veronica. 'Not a good time for her to be uprooted, given her ...' she hesitates, then mouths, 'problems.' Watching her son as he picks up a sandwich, she adds loudly, 'Edmund, is that prawn? I don't think you should, darling, you never can tell with prawn.'

Edmund pops the prawn sandwich into his mouth and picks up another one, 'Gran wants to come, I heard her say so earlier.'

'Did she darling? Well she doesn't always know what's best for her.'

Hannah continues with the drying of the glasses, stowing them into the boxes provided by the caterers. She keeps her head down, she looks small and pinched. Rose quickly exits. Aurora is pulled between staying and going. Ben moves to Veronica's side and touches her elbow as if to steer her to somewhere they can have a confidential discussion, only everyone, apart from Hannah, remains attentive. 'Veronica, it would be such a help to everyone if you could step in,' says Ben, with a hint of a bow towards her. 'Mrs Poole really needs someone to keep an eye on her and I am certain you can be relied on to be alert to the symptoms.' Veronica blushes and giggles. Ben continues this time, almost whispering, 'It's all been a great strain on Hannah, I'm sure you're as worried about her as we all are.'

Veronica is practically swooning into the hold Ben has on her arm, 'Well, of course, if you think, Ben ...'

Harry clatters into the kitchen. 'Come on Mum, Dad's waiting and Gran's in the hall. Rose has brought down her bag, says she's coming back with us or something. Hey,' Edmund is now tucking into a sausage roll and Harry tries unsuccessfully to swipe it off him.

'Does she? Is she?' Veronica straightens up quickly, her seductive smile gone. 'You boys put those down now, we don't want you sick in the car on the way home,' she snaps.

Then Stephen's voice bellows through from the hall, 'Veronica, Harry, Edmund, get out here, we're leaving in sixty seconds.'

And that is that. Val Poole, packed into the back of her son's four-by-four with her two grandsons, begins to nod off. Veronica's lovely features are screwed into a tight knot as she sits beside her husband who is making no attempt to hide his own fury at being given custody of his mother. *And Hannah doesn't leave the kitchen to say goodbye to any of them*, Aurora notes.

CHAPTER 10

Theo is glad of Suze's interruption. The atmosphere in the CID room is sluggish. Most people had taken some time off over the festive period and had, only just, managed to put away thoughts of a lost little girl for an instant. Now they are reluctant to remember fully the lack of development in the case. Theo has been to see Yvonne. The house was a museum for the moment her daughter went missing, the red and green swags now layered in dust. She had nothing to add to her previous statements, had the same set of the jaw as her ex-husband, who she continued to blame. 'We've had no Christmas in this house thanks to him.' There was something in her expression which suggested to Theo she found him and his officers equally culpable.

The family's computers have been checked, yielding nothing. Paul had been as good as his word, his sister's naive Facebook messages had only reached a small, contained audience, and there was no evidence of her being enticed somewhere by an adult masquerading as a child. So Theo is glad of the energy Suze brings to his corner of the office, which is demarcated by see-through walls not tall enough to reach the ceiling. He can see that she is a woman on a mission. She is looking well after her Christmas break; her knuckle joints less painfully swollen, she is using only one stick for walking. She has on a bright blue and turquoise knitted dress over her leggings and a glittery slide in her short, flat, mousy hair. Her pointed, child-sized face breaks open into a smile when Theo compliments her, she touches the slide, the gift her daughter had chosen for her. Suze's team of civilian administration staff has recently been pared back, with someone leaving and not being replaced and a stop being put on bringing in temps. She's, therefore, having to do the work of several, and, when she's this well, she has the force of many.

There's some overtime chits and expenses claims to be gone through, then she gets down to what she really wants to talk about: Vicky Everidge. Privy to management emails, phone calls and organiser of their meetings, Suze knows the detective superintendent has been putting pressure on the DCI who is prodding at DI Hoyle for more progress. And Hoyle will do anything to wriggle off the hook, including throwing DS Theo Akande in as bait. But more importantly for Suze, her own eight-year-old isn't sleeping well, worrying about her school friend. Her extended family includes the fishing community in the old town and, on her husband's side, the building trades and owners of the amusements. And she's heard through them that Theo has been given a line on the resident of number 41 Westedge Lane. She wants to find out more.

Theo is happy to discuss it with her, she understands what's confidential and her connections mean that she can often tell him things which would not come out in any other way. Only he's not got much to tell. Alexi Kestle is sixty-eight, he has no police record, is not on the sex-offenders register, lives alone. He is described by social services as vulnerable. They have put in place support for him, in the form of house cleaning and meals prepared for him a couple of times a week. He became known to the social services several years ago after he collapsed in the street; his mother had died six months previously and without her care both the house they shared and his own health had deteriorated badly. Since then he has been moved several times: from hospital to residential home and back and then into a maisonette and finally into number 41.

'Alexi? Kestle?' Suze questions.

'German father, I believe, refugee in the war. Long dead. British mother.'

'Why all the moves?'

'From what I can gather, he doesn't get on with people easily.'

'And how did you get on with him?'

'I haven't spoken to him. He's gone.'

'Gone? When? Where to?'

'I don't know,' Theo admits uneasily. Another misper, this time a vulnerable adult. 'The last sure sighting we have of him is in the corner shop on the morning of the 16th of December.'

'The day Vicky went missing.'

Theo doesn't need reminding. 'We've nothing to tie him to Victoria or her disappearance. Just his neighbours pointing the finger and you know how rumours get started.'

Suze pinches her lips together. Her navy eyes become crushed under her heavy dark brows.

'If you've got something to say, Suze, then say it.' He can see she's weighing up whatever it is.

Slowly she begins, 'My niece, she lives at number 13, says he approached her, said he'd like to take a photo of her. About a month back. She told him to get lost. She's a good kid, she wouldn't make something like this up.'

'How old is she?'

'Fifteen, looks older most of the time,' there's a hint of disapproval in Suze's voice.

'Was he inviting her back to his house for the photo?'

She shrugs stiffly.

'When was this?'

'Beginning of December.'

'Did she tell anyone one about it?'

Suze shakes her head. She always brings with her a faint scent of the rolling tobacco she smokes and peppermints. It reminds Theo of a couple of his aunts who were a soft touch for sweets and loose change. 'She didn't think much about it until Vicky,' she looks uncomfortable.

'So that's the gossip at Westedge? Mr Kestle has taken Victoria Everidge?' Theo snaps. He could do without this. 'Just because he's an incomer and a bit of a loner. Come on Suze, you know better than that, you know the key to a misper lies within the family. The idea of the predatory paedophile being to blame is most often a diversion, helps people project the nastiness out there, away from themselves. In any case we have absolutely no evidence Mr Kestle is interested in little girls.'

Suze responds sulkily, 'You won't talk to her, then?'

'Of course I will, if she'll talk to me.'

'I'll make sure she does.' Suze stands with surprising grace, then pauses a little shakily. 'You find her, DS Akande, you find our Vicky.'

He sees the worry on her face and softens his tone, 'I intend to, Mrs Irvine, I intend to.'

Chapter 11

Hannah hasn't seen Izzie since before ... since before ...

Since before her father's death. Since before Christmas Day when, Lawrence being away visiting his mother, dinner had been fried eggs and oven chips accompanied by gin, for her mother, and a cheap unremarkable bottle of wine for her. The alcohol had, at least, dampened any potential arguments. Since before the funeral. That's an awful lot to condense into a response to Izzie's usual opening enquiry of, 'So?'

Hannah wishes she could remember it all better, to give some kind of complete narrative. What she's left with are episodes, which don't link together, as if she wasn't quite in her body at the time but was observing herself. She recalls to herself, *Ben has been kind, he's been kind to visit me. There's been no sign of Maya, of course. I'm not going to tell Izzie about it, though. I don't want to admit I've been back with her. Izzie will give me her look then, oh so gently, get me to admit how unhealthy Maya is for me. I could talk about the not sleeping at night and the tired fug which drags about me during the day. Have I really not seen Izzie for only a bit over a fortnight? It feels like a century.*

And still she hasn't replied. Her therapist is waiting patiently, relaxing into her armchair, her blue eyes keeping watch. The freckles that scatter down from her well-defined nose to her cheeks are more distinct than Hannah remembers them, *Perhaps she's been away?* She is wearing a plain cream blouse with a navy skirt and long cardigan. Her pale hair is short. Lilac earrings hang from her ears.

'It was weird sitting by the coffin, during the funeral,' Hannah begins croakily.

'Weird?' Izzie's tone is encouraging, always that, but she's not going to let Hannah get away with generalities like 'weird'.

'I thought maybe he'd get out again, it wasn't strong enough to hold him, the wood, I mean, the wood was too flimsy to keep him in there. Only he's gone, hasn't he? I suppose what I'm saying is, I can't believe he's gone, finally.' She pauses. 'I'm glad. I'm glad he's gone.'

'It's been tough these last few months.'

'Yes. It's not because of that though.' She gathers herself for the revelation. 'I'm glad he's gone to somewhere he can't touch me anymore.'

'He was demanding of you.'

'He was always disappointed in me. Well not just in me, in Stephen too, and in Mum.' *Is that true? Am I telling the truth? Do I want to tell the truth? We could have a laugh, me, Dad and Stephen. Didn't we? Sometimes?*

'He strikes me as a disappointed man.'

Hannah considers this slight twist in meaning, 'Maybe.'

'He can't touch me anymore,' Izzie says, eyeing the phrase speculatively. 'How did he touch you Hannah?'

'I don't mean he touched me physically, I mean he can't get at me. He'd try to get at me, wind me up, punish me in some way.'

'Punish you, for what?'

'Being a disappointment, I suppose.' Hannah is beginning to lose a sense of where she is. It's hot in the room. She's tired. Maybe that is all it is.

She looks round at the familiar room, it's on the second floor of a converted garage, a square window is punched into one wall through which trees are visible. Some books are on a small set of shelves, she recognises a few of the titles as texts she's read for her counselling training. A basket of stones are on a low table with the box of tissues. There's a large cushion on the floor. Somewhere there'll be a tennis racquet for hitting the big cushion, as there was in the training room. Though she only watched others use it there – with fear and envy – and she's never seen it here.

Now she looks down on herself sitting on one of the couches with its squashy black cushions, small and insignificant. She is scared, tearful, afraid to make a sound. She hears herself say very quietly, 'I think I did something very bad once.' She sees a caved-in face, bashed to a pulp with a hammer. It is the face of psychotherapist Dr Themis Greene. *But I didn't do it. Did I?* She tries something else out in a whisper, 'I made him do it.'

Izzie leans in to hear. 'Who do what?'

She cannot say. *I must not say it. It's a secret.* She curls up inside the reinforced walls of her body. 'All I know,' Hannah says suddenly, wildly, 'is I'm very bad, evil.'

'Evil is a big word, what makes you say it?'

I can't say. I must not say. It's a secret.

The silence may have lasted a short or a long time, Hannah is not sure. Izzie says gently, 'You're rubbing your arm. Have you been cutting?'

Hannah looks away at the trees, black against the cobalt sky, there's an answer scribed in their branches.

'Can you show me?'

She shakes her head.

'Hannah I don't want you to hurt yourself. I want you to express the hurt outwards. Do you think you can try to do that? Can you try hitting the cushion?'

Another shake of the head.

'Are you still writing?'

'Sometimes.'

'Does it help?'

'Sometimes.'

'Can you promise the next time you want to cut you'll try writing first?'

Crossness bubbles up, she plants her feet determinedly on the carpet, 'I'm fine.' She ignores Izzie's pitying look and hurries on, some rubbish about she's fine now her mother has gone off to her brother's. And she has plenty to do: sorting her father's files for Lawrence to write some kind of short biography; getting the house straight; working on her case study. *All lies. I haven't been able to enter Dad's study. Without Rose's intervention, the house would be fast becoming a hovel. And I haven't been able to put fingertip to keyboard for my case study.* She talks about being (wasting time) on Facebook. How she scrolls through Rickie's and Steff's pages, sees their updates. 'How could I ever imagine I was part of their sparkling lives?' Her own page is looking distinctly abandoned as she finds it impossible to do anything. Steff had sent a text, 'Soz to hear about your dad. Great guy. You coming down for Rickie's New Year bash? Should be a LOLs. Sx'. Then later, 'Hey Hannah, u missed a fab night. Cu S x'.

'I guess,' Hannah now says, 'it's the best she can do.'

Izzie looks unconvinced, 'You're getting support elsewhere, though, aren't you?'

'Agatha's been kind, Aurora and Rose have been around helping. And Tina sent me a lovely card. She's not going to complete, qualify, after the work she put in, what a waste.' So that's how she finishes, talking about Tina, a fellow counselling trainee, and how she'd given up her dreams to be a therapist to follow her husband to somewhere. *Chesterfield, was it?* 'What's she going to do down there? She'd have been a good counsellor, too, if only she'd felt more confident in herself.'

'Maybe she'll come back to it,' Izzie sounds uninterested, she looks undecided about something, but Hannah has successfully chatted her way through the last ten minutes of the session and there is no time to delve more. So Izzie merely says, with a real warmth in her voice, 'I'll see you next week, Hannah, take care of yourself until then.'

Hannah leaves, congratulating herself on having 'got away with it'. Though what it is she has got away with she cannot precisely define.

CHAPTER 12

The first Wednesday of the New Year and Aurora is back in her old office. It feels as if she left it a generation ago, though it's been less than a year. It could belong to someone else. She moves around it cautiously in case she disrupts something for the real owner, the proper solicitor to whom the desk, the chair, the computer, the shelves of legal tomes, the filing cabinets and the fiery Georgia O'Keeffe on the wall belong.

'Take your time to settle in,' she's been told. 'Organise your hours to suit you.' She's having a graded return, working up to full time over the next month and a half. She's finding it hard arriving before 10.30 a.m., what with getting Oliver up and ready, herself dressed into the one suit which still fits after a fashion and delivering her son to his nana's in Malton before driving to York. This morning it was 11 a.m. It hadn't been Oliver, he'd been eager to have his breakfast and be washed and cleaned, into his clothes. She had been the one to dally, reluctant to have her shower, putting on a load of washing which could have waited until the evening, being distracted by the breakfast TV. *Only a few days in and I already want to play truant.*

She hasn't been handed any new cases. Her job is to acquaint herself with what has been going on since she left and with any changes in legislation or regulations. She reads through the email alerts and e-newsletters, constantly having to bring back her thoughts from wandering. *Will Oli eat for his nana? Of course he will, when did he ever refuse food? Will he sleep? Play nicely?* She imagines him going out to the park near her mother-in-law's house, pointing and reaching out to each new discovery – a gate which creaks, a blade of grass, a bird landing on a bare branch like a swinging trapeze artist – and chattering about it in his yet unformed language. *Will his nana respond to him? Encourage him? Of course, she will*, Aurora reassures herself. *Max's mum dotes on her grandson.* Aurora turns back to her screen and taps through some more paragraphs, pausing to make notes on the colour-coded reference cards she has beside her. She remembers doing this for her exams at school and then at university. Meticulous, methodical, *It got me through then, it will get me through now.*

Her leaving work had been abrupt. She had expected to carry on almost to her delivery date, as her GP mother had done with her. *But I had to accept defeat. Reluctantly. Very reluctantly.* She'd had to accept that tiredness of mind and body was making her ineffective, and had taken to her bed for several days and not returned to the office. She had, therefore, left cases uncompleted. These had been taken on by her colleague in the family division, *Probably grudgingly, he'd not off-loaded on me when his wife had a baby.*

The folders are in her tray. They are all different colours, she's always flouted the unspoken rule of the firm so as to have reds, greens and blues instead of manila. She sorts through them, filling in the front panel with what's been done and what remains (if anything) to be completed. Sometimes files will be 'pending' for years, will never be resolved; the involvement of a solicitor in a family dispute, the instigation of divorce proceedings, distilling for people what they may be about to lose.

She begins to file away the paperwork. This she can do with ease. *I have not lost the capacity to sort alphabetically.* She laughs at herself, *I used to do this without thinking, now I congratulate myself for remembering 'me' comes after 'ma'.* The drawer is becoming tight for space, so she begins to sift: cases which are over four years old can go to the store and there is excess capacity after 'z' so she can move folders down the drawers. In doing this, she picks up a turquoise cardboard wallet marked 'Marchant, R.' with a cross-reference to 'Everidge, V.' underneath.

The impression of the mother, her pinched, anguish-contracted features, sweeps through Aurora as if the pain is hers. She sits down, because she has to, and begins to leaf through the folder. The story comes back to her as she does so. She remembers

Ray Marchant, a taut little man, prone to blustering and demanding his rights. She had had to calmly keep reminding him that he had gone a long way towards forfeiting these rights by his previous behaviour. 'She drove me to it,' he replied, his tone aggressive. 'Maybe Mr Marchant,' Aurora had said firmly. 'Only the court won't see it that way and that's what we've got to worry about.'

She had got him some of what he'd been after. The file was not marked 'R.' for 'resolved' lest Ray decided to push for what he said he really wanted, joint custody. *I did it because it was my job to do so and I was (am?) good at my job.* Now she sees the mother's parched face and feels winded. *What if Ray has something to do with the disappearance? And I was instrumental in bringing him back into his daughter's life? Giving him access? Regulated but unsupervised access? I did it for, why? Because I could? To prove how able I was (am)? It's the fathers you have to be wary of.* Years of experience have shown her this. *Mothers can be manipulative, neglectful, easily led, stupid, but they rarely wreak the havoc the fathers manage.* 'If I can't have her, then no one will,' she's heard those words a few times in her career. Once they'd been the precursor to a man killing his two toddlers just so his wife could feel as bad and as hard done by as he did.

Aurora feels cold, her mouth is dry. She has an overpowering urge to rush over and take Oliver in her arms, hold him tight, keep all evils from him. *I let Ray back into Victoria's life. Was it a job well done?* A knock at the door brings her sharply back into the present and sends the bright blue folder to the floor, the sheets scattering at her feet. The new paralegal in her section pops his head round and offers her a coffee. 'Goodness, Aurora, are you OK?' he says, coming further into the room. 'You look like you've caught someone digging your grave.'

With an effort she smiles. She nods to the offer of coffee and scrabbles to get the papers together again. She shoves them all in a jumble into their cardboard jacket, puts it back into the filing drawer and slams it closed with a satisfying clang. Then she says quickly, 'Wait up, let me come with you. You said you wanted me to look at something you are working on, and now's a good time for me.' She follows the young man out.

* * *

The New Year and the same old preoccupations. Hannah is awake at 2 a.m. again. She's generally a restless sleeper, but it's become worse since the beginning of her father's final illness. Normally she falls quickly to sleep at 10 p.m., then wakes at around one, drifting into a fitful slumber around six, only to be snapped into consciousness by her alarm at 7.30 a.m. The one time she left her alarm off, she'd slept through till midday and almost missed an appointment with a client. Besides she has stuff to do: her counselling case study and some copyediting for Lawrence's book on Baruch Spinoza. Sometimes she is able to do these in the nocturnal hours, though she is left with a limp dishrag where her brain should be during the day. Sometimes she lies still trying to usher in sleep and halt the thoughts which rattle through her head: marbles on a wooden helter-skelter, one chasing after the other. Always there is the remembrance of mistakes she has made, occasions when she has felt a fool (recent or long ago) which grow and accumulate until she feels the rottenness in her marrow. *A rottenness I was born with, no doubt.*

There are the nights when she tries to cut it out of her, a sharp nick with a razor blade across her arm, then she can watch it ooze from her with her blood. Other nights she holds true to her promise to Izzie and scribbles into her notebook, words, invective mostly. They make no sense, they are huge, capitals, the pen scratching through to the pages below, then they become tiny, a child's scrawl. Once she tried reading it back during the day, squinting to get the meaning left by this nocturnal scribe. Afterwards she noted:

I am no writer. This isn't creatively writing, this is vomiting on the page. Word after word after word scrawled in some desperate attempt to make sense of it all. Sometimes it feels better to have it out, like sicking up a poisonous piece of meat, though I never seem able to quite get rid of all that's rotten. At other times it all appears such a waste of time. And so it's written, so what? What does it change?
I chart, I chart my moods, list my unconstructive thoughts, mouth more balanced ones, detail my achievements, call failures feedback, count, count up my blessings like a miser fingering her coins, testing them with her teeth: are they gold? And all this time, behind my back, the rats and cockroaches gnaw and gamble in what I have chosen to ignore, the putrid stench of my lack of success, my inabilities, my deeply unlikeable self.

At 2 a.m. this night, she thinks about her mother. Stephen has shipped her off to her cousins, a couple who Hannah never knew existed and who had apparently refused an invitation to the funeral, such was their dislike of Stan Poole. Then there's her father for whom she does not grieve. *What an ungrateful daughter I am.* She knows that not all families are like her own. She has met Aurora's parents, up from Devon, who are quietly kind and solicitous. And Theo's, more raucous but equally caring. Even Lawrence's mother is, in her own laidback, hippy-ish way. *And – and here's the clincher – Aurora, Theo and Lawrence are fond of their parents, Theo says he loves his! What is so wrong with me? I have nothing but distaste for mine.* The pressure begins to build up inside her. The pressure to punish herself. The pressure to blood-let.

Instead she forces herself out of bed and pulls on a dressing gown, slippers and leggings to supplement her nightshirt. *Distraction*, it's the only answer. She goes out onto the dark landing. A ghost ship's rigging creaks below. It's cold. Ice coating the sails, rendering them useless. The skylight is a square of indigo pricked by silver-headed pins. Hannah had told Lawrence about the witches who had lived here once. He had looked at her questioningly, his sardonic turn of the lips sitting uneasily with worry lines appearing between his pale blue eyes. He objected: the house was only built in the 1920s.

'In a hovel on this spot, then. I hear them, the spectres of witches,' she had finished quietly.

'Nonsense.' Lawrence passed his irrefutable verdict and the house knew to remain taciturn. This night it may not be so accommodating. She creeps down a floor to her father's office. Lawrence had helped her begin to sort the contents before he returned to London. He intends to write at least one, maybe more, biographical pieces about Stan Poole, and Hannah has been given the task of organising and cataloguing her father's papers so that Lawrence will have original source material to work from. She has done this for him many times before, she didn't think it would be different just because the subject is her father. It is different.

Her job is made easier as Stan Poole was meticulous in his filing, his categorising, his archiving. Every scrap of paper sorted, labelled and stored in the appropriate buff envelope. There are first editions of everything he wrote and the prize-winning pieces he had produced, articles about him and his career, background information for his local history and walking guides. Hannah is slowly making an inventory on her laptop of all these.

She sits cross-legged on the floor, turns the fan heater on by her side, leans up against the wall, behind the solid mahogany bureau and its large leather swivel chair. She can't bring herself to sit at her father's desk. Though she wiped it over, being careful not to disturb the few accoutrements he had kept there. In particular, the bronzed metal stand in the shape of a typewriter which still holds his favourite pens, sleek and expensive Parkers, and the matching letter opener in the shape of a quill, both given to him by his son.

Hannah remembers giving her father a glass paperweight – all colours and swirls – one birthday. She cannot unearth it, however, even after searching through the drawers where she finds spare paper, pencils, a sharpener, an eraser, paper clips in a tin, stamps, a cache of little red sweets and a desk diary which has been hardly used, just a few medical appointments noted earlier in the year, then nothing. She remembers Maya once telling her she'd counted the photos in the house, twenty-three of Stephen, two of her, and one of those with her brother. She dismisses this thought. *Get on with something, Hannah, stop wasting time.*

Stan Poole loved all the newest gadgets. Lawrence has taken her father's swish computer with him. He's told Hannah there are folders secured by password, but he knows someone in IT who should be able to release them.

She has already worked her way through one of her father's filing drawers. When she tried to shut it the other afternoon she found she couldn't. After much wrestling, she discovered a folder had got stuck down behind. She finally managed to extract it and it lies on the carpet before her now. The cover is mottled and brittle, made ragged by her efforts to free it. Inside are pairs of images torn from magazines. A photo of a flower or animal with one from a car magazine held together with rusting staples. She can't say what their connection might be to Stan Poole, who, as far as she knows, was uninterested in all three. On examination she finds the pictures are sometimes duplicated and the mix of flower or animal and car replicated. They are all dated in Stan's handwriting and are all over fifteen years old. *What has this to do with Dad? It doesn't make sense.*

From her position, Hannah can just see through the window, the naked branches of the lilac creating an intricate pattern against the sky, a paper-cut picture from a fantastical Eastern European story. Hannah knows the snow (turned to slush on the roads and pavements) still thickly covers the garden, its white mantle decorated by the footprints of robins and squirrels. She can hear the sea, its mutterings rising up the cliff not much beyond the end of the garden.

A chill begins to thumb at her neck and draw down to her shoulders. Hannah hugs her knees up to her chin. Far off, a sensible voice tells her to go back to bed. Only it's too late. She's shaking now, the cold a blade digging at her stomach and then ripping at her spine. She's finding it hard to breathe as something – no, someone – is pushing on her chest. She's being torn apart, slowly, from her legs up to her throat. She wants to scream, but then the hand comes down, a big hand, the skin hard and unyielding, smelling of paper and ink. Someone is telling her to stay calm, this will be over in a minute, the words are accompanied by a spray of hot aniseedy saliva. She closes her eyes and lies very still. 'That's a good girl.'

When Hannah pulls herself awake, the window frames a sky shot through with citrus pink, everything in the room is gilded, even her skeletally cold fingers. She wipes her hand across her cheek and finds it to be dry. There is silence apart from the hysterical clicking of an over-wound clock.

CHAPTER 13

The snow melt causes streams to run where there'd been none before. Chilled water through soft earth, cutting a course for itself to join up with already swelling rivers and (eventually) the sea. Chilled water through soft earth, its way will not be denied, insistently goading stones and tree roots, cleaning out rabbit burrows and field mouse nests, churning up what has been secreted beneath the top soil. So it is that the leg bone is found by an inquisitive dog, up to its haunches in mud, on the edge of a field by the side of the A64.

Theo is sitting with Yvonne Everidge when he gets the call on his mobile. Almost a month on from her daughter's disappearance, her focus remains on Ray Marchant. 'He's got her, I know he has, kept somewhere, away from me. She's not dead, I would know if she were dead.' Yvonne sounds like a cracked record, the repeated statements going round and round, her voice hissing and jumping awkwardly from her normal tone to a high-pitched squawk. It sounds dry, perhaps from a throat infection or overuse or panic. She is looking worn, though today she is made-up and her hair has an artificially induced bounce to it. The work of her next-door neighbour, Theo has already learnt from the woman herself, when she rushed out from her house to greet him on his arrival with, 'Any news honey?'

Yvonne continues, 'You've found stuff on Ray's computer haven't you?'

We have, some adult soft-porn, nothing worse than would be found on some of the investigating officers' machines. How does she know? Has Victoria told her? Has Ray been showing his daughter? Theo remains placid.

Yvonne rushes on, 'And he's got some whore holed up in Huggate.'

Not technically a whore, a married woman who Ray had met at a hotel in Scarborough the afternoon of his daughter's disappearance and ironically, from Yvonne's point of view, almost gives her ex an alibi. Almost, but not quite. However, Theo now gets the sense that, with the admission about his lover, Ray has finally come up with what passes for the truth. *It's Yvonne I'm not sure about. She's impenetrable.* And there's the question of the missing clothes, identified by the ever helpful Paul. *Victoria left with clothes in a bag. Did that mean she left willingly? With her dad? With Mr Kestle, also, for now, a misper? With someone she met through her Facebook page, though there are no hints in her messages, maybe a communication had gone off-line? By herself?* None of these options fill Theo with much hope, except, perhaps, if Ray is involved. *And what exactly does Yvonne know?* He is returning to this question, watching her flint eyes which are not looking at him, trying to see through them into what she is withholding, when his mobile buzzes.

He would have let it go to message, except his interview with Yvonne has been going in circles for at least twenty minutes and it is only a re-run of previous ones. He excuses himself and takes the call in the cramped hallway. A body has been found. He takes a moment to steady himself, his fingers seeking the support of the textured wallpaper covering the wall. There's a photo beside him, a little girl with brunette bunches grinning up at the camera. Grinning up at him. He closes his eyes for a second, *This may not be Victoria*. Then he goes quickly back into the sitting room to take his leave and tell DC Shilling to come with him. Yvonne is curtly polite saying goodbye and showing them out. She is uninterested in their rapid departure. She does not ask: 'Have you found her?'

* * *

'Just start writing, it doesn't matter where you start, as long as you start.' This is the advice her supervisor, Orwell Winters, gave Hannah for getting on with her case study. So she now has some words on the screen. Basic information about Julia: name, age, job;

how she came into counselling; and the 'presenting' issues. Like everything about her client, these are difficult to pin down. She doesn't appear depressed exactly. She's got too much energy, motivation, purposefulness. Anxiety was something she talked about initially. More recently she's not troubled by it, even when chairing high-powered business meetings or talking at conferences, which Hannah hears about with increasing apprehension. 'Projection?' she types. Julia has only four stable relationships in her life: her accountant; her lawyer; her PA; and her sales manager. They've all lasted since she started her first company fifteen years ago, but rarely seep into her personal life beyond the occasional after-work drink or dinner during work-related trips away. Everyone else in her life is 'easy come, easy go', including most of her staff in her growing portfolio of businesses. 'Who do you talk to about how you're feeling?' Hannah had ventured once. There'd been a silence, then Julia had responded tentatively, 'You?'

What can she say about Julia's relationship with her? Hannah is hesitant. Finally she notes, 'Julia turns up every week, on time, has only cancelled once. I'm constantly surprised she keeps coming back. She must want something.'

The last few sessions have been filled with a dispute Julia has become embroiled in with a young woman she employed recently. 'I took a risk with her, I told myself I shouldn't do it, I knew she'd let me down, but then I thought, give her a chance,' said Julia, sitting, as she nearly always does, upright yet relaxed. 'I felt sorry for her, isn't that what you want from me? A bit of empathy?' she smirked. 'Well, I should have known, that cat-on-heat's got it in for me, a disability discrimination case, says I didn't take enough care of her mental health. Got bipolar or some such nonsense.' Hannah winced, only she didn't have the impetus to intervene, Julia was onto the main point she was trying to make about how 'the loser' (her ex), a solicitor specialising in employment law, was behind it all. 'Wants to get his own back on me, just cos I dumped him after that awful weekend with those revolting children of his. Well no one beats Julia. No one.' Her eyes were electric and her chin jutted up to the ceiling as she delivered this final declaration. Hannah believed it was as much for her as for 'the cat' and 'the loser'.

She looks at the next heading in her guide on how to write a case study and types, 'Diagnosis: Personality'. She underlines it. This is easy. She adds in, 'Julia has strong narcissistic traits.' *And how.* Hannah has had the classic 'I'm not good enough' counter-transference from the beginning. Not that she recognised it at first, it being so close to her usual sense of herself, it was easy to take it as gospel, that she wasn't good enough for this client, could be of no use here. As usual, it was Orwell who pointed out the bleeding obvious in his gentle voice, delivering a warm smile which reached Hannah with a tinge of mocking. She feels tired, aware of all the energy it takes her not to see criticism at every turn. She takes a gulp of cold coffee.

She is cosseted up here in her attic room. Nothing bad has ever happened up in the eaves. Her childhood bedrooms were never in attics. From the skylight she can see the hard blue dome of the sky, the crystal casing of a snow globe. Everything is dripping outside. Over the last days and nights she has heard the shift of the snow as it lost its grip on the roof and descended with a thud into the garden. Now a seagull lands heavily and gives out a guttural 'ha-ha', derisive of the human world he surveys. She knows at some point she will have to add something about her own personality traits and how they interact with Julia's. 'Borderline'. She recognises the label for herself and that it usually comes under the index heading of 'disorders'. She recalls one eminent psychotherapist writing about the sinking feeling he has when faced with a borderline client, about how they are 'manipulative', 'selfish' and working with them is a 'very long haul'.

Hannah pulls her focus back to the screen in front of her, 'If there are narcissistic traits then there must be the narcissistic wound.' *Not that I've seen it yet, it is typical that it is firmly covered.* She puts a question mark for this. There are many question marks with Julia. *I still doesn't know why Julia has chosen to come to Scarborough for therapy, I don't buy the explanation of the recommendation from a former client. I suppose it cuts down on the possibility of being seen by someone Julia knows. But there's something else, I'm certain.* Once, briefly, Julia talked about a walk she took along the beach before coming to her session. She let slip that she'd visited the town as a child, on holidays. Her family weren't rich, were from Leeds, though her accent doesn't betray this. Her upbringing was 'ordinary, boring, I wanted more'.

She wouldn't explain further and snapped back to the present difficulties with 'the cat' and 'the loser'. The section entitled 'Childhood' is looking rather bare. *Then there is the big question mark, who is Meech?* Short for Michelle, Hannah has at least ascertained. *How does Meech fit into Julia's story?* As she types, Hannah has the impression she is entering a fairground house, the mirrors fooling her about where the doors and traps are. She looks down at the scribbled notes she makes at the end of each of the sessions with Julia, on several she has doodled in yellow, once or twice these doodles have manifested into buttercups. A flower, Hannah now remembers, Julia once declared she detests. Detests? A harsh and extravagant word for such an unassuming bloom.

* * *

Buttercups. The bank would be covered in buttercups in summer. Now it is a soggy mess of leaves and paper and cans tossed from cars passing on the nearby A64. The CSIs' white suits are becoming rapidly splattered with mud the colour of tar. Theo doesn't need a pathologist to tell him the body should really be termed remains, and they do not belong to a little girl. He allows himself to feel the relief before taking on the realisation that this is still a human being, a dead human being.

CHAPTER 14

Hannah is quiet. Not that Hannah is ever what you might call gregarious – she can make conversation, but just as quickly she can also retreat, as if what's going on in her own head is more absorbing, perhaps, or overwhelming. Aurora is serving them coffee and cake in her kitchen. She is pleased with herself. The house is clean and tidy. *OK, Rose had something to do with that.* The kitchen is bright and warm against the drab day. Oliver is playing on his mat on the floor, singing softly to himself. *I have got through my first week of work without making a fool of herself. And the cake is homemade.* 'It's edible,' she says as she puts it down, having a vague memory of dishing out unpalatable baking to Hannah once, *back when*, Aurora struggles to find a descriptive term which she's happy with. *Back when things were unbearable.*

    Hannah grins briefly, she agrees it is more than edible after taking a forkful of her slice, though the rest remains uneaten. *She looks thin, small, however, that may only be in comparison to me.* Aurora is tall and curvy and now feels big. *I'll start going to the gym a couple of times a week. Not now, in a few months' time, I can't spare the time away from Oliver right now.* Hannah, Aurora is sure, has been more rotund, especially in the face. Hannah has given up wearing make-up most of the time, has stopped straightening and tinting her hair, which Aurora thinks is a good thing, she likes the ruddy curls which result. She's begun dressing more casually; the layers of polo neck, pullover and fleece bulk her out, however Aurora can still see the snapping thinness at Hannah's wrists.

    Hannah has been encouraging Aurora to talk about her return to work and somehow they've come round to the Everidges and the discovery of the bones. 'It must have been awful for the mother,' says Aurora, the coffee hot and bitter on her tongue, real coffee with cream, the way she likes it. 'Thinking it might have been her child, even for a short while. If I ever lost Oli, I couldn't …

It would be unendurable. I don't know how she carries on.' The other woman does not reply, her attention moving back and forth between the grey on grey scene outside and the child on his playmat. Oli smiles, Hannah does not smile back. Aurora prompts, 'Don't you think?'

'Yes, I guess.'

'Of course, you wouldn't understand, not having a child. I didn't know, until I had Oliver, it changes everything.'

'Yes.'

Aurora is flustered, hot. Hannah knows more than anyone (except Max) how it changed things, how Aurora struggled. At first. She's making up for it now. *I'm a good mother now.* 'The poor woman,' she says, not entirely certain she's talking about Yvonne Everidge anymore.

Hannah is looking down at the coffee mug she's gripping between her two hands, 'There's something a bit odd about her, though, a lack of emotion somehow?'

'Odd?' Aurora retorts. 'She's lost her daughter, of course she's acting weird. She's probably only just holding it together. Someone's taken her daughter.'

'Have they?'

'What other explanation is there? The dad or some Schedule One, it has to be.'

'Schedule One?'

'Someone convicted of an offence against children.'

'Mrs Everidge could have ...' Hannah's voice slows, each word carefully placed, 'She could have done something. Killed ... an accident ...'

Aurora storms in, 'No way, no way, she's a mother, she couldn't have.' *I'm a good mother now.* 'If you haven't had a baby, you don't get it.'

There's a moment's silence, then Hannah shrugs, finishes her drink, says she should be going. Aurora checks the clock, ten minutes and Max will be back from his Saturday morning footie,

Bringing Ben as instructed. I'll not have my plan disrupted. She asks about Hannah's week. Her shoulders sag, her replies are concise. She's seeing clients. She's doing some research for Lawrence's book to get money. She's got her case study started. Her mother has gone to stay with one of her cousins. 'Is he alright?' her gaze comes to rest on Oliver.

Aurora looks over, her son is chewing on a wooden farm animal (certified safe for being put in the mouth). 'He's fine. Aren't you my love? Yes, you are, aren't you?' Her tone lilts and Oli responds, clapping his hands together.

'He's making a strange noise.'

'Is he?' She listens, can't hear anything unusual.

'A gurgling. Hasn't he been sick? Maybe he's choking. Don't you think you should do something, pick him up or something?' Hannah's voice is taut, her body pulled in.

'What? Nonsense.' She goes over and wipes her son's face with a tissue, there's a bit of snot and spit up, nothing to get excited about.

'They really are very fragile, aren't they, babies? One swipe and they're broken. I mean one misplaced something and they're a gone-er.'

'I used to worry about that, but they're really more robust than you think.' *I'm a good mother now.* She bends down and sniffs, he needs changing. She picks him up and he squeals. She turns. Hannah has her hands over her ears, her eyes screwed shut. 'Are you OK?'

Hannah opens her eyes, swiftly stands and backs up to the French windows, her arms tightly crossed, mutters, 'It's the crying, it goes right through me.'

'He wasn't crying. He didn't want to be taken away from his toys that's all.' She softens her response with a smile. She's irritated by Hannah's behaviour, has to remind herself of the woman's past kindnesses, and that it won't be long before Ben is here. She'll be shot of her then, will be able to enjoy time with her son. She hugs him close and rubs her nose into his warm soft neck, says she has to go and change him, asks Hannah to stay while she does so. When it looks like Hannah might flee, Aurora adds, 'Please, I won't be long.' She is rewarded by a stiff acquiescence.

* * *

Hannah is glad to be away from the over-heated dazzling kitchen and into the muted colours and cold of the outside, even if it is in the company of Ben and with the knowledge that this was all part of Aurora's little project. *Her project to what? Cheer me up? Get me away from Maya? Not that she's been in touch since death came a calling.* It takes less energy to submit to Aurora when she's got a plan than to resist. *And at least it gets me away from that enormous baby and its cooing parents.*

One good thing about Ben is he doesn't immediately demand attention or talk. He has a companionable way of walking next to her which is reassuring. She has an image of herself as a discarded balloon being blown hither and thither, and Ben being the tether, the only thing stopping her floating away and quickly losing height to be dragged into the churning steel cogs of the sea below. When the waves hit the sea defences at the base of the cliff, where they are walking, she can feel the vibration through the path under her feet, hear the boom echoing up to her. It is invigorating. The sea's fury is her own. 'Aurora's getting impossible to talk to,' she volleys forth. 'She's like a lioness defending her cub, even when there's no threat, anything I say about mothers she takes as a personal insult.'

'She's had a tough time,' says Ben mildly. 'It's good to see her enjoying Oliver.'

I've had a tough time, can't you see? 'She used to be more open, to hearing stuff, about how I'm feeling.'

'Then that's not easy for you.'

No it isn't. And, oh my lord, what an ugly kid, an ugly, ugly kid. 'I don't get it, I don't get it, why bring a child into this shitty world, just to be battered and hurt and let down?' Her hand clenches into a fist, a battering fist.

'I suppose Aurora, and Max, think they can protect Oli from most of it.'

'They won't be able to. It's the parents who do most of it, anyway.'

'Is that right?'

Hannah makes an effort to calm herself and say with more humour, 'To mis-quote Larkin, it's your mum and dad who fuck you up.'

'He may have had a point, though it doesn't always have to be so. At least, not entirely so.'

She stops, 'Is that right?'

He faces her. He's wrapped up, his black hat has ear flaps and is pulled low over his brow, his skin is white, his nose and cheeks are pink veined from being chafed by the wind. His dark eyes, they are searching through her. He pulls his hand out of his glove and touches her cheek with his dainty fingers. 'What's happened?'

Boom. It ricochets through her. Dislodges. 'I don't know, I don't know.' A small bird flaps behind her sternum desperate for release. Tears are threatening, they too are caught. She is caught, in a grip, he won't let go and he is hurting her, inside. 'I don't remember, not clearly, I think he hurt me. She let him.'

'Who?'

Dad. Mum. She shrugs. 'I'm wrong, I'm wrong.' *To say it. To think it.* 'Ignore me.'

Again the intense look, the gentle touch, he shakes his head. 'I think that's what's happened too much already. Tell me about it Hannah, tell me what went on.'

She pushes away his hand, laughs harshly, 'Nothing, nothing went on. Now are we going to have lunch or not?'

'Hannah, tell me.'

'No.' Boom. She starts walking and shouts back, 'You coming?' She's ravenous. They're headed to a little café on the front in North Bay, a particular favourite of Ben's which serves local and organic produce and where the cakes and bread are baked on the premises.

On the way over, in between being buffeted by Arctic blasts and easy silences, they've talked about what's been going on in their lives. Ben says his private practice now includes a contract with the university and is going well. She can hear his enthusiasm for his work. It reminds her of her own eagerness when she thinks of her own clients, only hers gets tainted by reservations about her abilities. *Doesn't his ever?* He's talking about his first few times volunteering with a conservation group, clearing up and maintaining paths through a local wood, when she breaks in, awkwardly, to ask him, 'Don't you ever worry about getting it wrong?'

'There's a guy there, a ranger from the North Yorkshire Moors park, he knows what he's doing.'

'I don't mean in the woods, I mean with your clients. You always come across as so confident.'

'Do I?' He pauses. 'I suppose it comes with time and experience. And that's not to say I don't sometimes wonder what I'm doing, feel uncertain, I think it's part and parcel of being a therapist. It's more a confidence in the process, we'll get there in the end.'

'Wherever there might be.'

'Exactly. And I don't always know where *there* is going to be, it's not for me to define, it's for my client to work it out for themselves, preferably with me. I remember when I was starting out, though, I did have terrible moments of self-doubt, I thought I had to know, had to know what was coming next, what the outcome should be. I think I've become better at relinquishing control.'

'I certainly don't feel in control. I think I ought to be driving it all a bit more somehow.'

'It's a balance, I want to create the space, a safe, containing space, where things can happen, that's the bit I need to control. After that, well, there's two of us in that room, and we both play our part. You'll find your way.'

'Will I?'

'Certainly, whether it is continuing as a counsellor or not.'

Not continue as a counsellor? How dare he suggest it? I want to be a counsellor, a good one, more than anything. 'So you think I should stop?' she says sharply.

'I didn't say that.'

Only it's what she's heard. Crossness quickens her pace as they turn the corner on the Marine Drive and the full force of the wind slams into them. It's difficult to talk for a while. She can't maintain her rapid gait; it makes no difference anyway, Ben comfortably keeps up with her, her point is lost on him. She asks him whether he's seen Maya recently, *Because I bloody haven't.* He'd grown up a few doors away from Rose and her daughter Maya, and takes a brotherly interest in the young woman. *Blind, as some brothers might be, to her calculating, as Izzie terms it, nature.* Ben says Maya is in France visiting her wealthy father and his family. *No wonder Rose was reticent about Maya when I last saw her. She doesn't talk much about it, but I get the feeling she's none too happy when Maya sees her father. Of course, she gets terribly spoilt, and Rose can't hope to match what gets heaped on her daughter. But I'm guessing there's some guilt in there, Maya's father was married when Rose had her affair with him. Guilt and shame, they are terrible things.*

'She gave the impression it was all over between the two of you when I asked,' Ben says tentatively.

She did? The bitch. You asked? You're interested enough to ask?

He continues, 'I think it's probably wise. Maya can be a bit thoughtless at times.'

How dare you try to interfere? What's it got to do with you who I see? Pompous git.

'I'm concerned about you, Hannah.'

Really? Why?

'It's a tough time for you.'

Because I'm the grieving daughter? She knows what grieving daughters ought to feel. *Is that why you're bothering about me?* She's faintly disappointed. Like when people ask her how her mother is. *Why don't you ask her yourself? Oh that's right, you've never met her. It's me you know. What about me?* she thinks, even as a more courteous, more appropriate response comes out of her mouth. She doesn't reply to Ben. She changes the subject, probes him about Theo's intentions towards Lawrence. Ben knows Theo better than her, *Is he reliable, will he break Lawrence's heart?* It is Ben's turn to be evasive.

They reach the café, a glorified wooden beach hut in pale blue and white, with a veranda overlooking the sea. Inside is warm, suffused with the smell of fried bacon and eggs. It is busy, it is only by luck she and Ben are able to slide into a booth next to a spray-splattered window. She says she will have the all-day breakfast and he goes to order at the counter. While he is away, Hannah stares out the glass by her side. The retreating waves have left the beach a mirror. Grey clouds against a pale blue sky float improbably on the sand. There's a smudge of silver pressed into one of them. The dark moon reappearing again.

Rose has invited her for the Awakening, Brede's festival. The goddess of healing and writing and the quickening of spring is Rose's description. Hannah knows Aurora is going, attends regularly. It feeds something spiritual in her, she says. She brings back tales of the others who go, sometimes Ben is there. When he is, he leads part of the rite. But Hannah hasn't been for a while. The first time she went, midsummer last year, she'd felt a bolt of energy, of assurance: a conviction of her place in the world, of her right to be in the world. She hasn't been back since. Still, she feels drawn to try again. Ben returns with their cups of coffee and she asks him whether he will be there. When he says yes, she thinks more seriously about going. 'Do you really believe?' she asks.

He doesn't reply immediately, his gaze also on something beyond the window, perhaps the shimmering crescent bathing in her sandy pool. 'It touches something in me,' he says quietly. 'There's a sense of harmony for me in making the connections with the changing seasons, in acknowledging the different aspects of me, the male and female aspects if you like to call them that.'

'What about the magic?'

He smiles, looks at her, 'I don't do spells, if that's what you mean, wave wands about, mix up potions. But there's magic in the world, isn't there? Things we don't understand. Magic between people. I believe that. Don't you?'

She is held by his eyes, the colour of iron-infused moorland water, she could dive in them, their coolness against her flushed skin.

'Breakfasts, two breakfasts, one veggie,' the waitress yells out and Ben turns to wave. The steaming food is delivered on two large plates with questions about what sauces they might have, whether they want more coffee and a final signing off, 'Enjoy!'

After the bustle, Hannah looks down at her meal. She can no longer eat it. If she puts anything into her mouth, she will choke, she will suffocate. *Come on,* she tells herself severely, *you're hungry, cut it up small and it'll be OK.* She tries. She still cannot lift a fork to her lips. Ben is digging in with gusto. She watches some egg drip from a piece of veggie sausage as he carries it to his mouth, and feels nauseous. He notices and asks her if she's alright. She nods and nibbles on some toast, the crumbs just about making it down her throat. It would be too ridiculous to tell him that consuming this ordinary array of foodstuffs will kill her. She tells him instead about the research she is doing for the biographical tribute Lawrence is planning for her father.

Ben encourages her with questions while still eating, only with less zest.

Finally she says, 'I don't feel anything, about him. I don't miss him. I don't understand when people say, "He's my father, of course I love him, whatever he might have done as a father." I don't feel anything. Never have, when I think about it. I ought to feel something. Don't you think?'

'You feel what you feel. That's the starting point, to feel what you feel.' He puts down his knife and fork. 'You're not eating.'

She crosses over her cutlery, 'I'm not hungry.'

'No, I mean, in general, you're not eating. You're losing weight.'

'A bit.' Another waitress comes over, this one has a pronounced Polish accent and exclaims over the uneaten meal, was it not good? Hannah assures her it was very good, only too much for her. The waitress begins to point out Hannah has eaten nothing at all, and would have stayed to remonstrate if Ben had not politely and firmly ushered her away. He asks Hannah if there is something she thinks she could eat now. She shakes her head. She tells him about the file she's found in her father's office, 'Everything else makes sense except for this one. It gives me the creeps.'

'A code?'

'What?'

'It sounds like maybe it's a code he's using.'

'What for?'

'Something he doesn't want others to know about? An undercover story he was working on?'

'My father an undercover reporter? I don't think so. Not his style.' The warmth is getting oppressive. *I'm going to faint.* She tells him she needs some air. She is revived a little once outside, *Though oh so tired, I'm not sure I can manage the walk home.* She closes her eyes, *It's all impossibly heavy.* Her arm is taken by Ben who guides her to a seat on the pavement. They sit side-by-side for a while.

'Let's get the open-top bus back,' Ben says. 'My treat.'

'What?' She's sleepy. In her dream his arm goes round her shoulder, squeezing it, he gently kisses the crown of her head and tells her not to worry, he's going to take her home.

CHAPTER 15

Date: 10/01/10 10:03
This message will be sent via BenedickCartwright@therapy.co.uk
To: LawrenceFielding@LawrenceFielding.co.uk
Subject: Re: Hannah
Hi Lawrence, as promised I saw Hannah. I am a bit concerned about her. Of course, I'd expect some fragility while she's grieving, and in some ways she's coping very well. I do think making sure she gets the support of friends is key, especially as it doesn't seem like she can rely on family. All the best, Ben

Date: 10/01/10 13:11
This message will be sent via
LawrenceFielding@LawrenceFielding.co.uk
To: BenedickCartwright@therapy.co.uk
Subject: Re: Hannah
Ben, unfortunately I'm busy this week, I've got an interview to do with Cameron, probably our next PM. But I will arrange a trip up, until then I hope I can rely on you to keep an eye. She looks to you in a funny sort of way. I hear you stayed over. I'm surprised she's grieving, she and old man Poole didn't have much of a relationship. Regards Lawrence.

Date: 10/01/10 17:30
This message will be sent via BenedickCartwright@therapy.co.uk
To: LawrenceFielding@LawrenceFielding.co.uk
Subject: Re: Hannah
Hi Lawrence
I thought I'd better stay over to assess how she was overnight, <u>and</u> to make sure she ate some breakfast! Purely platonic. Grief is a

very complex thing, can take people by surprise, is often hardest where the relationship is unresolved.
Think about coming soon. All the best, Ben

Date: 10/01/10 17:41
This message will be sent via BenedickCartwright@therapy.co.uk
To: URBORINGME@virgin.com
Subject:Re: Where the fuck are you?
Hi Maya, you know I don't check Facebook often and I was busy last night. I'm glad you're having fun out there. Ben x

Date: 10/01/10 17:54
This message will be sent via URBORINGME@virgin.com
To: BenedickCartwright@therapy.co.uk
Subject:Re: Where the fuck are you?
What d'ya mean busy? You still haven't told me where you were. I text you too, a gazillion times. Not that I can't guess where you were, with Hannah, strays with broken wings are just your thing. You could at least choose someone who's a bit better looking and isn't a complete gonzo. I'll be back soon, then we'll see about it all.

Date: 10/01/10 18:02
This message will be sent via BenedickCartwright@therapy.co.uk
To: URBORINGME@virgin.com
Subject:Re: Where the fuck are you?
Maya
Don't be unkind. Who I spend time with is none of your business. You'd planned to spend a month with your father, I think that would be best.
Ben

Date: 10/01/10 18:06
This message will be sent via URBORINGME@virgin.com
To: BenedickCartwright@therapy.co.uk
Subject:Re: Where the fuck are you?
Fuck you!

CHAPTER 16

'What do you think about false memory syndrome?'

Sometimes – often – Julia catches her off-balance, not knowing what to say. On such occasions Hannah tries to imagine what Orwell or Izzie would say, rather than rely on her own instincts. 'What makes you ask?'

'There was something in the paper about it.'

Curious, if it's not about business Julia wouldn't normally pay any attention.

'Some bloke saying there is no evidence memories can be repressed and that experiments have shown people can be induced into recalling traumatic incidents which never happened. What do you think?'

'I've read about the experiments. I believe the participants were being *deliberately* induced by researchers to think an incident has occurred.' *I don't want to be talking about this.* Uneasiness burbles in the base of her stomach. *It's too close, too close.*

'Isn't that what you therapists are supposed to do?' she says with a mocking smile. Then with a tone which sounds grudgingly respectful, 'Only you haven't.' She faces front, at her most statuesque, encased in toughened bark, 'So you think memories can be repressed?'

'I think ...' Hannah begins cautiously. *Yes. Yes? Maybe.* 'I'm wondering ... I'm wondering what's troubling you?'

'Me? Nothing.'

Then what are you doing here?

'I just read something, that's all.'

'And it's stayed with you, you're troubled by it?'

'Not exactly troubled.'

Stay with her, don't push, Orwell's words come to mind. She waits.

Julia folds her arms tightly around her chest. 'Dreams, nightmares, only more when I'm awake than asleep,' her tone is uncharacteristically faltering.

All at once, her client comes into focus for Hannah, it's no longer as if she is seeing her through a telescope held the wrong way. She waits, breath shallow.

'I'm sure it's nothing.'

'Tell me, I'd like to hear anyway.'

Leaning forward, Julia rests her elbows on her knees, her eyes are squinting. 'It's not true, I mean we don't dream the truth.'

'I like stories, true or not,' Hannah says softly. They're held together in this moment, any ungainly move on her part and the connection will snap, the slender thread of a spider's web broken by an oblivious shin or elbow.

'It's a beautiful day, a summer day, hot. I'm sweaty, uncomfortable, feeling sick, bruised. I pick up a stone. It's covered in sticky red stuff. I drop it. Sometimes I run. Sometimes I can't.' She shrugs, gives a wonky smile. 'Stupid, eh?'

Wait, Hannah, wait. Someone is pressing down on her own chest, into her own mouth. *Stop, stop. Stay with Julia.*

'And Meech is there, daft mare, she's whining. Always whining.' Her voice becomes hardened, she shifts her posture, she's almost a stately elm again.

'Tell me about you and Meech. You're fond of her?'

'I wouldn't say that. We grew up together, always in each other's pockets.' She suddenly hums a few bars and then laughs, '"Coal Miner's Daughter", Loretta Lynn. Meech loves it. Not that we were. At least Meech's dad grafted. Scrap metal. Never made nothing of hisself. Mine never turned in a hard day's labour in his life. Made, and lost, all his money at the bookies. Is that ironic or predictable? 'Course Meech wasn't strong enough to get herself out of our estate. Not like me. I wasn't sticking around for no one, I was on my way. Didn't look back.' She smirks.

The thread has ruptured. The moment has gone. *I won't be able to drag her back now. It will wait for another day*, Hannah reassures herself. *The past is always there waiting for us. Didn't look back, Julia? The past is in front of us.*

CHAPTER 17

'Congratulations DS Akande. Theo, you've hit the jackpot, haven't you?' Hoyle's office is a plain, airless box halfway up a five-storey concrete tower, the triple-glazed windows shut tight against the fermenting gale and the traffic noise. On the walls are a romantic view of a Scottish glen in thick oils and a photo of Hoyle (at least ten years younger) with colleagues arrayed in DJs, cummerbunds and dicky-bows, drinks in hand, at a force dinner. It is hung just behind Hoyle's large head and is a good focus for Theo's gaze. He doesn't want to see Hoyle's heavy-lipped mouth chewing him over. The words are enough. *Missing girl. Missing paedo (unproven) with, according to Suze's niece who Harry spoke to, an inclination to take photos of pretty young girls. And now a twenty-five-year-old unexplained death.* 'So me lad, what's your next move?'

Not 'our', notice, even though technically the responsibility rests with the DI. Theo would like to ask for some advice, some support, but knows this would be unwise as well as not worthwhile, Hoyle's skills being marginally less than his negligible interest in the investigation. What he likes is results, simple and quick results, he doesn't like complex. 'If it smells like bacon then you're on a pig farm and up to your arse in shit,' is one of his phrases which he drags out periodically, usually at random. Theo blames the premature closure of his first case in Scarborough on Hoyle's impatience, the murder of the psychotherapist Dr Greene. *If I'd had enough time, I'd have got to the truth. But no, you wanted the easy option.* Theo works hard at keeping his dislike of Hoyle out of his face.

The DI is waiting, his hands, the size of hams, toy with a dagger-shaped silvered letter opener, 'Nothing, lad?'

Theo knows Hoyle could still do some damage to his career if he fancied it; as a laugh, his last before retirement. It doesn't take much to rile Hoyle into this kind of action. Theo has seen Harry

Shilling leave Hoyle's office and head to the Ladies in the hope of not being spotted crying. When he asked her about it, she said nothing had happened. Theo doesn't believe her. She fears saying something could jeopardise her promotion chances.

He rouses himself. He tells his superior he'll be going over to the Everidge's this afternoon – *Hadn't planned to, maybe I will now* – as something's come up from the IT search of Paul's hard drive. *Not true, but anything vaguely techie puts Hoyle off asking questions.* There's a lead on Alexi Kestle, *True, a sighting in Hull which DC Shilling is following up.* Then he goes on to list the pertinent elements of the pathologist's report on the remains: 'Male, probably in his twenties or thirties, slight build, reddy-blonde hair. He was wearing denim, cowboy boots and a thin leather tie. No wallet. No watch. He's been dead over two decades, decay, and some dismemberment, probably by foxes, will make identification difficult. Death was most probably a violent one given the state of the skull, though this might possibly have been due to a fall or, very improbably, post mortem with the action of rocks or tree branches. DC Chesters is working on an ID.'

'Ah the eager young Chesters. He'll go far.'

Theo has the impression Hoyle is saying this to irritate him, somehow knowing Theo finds Chesters' excitability wearing and thinks Shilling should go further.

The DI puts down the miniature dagger, maybe he has given up on going for the kill. He sits upright and his large leather chair creaks forward to accommodate his new stance. He smiles with what could be a genuine warmth. 'Good, good,' he starts slowly, then, 'It's the girl, the girl I'm worried about, Theo. We can't have her missing for too much longer, we need to find her.'

'I am aware of that.'

'It's awkward for us, of course, but the main thing is think of how the mother must be feeling, DS Akande, think of her.'

Theo is flabbergasted. He would have sat there a long time trying to work out Hoyle's latest incarnation if the DI hadn't dismissed him with a curt, 'I think we're done.'

Instead of going back to his desk, Theo grabs his coat and keeps on walking out of the back of the station down a snicket and into the cemetery. He doesn't need reminding that they need to find Victoria Everidge. *Whatever has happened to her, if she's still alive, she will have been traumatised. Poor little thing.* He can see her scared and alone. He wanders along the paths between the gravestones, mostly Victorian or Edwardian, some elaborate, decorated with carved anchors, some listing the demise of generations. Dead babies, dead children. 'Passed away.' 'Fell asleep.' Their deaths were probably not as tranquil and nor would Victoria's have been if she has met it. *Poor little thing.*

He comes to the restored mortuary with its extravagant brickwork and tiling, and realises he had been hoping to find Suze there as she often uses it to sit quietly and smoke during her breaks. Suze, normally a mine of local information, has not been able to offer anything on this one, *Could she be avoiding me because of it?* He sits down inside on one of the tiled benches which jut from the walls. He is glad to have some peace from the rawness of the wind. He checks his personal phone, another email from Lawrence asking him to check up on Hannah, make sure she is eating. Theo turns off his phone without replying. *I have my own victim to worry about and Victoria is in more danger than Hannah.*

He stomps back to the CID room, nevertheless feeling refreshed from having escaped for a short while. *I'll find out how Chesters is going on, be encouraging to the young man, it will be my good turn for the day.* Before he can set off to find the DC, he gets a call from reception. Paul Everidge is down there, he says Victoria wants to come home and can Theo help?

CHAPTER 18

Paul Everidge is seventeen years old, so technically Theo can talk to him without calling in his parents or an appropriate adult. However, Paul looks young, doesn't have any of the bruising assurance of most of the seventeen-year-olds who end up at the police station. Theo suggests phoning Ian or Yvonne. Paul refuses. He will only talk to Theo. They go to one of the interview rooms, drab and serviceable with its small window high up. Theo switches on the harsh light. Paul is already talking, they stand awkwardly, he wants them to go, quickly, pick up Vicky who is at Hull railway station, waiting for them. Paul'd had a phone conversation with her twenty minutes previously. He'd rushed over at once, certain Theo would know what to do. Paul's anxiety lines his face, he licks at dry lips. Can't Theo get them a police car, with a blue light and a siren? They have to get there fast because his sister is already scared and lonely.

Theo makes his decision. He calls Harry, ascertains her search for Kestle has been unsuccessful and she hasn't left the city yet. He tells her to go to the station and find Vicky, then call him. Meanwhile, he ushers Paul out to the car park and into his car; no blue light and siren, but a sporty engine and Theo has done his advanced driving training, he knows he can make the journey quicker than any marked car.

The drive is completed mostly in silence. Theo puts on the local music radio so there's a background of seventies and eighties hits interspersed by ads for a drain-cleaning firm and local wedding venues. About ten minutes out of Scarborough, DC Shilling calls, Theo picks it up hands-free; she has Vicky, the little girl seems unhurt and Harry has taken her to the station café where she's drinking a milkshake and eating chips. After that, Theo feels some of the stiffness go from his shoulders, while he maintains his focus on the road ahead. Paul is perched forward on the passenger seat, as if his concentration will get them there faster.

The road is flat as it follows the coast, though it twists and switches from single to dual carriageway and back again. The dusk is not hanging around. The undulating Wolds gently rise and swell to their right. For a brief moment, the tops are crowned in gold, pink spits up into the base of the clouds, then the brightness is gone. Theo switches on his headlights. His priority now is to get them there safely. He allows part of his mind to thumb through some of the possibilities. *Did Victoria leave of her own accord with her brother's help? Surely it would have been too complicated for an eight-year-old girl and an unworldly lad to organise, especially over all this time? Then someone else has been keeping her somewhere? Who? Ray? Kestle? A person or persons unknown?* He slows for traffic, another part of his brain calculating speed and braking distances. *She's safe.* He smiles. *I'm not going to find a small broken body. And, on the surface at least, she is unharmed.*

It's all nose to tail from here on in and Theo switches on his sat-nav. He doesn't like the thing, only he doesn't know his way and, when asked, Paul says he doesn't know where he is either, before going back to his silent vigil. They pull into the station's short-term parking and Paul is out of the car before Theo has fully stopped. Theo doesn't bother with a ticket, hoping his police permit in the window will be noticed. He has to scurry to catch up the youth. Even so, Paul gets to the café first and a lass with brown pigtails bounces up and is gathered into her brother's arms as Theo arrives. *Should I be allowing this? Is Paul a suspect?* But watching them he is convinced of the genuineness of the relief and pleasure they display in greeting each other.

Harry is more chipper than she has been in a while, almost maternal as she clucks around Paul and Victoria, getting drinks and snacks for them all after they sit down together at the table. Theo needs a coffee, he also needs to think. *Where to take his brood? Paul had said Victoria wants to come 'home'. Is that Ray's or Yvonne's? And what if 'home' is where the problems are? I'm not qualified to say.* He will hand all this over to a specialist team for the questions to be asked of the child as soon as he can. Now, however, he is in charge. *It's my call.* Paul introduces Victoria to Theo and says he will take her home. She smiles, yawns, looks tired.

'Is it what you want, Victoria?' asks Theo carefully, unsure of what the right enquiry might be.

She nods, leans her head against Paul's shoulder, her eyelids droop. Her brother provides the words for her, 'We'll be home soon, Vicky, you should see the sergeant's driving, it's amazing, won't be long and you can be tucked up in your own bed.'

'And tomorrow I can go to school?' she says quietly.

Paul is hesitant, 'Maybe.'

'I want to see my friends. I miss my friends.'

'We'll get them over, if you can't go to school straight away.'

'And it's all over now, isn't it Paul? We can just forget it. We won't talk about it again.'

Again Paul's voice is uncertain, 'You might have to talk a bit about it. People have been worried about you, the sergeant and everyone have been looking for you.'

She shakes her head, 'Don't want to talk about it. It's all over now. We can put it away and forget it.' She's asleep, the second milkshake untouched in front of her. Theo takes another gulp of coffee before picking her up and carrying her to the car, her head weighty against his chest, his chin tickled by her silky brown pigtails. He is reminded of having one of his nieces in his arms, slumbering after a day out. Paul sits in the back, holding his sister's hand as she flops against the seat belt Theo insists she wears. In the front, as Theo drives, Harry makes phone calls. She ensures the family liaison officer who has been with Yvonne before is at the Everidges' house. She arranges for a DI from York and a specialist team to come over the next day to work out how to handle the questioning of Victoria. Then she has to talk to the family liaison officer again to emphasise that Yvonne will have to accept a police-arranged doctor looking at her child tonight and, no, it can't wait till morning. She talks briefly to Hoyle and Theo can hear his brusque responses, he sounds pleased. He has something to tell the press, at last.

The Everidges' drive is bathed in light when they arrive and Yvonne, with Ian close behind, rushes out as Theo stops the car. She is opening the back door and unbuckling her daughter as the engine cuts out. Victoria stirs and submits to her mother's embrace. She mutters something. Theo thinks he hears, 'Sorry Mum.' Yvonne shushes her, 'Don't say anything, honey.' She sounds brittle. She extracts her daughter and walks into the house without another word.

It is left to Ian to thank Theo and Harry and to try and prise the story out of the taciturn Paul, who shrugs away his father's queries. 'OK,' Ian says finally, giving his son's shoulders a quick squeeze. 'It's late, you've had a bit of an adventure, eh? Let's get to bed and then we can talk about it in the morning. That'll be alright, won't it sergeant?'

Theo agrees it will be and then it is just him and Harry left on the kerb. He takes her home and goes back to his house. It is after showering and turning in himself that he remembers Victoria's words at the station and he wonders, *Why didn't she say she'd been missing her mother?*

CHAPTER 19

Aurora is about to leave when the call comes through from reception. She is already thinking about the journey home and seeing Oli. Max is in charge today, of getting her – *their* – son to his grandmother's and back again, of feeding him and bathing him. She had planned to be back for Oli's bath, for the moment before bed when she can hold him, warm and clean, and tell him a story, his eyes watching her as if she is the only person in his world. And now the phone is ringing.

She looks at the clock. It's only touching five o'clock. *'BM', before motherhood, I wouldn't have hesitated in answering, wouldn't have flinched at working on.* And she doesn't want to have changed (though she has) so she picks up the receiver. A Ray Marchant is downstairs asking to see her, has she a minute? She swears silently. She agrees to see him. Her day has gone well up till now. She has successfully facilitated a mediation session this morning between separating parents warring over what it should cost to bring up their children. *I haven't lost my touch in handling that kind of situation.* She has drafted some letters this afternoon. The thought of staying late, *and staying late to see Ray Marchant*, flattens her spirits. She does, however, raise a smile when she greets him. She takes him into her room, even offers him coffee, though is heartily glad when he refuses. *Perhaps he won't stay long and I can still get my early train.*

She remembers him as a confident, brash man. He has lost his bravado, his face is more weary, a patch of white looks as if it is spilt paint over hair the colour of his daughter's. She has to prompt him to speak. He makes a couple of false starts before saying she's probably seen on the TV what's been happening with Vicky.

'She's at home now.' Aurora recalls her relief that this time there wouldn't be a sad procession behind an under-size coffin. She had been wondering, in the snatched moments when she hasn't had to be thinking about anything else, what the story is.

Where had the little girl been? Who had taken her there? What had happened to her during the month of her disappearance? None of this has been reported on the news.

Ray nods, 'She's with Yvonne. They're not letting me see her.' Sadness nips his face.

'I'm sure it is only temporary, until they've sorted out what happened.'

'Ian tells me, on the q-t like, she's not saying nothing.'

'At least she's safe now.'

'Maybe.' The whites of his eyes are cloudy with pink. 'It wasn't nothing to do with me. I know people are thinking it was, but it wasn't.' He pauses. 'You believe me don't you Mrs Harris?'

She has to struggle to keep her suspicion out of her features, out of her voice, summon up the professional front she used to assume effortlessly, 'It's not for me to say Mr Marchant. I'm sure the police are clearing things up as quickly as they can.'

He loses any substance in his core, folds in on himself, 'If only they'd let me see her, I know she'd tell me what happened. My poor little lass.'

There is silence. Finally Aurora breaks it, 'What is it you want Mr Marchant?' She's missed her train. She's cross about it, cross with the man in front of her, who she is more than willing to believe is hiding a bizarre plot to keep his daughter from her mother.

He rouses himself, his voice is stronger, 'You were so helpful before, got me access, I want you to do it again.'

She takes no time to respond. 'I couldn't do that, not while the investigation is going on. Once the full details are known, well then, we'll see. If you've had nothing to do with your daughter's disappearance, then I'm sure access will be resumed as before. There's no reason for it to be altered.'

His head snaps upwards. 'If? I'm telling you I haven't done nothing. It's her, Yvonne, I don't know what she's been up to, but she's been up to something.'

Aurora is reminded of her morning's clients: it's not me, it's her; it's not me, it's him. She sighs, *Me and Max are not immune to such sniping.* She focuses on Ray's face, sees the wretchedness, feels a smidgen of compassion. *Anyway, I'm on my way to missing another train, I have to get him out of here.* However, before she can say anything he's continuing, something about Yvonne's car, how it's got itself into a state. 'She's been driving long distances, had some scrapes, dents on the door. Ian asked me to have a look.' He concludes, 'She's been up to something.'

Aurora sighs louder and more definitively. 'Maybe she's been driving round looking for her daughter. As I've said, there is really nothing I can do until the police have finished their investigation. Afterwards, if there's a problem to be sorted, come back to me.' She mentally crosses her fingers hoping he won't (be able to or need to). 'Now I have to go, I have a train to catch.'

He opens his mouth, maybe to protest, then closes it and nods. He leaves. If a chin could be said to be dragging along the ground, his could be described that way. Aurora gets ready to go. She wishes she could have a shower before returning home, to wash away Ray Marchant and to ensure she doesn't contaminate her son.

CHAPTER 20

'You're not here to ask questions, DS Akande,' says DI Pippa Wiltshire. 'You're here to listen and learn.' She heads up the specialist team from York brought in to question Victoria about what happened to her.

Theo had met Pippa at the fag-end of his first case in Scarborough, the murder of Dr Themis Greene. He had got on well with DI Wiltshire then. A trim, pear-shaped woman, with short, dark hair, who habitually wears navy-coloured trouser suits while working. She'd struck Theo before as being calm and jovial. He is now encountering her abrasive edge.

They are standing in the kitchen at SC4Tea. It could once have been a bathroom with creamy tiles on one wall and a dumb-waiter to bring up hot water from the scullery below. Theo hasn't been back in the building since his investigation into Dr Greene's death which had occurred here. Pippa had wanted a neutral setting for her talks with the Everidges and Hannah had brokered a deal whereby they could use one of the therapy rooms. This will be their fourth meeting with Victoria and her mother, and it's ten days since the little girl came home.

'Slowly, slowly, it's how we'll tackle this,' DI Wiltshire had said right from the start. And Theo can see the sense in this approach. Each encounter has been under an hour and Pippa has spent most of the time chatting to the little girl about her likes and dislikes. Most of the time Victoria is articulate, until, that is, near the middle of the last session, when the DI dropped in a question about the recent Christmas. Then the youngster was suddenly tired, didn't want to talk anymore, was clamouring to go home.

And her gaze was immediately on her mother. It was as if she was searching for answers, the answers she was supposed to give. Victoria's a smart girl, no question.

In Theo's opinion, Yvonne has shown a remarkable lack of interest in finding out what happened to her daughter during those four weeks. *She has not helped the questioning along, not encouraged her daughter to say a little more. And at the first opportunity on each occasion has closed the proceedings down.*

'All conjecture,' Pippa had said this morning when Theo had raised these observations with her. Then she had fixed him with something akin to a glare, 'You don't have children, Theo, you have absolutely no conception of what it would be like to have your daughter go missing. Yvonne Everidge is merely protecting Victoria from more upset.'

'So a mother can never be a perpetrator?'

'I didn't say that. But I'm the one with experience and training here, it means I can read the situation with some degree of certainty. When the mother begins to trust us, me, we'll begin to get somewhere. And there's no space in the room for someone giving off counterproductive signals to either mum or daughter.' She sips from her mug, the astringent scent of ginger emanating from her herbal tea. It's then she delivers her decree about Theo's role.

I'm only here on sufferance, I know.

She smiles, a tight, sharp smile. Noises from the front door and hallway tell them Victoria and Yvonne have arrived with their family liaison officer. 'Shall we go?'

They cross the landing, where a weak sun through an arched, stained-glass window is throwing a mosaic of reds, blues and yellows onto the floor. They mount a short flight of stairs and go into the room where Victoria and Yvonne are getting comfortable. It is a high-ceilinged space with a bay window and a fireplace, a reminder of the swanky residence this used to be. As with most of the building, the decoration is bland, there is one picture on the wall, a large-format photo on canvas of a shady path disappearing into a wood. The smell is of polish and carpet shampoo.

This is a training room and there is enough furniture to accommodate upwards of twenty people, plus there is a flip chart on a stand and a whiteboard on the wall. Theo has already helped

Pippa pull forward a settee and a couple of armless, sitting-room-style chairs to create a more intimate setting in the middle of the floor. The family liaison officer, a middle-aged PC who has the archetypal maternal demeanour, sits quietly in the corner behind the Everidges. Yvonne is upright on the couch with Victoria curled up beside her. Pippa sits in the chair directly in front of them, Theo in the one slightly to one side.

'I shouldn't have brought her,' Yvonne says immediately. 'She's not well. But she,' she jerks her head backwards, 'said it was better to try just for a little while.'

Victoria does indeed look peaky. Her complexion is pale and she is lying with her head on her mother's knees. Her eyes, dark like her father's, are huge and round. They are open. *Alert.*

After thanking Yvonne and Victoria for coming and asking some solicitous questions about the nature of the illness and getting perfunctory answers from the mother, Pippa begins to try and cajole something out of the daughter. Even on subjects which she would normally happily talk about, such as school, her friends, weekend outings, the little girl is taciturn.

'I imagine it must be hard to catch up on the school work you missed when you were away,' says Pippa gently. 'Are you finding it hard?'

Victoria doesn't respond, she looks up at her mother.

Seeking permission?

Yvonne strokes her daughter's cheek and the smiles which are exchanged between them are genuinely warm and tender. 'Don't worry honey,' she says softly. 'You don't have to say anything you don't want to.' Mrs Everidge's brittleness returns as she snaps at Theo, 'And you wouldn't have to if he'd done his job proper.'

Theo ignores the jibe. He is watching Victoria, she tenses.

'Yvonne,' Pippa says evenly, 'we all want the same thing, to ensure Victoria and other girls around here are safe. And to do that we need to find out what happened.'

'My daughter is safe.'

'Now, of course. But what about other little girls? We need to know, so we can be sure they are safe.'

'He wouldn't take anyone else would he?' says Yvonne, shooting another glare in Theo's direction.

Theo wants to shoot back, instead he says coolly, 'We followed up every lead, Mrs Everidge, very thoroughly.' He can see Pippa isn't pleased with even this intervention.

Yvonne is as taut as a bow string, 'Not thoroughly enough.' Her daughter no longer looks comfortably cradled in her lap and begins to push herself to seated. Instead she is pulled closer to her mother's bony chest. Yvonne coos, 'There, there, Victoria, you're not well are you my darling? We'll be going home soon.'

DI Wiltshire takes a deep breath, 'Mrs Everidge, perhaps if I could ask Victoria a couple of questions?'

'Mum, please.' Victoria's voice is unexpectedly strong, *With exasperation?* She tugs herself away and sits up straight. Her hair is pulled back with a large clip this morning rather than in bunches.

She seems older, than she was at the session last week, than her eight years.

Victoria smooths down her top and clasps her hands into her stomach. 'I'm sorry DI Wiltshire,' she says, very politely, very clearly. 'I don't want to talk about it. I won't talk about it. I won't tell you what happened. I don't want to see you anymore. I'm fine. I would tell you anything I could to stop other girls being hurt, but I don't know anything. That's the truth. I want this to stop. Now.'

So it did. *It had to, I know that. Even so ...* Theo watches Yvonne leave, *You know more than you're letting on. Why?*

Pippa is furious. 'I thought I told you not to say anything. Don't you know when to take a direct order, DS Akande? You've set us back right to the beginning. Well done.'

Theo doesn't bother to argue. He lets the DI flounce out leaving him to wash up and lock up slowly. *No, other children may not be in danger, but how about Victoria?* He pulls his duffle closer around him as he begins to walk towards the station, the heat in the room had belied the chill outside. *Not my responsibility, not my responsibility,* he tells himself, not believing it for a moment.

Chapter 21

> Angry, *angry*, ANGRY. RAGING INSIDE. Keep the smile on your face, Hannah, don't let it slip. People don't, won't, understand. You must be sensible, rational. It is only a story.

Hannah looks back at the pages of writing she has done, scribbles, indecipherable, some of it, and wonders where it all comes from. *I don't remember writing half of it. And it is only a story.* That's what she tells herself. *His thing shoved in my mouth. The pain. Being torn apart. It all happened to some other little girl. Not Hannah. No. Not me.*

She closes her writing journal, afraid the written words might prove something. Might become concrete. As heavy as. Then she'd never lift them. Never stand up again and carry on. *Because that's what I'm good at, carrying on. People – parents, Lawrence, Steff and Rickie, Aurora, maybe even Ben – they all think what I'm good at is giving up, never getting to the finishing line, quite. Only they are wrong. What I'm good at is carrying on.* She puts her journal away, a velvet-covered bomb in her bedside drawer.

She goes downstairs in search. In search of something. Something to numb the pain. She rejects the knife, the bloodletting, and finds instead the bottle of wine, cheap and nasty. And when it's finished there's what's left of her mother's gin, her father's whisky. The flavours don't mix very well. After a while the taste doesn't matter anymore. She's lying down in the sitting room, the bright yellow walls, the cabbage-green upholstery she's collapsed on, the dark brown rococo-style occasional tables all begin to zing and clash. She feels nauseous. She closes her eyes.

She wakes. It's mid-afternoon. *I'm glad. Hours gone. I don't need to live them.* She stretches out her stiff limbs. She's cold. She gets unsteadily to her feet. Her mouth is dry. *I need to replace the* bottles. *I'll get some nice wine, wine Lawrence would approve of. Drink it to enjoy it.* She knows she won't. It's volume which matters. She uses the bathroom, notices her clothes look dowdy and ill-matched, does nothing about it. *I need a shower.* Instead she pulls on an old jacket, a woollen hat to hide her unwashed hair and her walking shoes. It all takes time. Nothing is easy. Her head and joints ache. She feels tired. Still she pushes herself towards the door. *I need a drink.*

On her way out, she finds the post. Most of it is junk, there are a couple of bills she shoves on the hall table and then there's a postcard from her mother. On one side is a cartoon of some sheep huddling together under a dark rain cloud. 'Wish You Were Here!' the caption says. On the reverse, Val Poole has written: 'Dear Hannah, having a lovely time. Weather good. Food excellent. You know your dad and I were always proud of you. See you soon. Love Mummy.'

Hannah drops it as if it has burnt her. She rushes out. *See you soon? Dad proud of me? Love Mummy? Love?* The words repeat and collide inside her already addled brain. *See you soon? Dad proud of me? Love Mummy? Love? Another story. Another fiction.* She's hurrying somewhere, anywhere, away from those words. She does not go in the direction of the shops. She goes down the cliff path, skidding against the chalky pebbles, trying to escape those words. *See you soon. Proud. Love.* Until she reaches the old South Bay lido, where the sea wall pushes out into the waves. She's run out of breath, her heart is bashing itself against the inside of her sternum. She holds onto the railings certain she'd fall if not.

It's drear, the water flat platinum, a mirror to the darkening sky. The cold eases itself around her inadequate clothing. Her fingers are rigid and raw. Beside her is the notice, twisted by the action of the waves. 'Danger from Heavy Seas' it warns. *Love? Proud? Love? I don't know what these words mean. I never felt it.*

She lets out a gasp, like she's been winded. *Now you're trying to re-write the story, only it's too late, it's far too late.*

The seagulls form a jury of grey-cloaked sages in the tumbling dusk. They silently glide in to take position, their muttering an integral part of the wind. *Judge me,* she voicelessly shouts at them. *I do not love my parents, though they love me. I am guilty. Judge me.* Their guttural sniggers skim the waves towards her. She stumbles away, the spit from the sea stinging her eyes. A tissue-paper version of the waxing moon, matte and without luminosity, rolls out from behind the castle headland which stands between south and north bays.

Walking helps. The solid, monotonous putting one foot in front of another. It brings a thought to her: *Talk to somebody. Text somebody.* She pulls out her phone. *Who? Lawrence? No, he couldn't cope with this. Ben? Maybe? No. I don't know how he feels about me.* Then it comes to her, she texts Izzie, 'Please can I talk to you soon?' She doesn't expect a response today, not on a Saturday, but the promise of a reply will lead her through the next hours: a moon-silvered path through a dense forest. Her mobile buzzes a few minutes later. 'Ring me Monday at 10.' It gives her a moment to aim for. *If I can get through until then. It's not so long. You can do it Hannah. You can.* She returns home slowly, avoiding anywhere she might be tempted to replenish her store of alcohol.

CHAPTER 22

Pippa has told Theo tersely, he is not welcome at any further meetings with Victoria and her mother and he won't be informed of future developments. He has to put it out of his mind as much as he can. A sociable weekend back in Manchester has been a distraction, now he is focusing on identifying the body; unearthed eighteen days ago by the A64, it still has no name.

Chesters has done a good job narrowing down a list of possible mispers from twenty-five years ago. The work now is in gathering information to try and puzzle out whether any of them could have ended up by the side of the road with their skulls battered in. Without viable fingerprints and nothing to match DNA to, it is about trying to dredge up people who might recall anything relevant from more than two decades ago. Thus far Chester and Theo have talked to: a sister whose brother went to buy cigarettes and never returned; a father whose son didn't come back from a trip to Spain; and a wife who thinks her errant husband had another family who he ran off to. It's dispiriting.

Then Suze tells him Alexi Kestle has turned up. Social services were supposed to inform him and hadn't got round to it. 'He's only been back a few days,' a harassed care manager says when Theo complains. Since his name hasn't come up in any of the conversations with Victoria, Theo would have preferred to let Kestle be. Hoyle disagrees, 'Where kiddies are concerned, we need to be seen to be doing everything, covering all potholes so we don't fall down any later on. Get over and have a word with him. Take Shilling. See how he reacts to a lassie.'

Theo puts it off. However, after another fruitless lead on the identity of the body, he and DC Shilling go to Westedge.

From the outside the house looks the same as it did when Theo last visited, unoccupied. It takes a long time for the front door to open, so long Theo begins to think there is indeed nobody home.

When it is pulled back, it is only by a few inches and there is a robust safety chain in place. Alexi Kestle takes several minutes to decide whether he will let them in, checking carefully the ID Theo and Harry present to the crack between door and doorstop. Eventually Kestle relinquishes his hold. He leads them into the front room and asks politely if they would like a drink. Neither of them do, but they've agreed beforehand that, if offered, they will accept and Harry will go into the kitchen with Kestle. She now, therefore, follows him through to the back of the house.

Theo sits on the hard sofa. Since it is such a gloomy day, Alexi has turned on the light, however, it is one of those early low-energy bulbs whose reach hardly goes beyond the shade; the heavy nets and curtains don't help either. The room is ordered. There are shelves filled with books either side of a fireplace breast, which holds a gas fire. Theo can see they are placed alphabetically, non-fiction in the one nearest the window, fiction in the one by his side. The non-fiction consists of several large-format coffee-table volumes on gardening, cookery and places in Germany, all in pristine condition. The novels are more thumbed. *Historical romances, so maybe the taste of the late Mrs Kestle?* He smiles to himself, *Shouldn't make assumptions.*

The mantelpiece holds an old-fashioned carriage clock plus one photo of Kestle and an elderly woman. Theo picks it up and studies it. The man is tall and broad, flabby around the waistband; beside the woman he is a giant. Today Alexi is conservatively dressed in blue trousers, collared-shirt and pullover, in the photo he is wearing an identical outfit with a blue tie added. In contrast the woman is a bright bird, wearing a jacket in pinks and yellows over a long cerise skirt. Theo searches for and does not find a family resemblance, the man has a large domed head, sparse in wispy light-coloured hair, the woman's features are petite, pretty even, her white hair still thick. He replaces the frame.

There are two hard-stuffed armchairs in the little bay and a low wooden table in the centre of floor. The carpet is brown, the walls beige. Another bookcase holds photo albums, neatly labelled by year. On the wall opposite the fireplace is a photo of the moors enlarged on canvas, the black silhouette of a leafless tree stands in purple heather and brown bracken against a stormy sky. Theo rather likes it. He is about to go over and pick out a photo album to see if the landscape photographer might be Alexi, when the man bustles in with a tray set with cups, sugar bowl and milk jug on a scallop-edged cotton cloth. Harry is behind him with the teapot. She will later describe the neat, clean kitchen and the slow careful silent placing of all the accoutrements on the tray. She didn't get the impression her presence was of particular significance. Theo seats himself back down on the sofa. Until this moment, he realises, the air has smelt of polish; Alexi brings in a waft of aftershave which Theo identifies as something generic from a high-street chemists.

 Kestle serves them tea, both with milk and sugar added, since he did not check their preferences. He then settles himself on the armchair left vacant by Harry. The large man waits expectantly, a little forward, his eyes focused on Theo's right shoulder.

 'You've been away, Mr Kestle,' Theo rouses himself.

 One unhurried nod and then the gaze returns to the right shoulder.

 'People were concerned for your safety.'

 A repeat of the nod.

 'Could I ask where you went?'

 A slight puzzlement knots the skin across his forehead, 'Why?'

 Why indeed. *Should have brought my fishing rod.* 'It would be helpful.'

 'I don't have to tell you?'

 'No.'

 'I won't then.' This is said without rancour, in a measured tone. Kestle has a voice a bit higher in register than would be expected from his size. However, it's not excessively shrill.

Attempts to draw out an answer with comments such as, 'It would really assist us if you could be more forthcoming, Mr Kestle,' get nowhere. Alexi remains unperturbed in his refusals to say anything further. Theo considers the pros and cons of inviting him to the police station. *Would the scare factor work in this case? Do I have grounds for arrest if he still refuses?* He's also reluctant to stoke further local rumours about Kestle. *Is it even my case anymore?* He feels his energy being dampened down.

They might have left after finishing their tea, if Harry hadn't mentioned how much she likes the picture on the wall. This elicits a broad smile, so she pursues the theme, asking him if he is the photographer, and, when he says yes, she adds more praise, probing his interest further. He takes out an album to show her, gradually turning the pages, giving details for each picture on what lens was used, the shutter speed and exposure, rather than of the location and memories associated with it. Theo feels like he has become invisible, an irrelevancy, as he listens to the deliberate even voice reciting the technical information. Then a very slight shifting in Harry's expression and body – a tautening – alerts him to something. In the pause while Kestle turns the page, she asks, 'Do you know these girls?'

Alexi looks up blankly.

Harry adds gently, 'Are they friends of yours?'

'Friends?' His fingers tap at the sides of album, he could be considering a difficult mathematical puzzle rather than Harry's query.

'Do they live around here?'

He nods, tries to go back to his ponderous recitation, tightly holding down the sheet which has got him into the situation of being questioned.

Harry interrupts, 'And they like you taking their photo?'

He shrugs.

'Why did you take their photos?'

It's a good while before he responds. Finally he says quietly, 'They were running and dancing.' A sadness seeps into his face, the pleasure of showing Harry his album has gone, he closes it. He continues, 'It's not easy to photograph people who are moving.'

DC Shilling looks briefly over at Theo. He mouths, 'Camera', and she wonders aloud whether she might see Mr Kestle's equipment. Again Alexi grins, it's quite an attractive smile for someone so unattractive. He leads her out the room and up the stairs. Once again forgotten, Theo follows to the hall where he can hear the man's heavy tread and then his convoluted explanations, though not the exact words. Theo knows Harry can take care of herself, is undoubtedly a match for the lumbering Mr Kestle, even so he wants to be in ear shot in case trouble erupts. It does not.

Later Harry will describe the upstairs, two bedrooms, doors tightly shut, a box room and a bathroom. The decor is mainly creams, beige and brown, though another of Alexi's photos adorns the landing's wall – this one of a waterfall surrounded by succulent ferns. His cameras and lenses are all tidily stored in the box room where there is also a computer and an A3 colour printer. After being given a mercifully brief tour of his equipment, Harry said she would like to use the bathroom so is able to report it is dated but clean, there is no medication stored in the cabinet above the sink beyond the usual pain killers, and those in small numbers, and Alexi is a wet shaver. She also manages quick peeks into the bedrooms, one contains a bed, the other quite a flash sound system and TV; both are tidy and plain.

While the DC is doing her surreptitious inspection of the upstairs, Alexi returns downstairs, and, ignoring Theo standing at the foot of the stairs, he takes the tea things back into the kitchen where he begins to wash and then dry up. He finishes as Harry reaches the hall. Theo says they will be going now, but if Mr Kestle wants to let them know where he's been for the last four weeks, he can contact them via phone or email. He hands over a business card with his contact details on. Alexi studies it for a moment and then follows them to the door. He says goodbye, he betrays no emotion at their departure and, when he closes the door behind them, they can hear a bolt and the chain being put in place.

Theo is surprised to be suddenly confronted by a brisk breeze, someone out of sight shouting the instruction 'don't be late' to another unseen somebody and the rev of an engine. It's as if he's been released from aspic. As they get into the car and he pulls away, Harry fills him in on what she saw of the house. He asks her about the photos of the girls.

'They were of girls from around here. I recognised the housing behind and one of them was Suze's niece.'

'Sexual?'

She shakes her head. 'Rather beautiful. Full of energy and exuberance.'

He has to wait at the junction with the main road to exit the estate, there's a pause until he finds a break in the traffic, then when he's driving towards town he says, 'So unless there was some kind of torture chamber in his downstairs back room, the only room we didn't get to see, our Alexi Kestle could be defined as a bit slow, a bit odd, a fine photographer and not really our concern.'

'What about his trip away? It's still unexplained and it coincides with Victoria's disappearance.'

He shakes his head, 'Mr Kestle enticing or forcing Victoria away? Not that there's much evidence of force. I can't see it, can you?'

She doesn't reply.

He sighs, 'No I think our girl went willingly, which points towards someone she knows.' Even though it might be the least traumatic for Victoria, this conclusion still does disappoint him. *But which one? Ray or Yvonne?*

CHAPTER 23

The next day, in pursuit of another cold misper, Theo takes Chesters with him to the Millstream estate in Leeds. It's only fair since he's done all the trawling through the paperwork. However, it does mean Theo has to put up with an hour and a half of non-stop commentary. Rangy and spiky-haired, with large ears, Chesters has something of the excitable whippet about him, especially when he's talking about his future plans. He's going to get his sergeant's exams, move forces, taking his current girlfriend whith him, who appears to have little say in the matter. He has quite a lot of thoughts about the case too. The person must have been hitch-hiking, why else would he have ended his life on the edge of the A64? Picked up, killed while being robbed, then dumped. A long-distance lorry driver, most likely, very difficult to trace, maybe it was even the Yorkshire Ripper.

'Hardly his MO,' offers Theo, glad the driving gives him something else to hold his attention.

This doesn't divert Chesters from his pontificating.

'Rough,' he pronounces when they arrive at their destination. And Theo can hardly disagree. The good intentions of the town planners to build a replacement for inner-city slums have long been thwarted. Two tower blocks of fifteen floors each dominate, while around the bottom brick terraces form crescents, petals to the stamens represented by the towers. All the buildings face inwards towards the patch of grass and the relatively well-kept playground at the base of the blocks, where a few toddlers are playing, watched over by some lethargic adults. The streets have their backs turned on the by-passes and the industrial estate which are encroaching and hemming the estate in, while, presumably, gobbling up the green spaces the builders had hoped would bring health and vitality to the residents.

Despite Hoyle's complaints about the cost, Theo now has a computer-generated facial reconstruction for their body. They go to the address of the misper Chesters has on his list and find it to be burnt out and boarded up. Neighbours look blankly at the image, they've only been on the estate for a few years, are hopeful of moving on, the face means nothing to them, nor the name Lenny Sharpe.

Theo and Chesters begin to work their way around one edge of a petal and then onto another. Finally, they come to an end property, its frontage a small area of concrete, covered over by a motorbike in bits which a slight-framed lad is working on. When he is addressed he reluctantly stands up; despite his stature he has some muscle tone, he obviously works out. His face is ravaged by acne, his skin pale and his cropped hair rusty blonde. It's not the temperature for working outdoors, however he only has a T-shirt on under a leather jacket with the words 'Steel Cowboy' emblazoned on the back. His responses are sullen and unhelpful, he hardly looks at the face in the picture.

His denial that anyone else is home is immediately undermined by the appearance at the doorway of a woman bearing a mug of steaming liquid. She is haggard, her ineptly dyed blonde hair has been hacked ineptly so it stands out in all directions. She is lumpy under ill-fitting sweatshirts and baggy jogging pants. She is unsteady on her feet and the milky drink slops onto the yard as she brings it over to the young man. He roughly takes it from her and tells her to go back inside.

'Wait a minute, I wonder if I could talk to you,' Theo interjects.

She is caught then between the two imperatives, to stay and to go. She looks hopefully for some guidance from the men standing before her. Theo gives her a broad smile and walks up beside her, as if he might take her arm, though he would not dream of touching her, 'Let's go inside and we can talk there.'

The woman is pleased she can thus obey both orders and takes them into the house. The house is messy, even so Theo can see there's been some attempts at cleaning. Ashtrays have been emptied into a wastepaper bin, beer cans have been crushed and put in a plastic bag hanging off the back of the door to the kitchen, the square of carpet between armchairs and table has been vacuumed, though dust and dog hairs form a layer everywhere else. Chesters is less tolerant in his later summing up: 'Dirty slut.' As he is of the woman's intelligence: 'Moronic.' The table is covered in neat piles of paper – mostly unopened post, some of it printed with red ink – and bottles of gin, vodka and value-pack cola and lemonade. The smell of cigarettes is prevalent, overlaying that of stodgy meals. The woman lights up and then offers them tea, both decline.

'What's your name love?' asks Theo, sitting back into the collapsed sofa. Chesters perches on the edge of one of the armchairs, his notebook on his knee.

'Michelle,' she says, sitting in a straight back chair next to the table, the hand holding her cigarette trembling. 'Michelle Davis. Mrs Davis. Mrs Michelle Davis.'

The repetition has a mechanical edge, raising doubts in Theo's mind that this is her actual name. Nevertheless he smiles. 'I wonder, Mrs Davis, if you could be so kind as to look at this picture. It's someone who may have lived around here. I'd like to know if you recognise him.' He holds out the sheet and immediately he feels it: she is scared. *No not scared, terrified. Absolutely terrified.*

'Lenny?' she says. She stares, her ciggie becoming ash in her quivering fingers.

'Lenny who?' asks Theo gently.

'Lenny Sharpe.'

'How do you know him?' Chesters' intervention is harsh, too brusque.

Her gaze snaps over to him and she shakes her head, taking a long puff from her smoke, she pushes the image of the man away from her. Scrape away those deep smoker's lines and those pouches under her pale eyes, there's a pretty face, a child-like face.

Chesters repeats his question.

She shakes her head again, 'I don't.'

'You just said his name,' Chesters says loudly.

'I was wrong. I don't know 'im.' She puts out her cigarette and lights another one. She looks back at Theo, 'You want a cuppa, honey?'

'No thanks, Mrs Davis. It would really help me if you could possibly tell me anything you know about Lenny Sharpe.'

'Oh? Well, I'm not too sure.' She taps her forehead, 'It doesn't work so well these days.'

'Tell me what you can,' Theo coaxes.

'He lived around here once, I think, that's all, maybe I saw him, on the street, yes that's probably it.'

'You know his name,' Chesters says with barely contained irritation. Theo glances over at him, wondering, *What's the matter with you, man? Why such hostility? Who does she remind you of?* A phrase he's learnt from Ben.

Michelle Davis shrugs. Any answer she might have given is interrupted by the sound of the door banging and a woman dressed in a business suit entering the room. A tall, elegantly turned-out woman, she says in a voice which is not used to being ignored, 'What's going on here?'

Michelle replies timidly, 'They want to know about Lenny.'

'Lenny? Lenny who? We don't know any Lenny, do we Meech?'

The other woman is practically shuddering, she looks down at a pile of envelopes nearest her and begins to finger them.

'And you are?' Chesters asks.

'None of your business. I think you were going gentlemen. Michelle, you need to ask these people to leave your house.'

'Is that what you want Mrs Davis?' Theo asks.

She nods. He gets up and indicates Chesters should follow him. For a split second the DC looks as though he is about to defy his superior. (Later they argue the toss in the car until Theo closes the argument with, 'We are not entitled to stay in someone's house unless we are arresting them for something, you should have covered that for your sergeant's exams.') Then Chesters gets up and stalks out. Before following him, Theo thanks Michelle for her hospitality and hands her his business card, says she should phone him if she remembers anything more about Lenny Sharpe. Theo hopes she can read enough to make out his number.

CHAPTER 24

'Tell me about Meech,' Hannah asks again without hope of a straight reply. She's feeling composed today. *I haven't drunk any alcohol since Saturday. Four days. Well done Hannah. I slept well.* Her brief phone conversation with Izzie on Monday helped silence some of her more critical voices. 'And we can talk more about this at our next session,' Izzie had said. *Yes we can. Only twenty-four hours to wait now.* 'Tell me about Michelle,' Hannah says to her client.

Julia doesn't respond immediately. She is very still apart from her clasped hands, her left thumb is stroking her right.

'What does your thumb want to say, Julia?' asks Hannah. She abruptly feels a fizz of excitement: *Something is going to be revealed, the dam wall is cracking.*

Julia looks down at her fingers, 'We used to be such good friends. Our families lived doors away from each other and our mams shared childcare from the beginning. We were like sisters. I only had brothers and Meech's sisters were a lot older than her. We did everything together. Our parents, you know, they weren't involved, not like parents are supposed to be nowadays. We were free-range kids, out there from morning to dusk, in the confines of the estate, sometimes ranging onto the bit of wasteland at the back where there was going to be the sports centre which never materialised. Meech taught me to swim, we took the bus to the local baths and she taught me to swim. I let her copy my homework. Words wobbled around for her, but nobody took much notice, just said she was a bit thick, it's what happened then, especially to working-class kids. And, lord, we would talk and talk, natter, natter, natter, I couldn't say about what, about something and nothing.' Julia pauses. Hannah waits, she notices Julia's slight West Yorkshire accent has become more pronounced. Julia resumes, 'I worry about her.' Silence.

'You're in contact?'

'She never left the estate, didn't finish school, got pregnant, the old story. Takes stuff, says it's from the doctor for her nerves, drinks too much, is always in debt. Sometimes we even talk, like we used to.' She chuckles quietly, 'I even told her about you. But mostly I help her out, with money. I get angry when I visit. So angry.' The last word is whispered.

'What about?'

The dishonesty of the answer, when it comes, feels like undigested mush in Hannah's stomach.

'The waste,' says Julia, bringing her gaze up to Hannah's. 'The waste of a good woman.' Her voice has gained most of its usual stridency. 'Though she's only got herself to blame, she didn't have to give up on herself. She knew where babies came from better than I did, her mam told her in no uncertain terms to stop her having any too soon, only she chose to ignore it all. Men, sex and alcohol, it's all she was interested in when she was fifteen. I left her to it.'

'And you got out.'

'Certainly I did,' Julia straightens her back and shoulders. 'I offered to help her, give her a job, but she wouldn't take it, so I left her to it.'

'Yet you keep going back?'

She nods. 'I help her kids, the older two, the younger three are in care somewhere. I haven't been able to keep track of them. Loretta Lynn, turned twenty-three last month, I make sure she gets a card every year and a little gift. And Steel Cowboy,' she smiles. 'Not his real name, obviously, it's his handle for the tables. I dib him a few hundred when I see he's losing.' Hannah knows Julia is talking about the virtual world of her online gaming empire. 'He'd be about twenty-five, twenty-six.'

Hannah does a quick calculation. Assuming Meech and Julia are of the same age that would mean, 'Meech was fourteen or fifteen when she had him?'

'Yes. Stupid, stupid girl,' Julia's voice has gone flat, with the harshness she uses when talking about 'the cat', 'the loser' and anyone else who has crossed her. Hannah wonders briefly, *Will I ever earn a pejorative term?* 'Whore!' Julia says suddenly, venomously.

Hannah takes a panicky moment to realise this is being directed at Meech rather than herself, then says, 'You sound angry. Tell me about your anger.'

Julia laughs harshly. 'And you want me to thump some cushions too?' This had been a suggestion weeks ago for expressing anger which had been summarily dismissed.

'I want to hear from your anger.'

'I told you, it's the waste, and the fact that she never learns, she's always letting herself get into trouble, she's so, so passive.'

Probably the worst sin Julia could come up with, being passive. Even so, Hannah isn't convinced. 'What happened to the two of you when you were fourteen years old?'

This enquiry might not have been uttered, Julia is cataloguing Meech's failings: her house is a mess; she's a mess; she doesn't use the intelligence she was born with; she has no self-respect; she's pathetic; always drunk or nearly. 'I was over there yesterday. There was some policeman asking questions. Poncy he was, his orange roll neck matched his glasses' frames for fuck's sake. Meech couldn't stop talking. I told her to keep her mouth shut or she'd be in trouble.'

Hannah has the impression the trouble would come from Julia rather than the police. 'What happened to the two of you when you were fourteen years old?'

Julia goes very still, there's a simmering in her voice, 'I told you, she got pregnant and I left.' Her tone becomes more diplomatic, 'We went our separate ways.'

'Who was the father of the baby?'

'I don't know, some oik from the local pub would be my guess. What's that got to do with anything? I thought we were here to talk about me.'

Hannah lets it go, though she is convinced she was on the right track and not everything Julia has said is the truth.

Chapter 25

Aurora had insisted she come along. It'll do her good to get out of the house, have a bit of fun. Having a bit of fun used to mean clubbing at midnight, not some hippy show in Rose's back garden shed. However, Hannah isn't strong enough to argue, especially when she can see Aurora is in a determined mood. Just getting up and through another day is taking all her energy.

There's more people than the first (and only) time Hannah had gone to one of Rose's pagan ceremonies. Then, at midsummer last year, it had been her and Aurora. Now Rose's small house in a village on the way to York feels crowded. Though there are only four extras. There's a large boisterous man with an overgrown beard, smelling of pipe tobacco and wheezing like the old squeeze box he plays. He's with his wife, who equals him in stature and noise levels, but with her toothy grin is immediately more approachable. They are both dressed in green, he has on a waistcoat appliquéd with an oak leaf, she a long flowing gown of crushed velvet and delicate silver crescent moons dangling from her ears.

In addition there is Ben, who Hannah expected to see, and, to her horror, Maya. The young woman is subdued, saying a brief 'Hi' from the doorway to the kitchen before going back to helping her mother. For someone who normally adores dressing up, Maya's costume is remarkably staid. A calf-length dress the colour of ferns hugs her slight figure. Her hair, close to its natural field-mouse brown, is tied into a simple plait which falls down her untanned neck. Her face is clean of make-up. She has on pearl stud earrings and a thin silver bangle around her slender wrist. She looks juvenile for her age, disarmingly innocent.

Ben greets Hannah and Aurora with hugs plus kind enquiries as to how they are. Hannah lets Aurora do most of the talking, *Once she is on the topic of Oli she is unstoppable.* It gives Hannah the opportunity to observe Ben. She's been thinking too much about him since he spent the night. He'd insisted, sleeping in a sleeping bag on the floor of her room. She would hardly admit it to herself, but she'd been glad. Had been glad when he'd been there to comfort her when she'd woken from a nightmare. Had been glad when he stayed long enough to bring her tea in the morning instead of rushing away. Now she admires the way his hair, as dark as molasses, curls at his shoulders, the litheness of his body, the slope of his buttocks. He is wearing his usual black, not a hint of green.

Hannah feels vindicated. How she was to dress for this charade was one of the reasons why they are late, Oli's bath time being the other. Aurora had tried to insist Hannah find or borrow something in the 'colour of the season' as she put it. Hannah refused out of pure obtuseness, she has a top which would have done. She chose instead a striped blue and silver mini-dress over navy T-shirt and leggings. Aurora looks magnificently curvaceous in a green silk salwar kameez, though Hannah has had to assure her several times of how fine she looks. Rose comes over and compliments them both, 'My, Hannah, you're the moon's handmaiden in that colour.' This pleases Hannah, despite her determination to be unimpressed by this nonsense. Rose looks different from her everyday in a flowing gown, her hair twisted up into an elegant whorl on top of her head. She tells Ben they can start now everyone is arrived.

They troop out across the back garden in the dark, clouds obscure any celestial light, and enter the gloom and cold of the shed. It smells of spicy incense. The one shrouded bulb in the corner mutely reveals the green of the draperies which hang about the walls and the shadows of objects: a metal cauldron in the centre of the space holding what could be a small tub of closed snowdrops and unlit candles in holders of every size and description. They all stand quietly in a circle around the cauldron. Hannah tries to relax, go with the flow, yet irritation prickles through her: *Why, oh why, did I allow Aurora to talk me into this?*

Everyone else has closed their eyes. She follows suit, the incense and smell of wax is heavy in her nostrils. Beyond the breathing (and wheezing) within, she can hear without the creak of a tree as it bows to the wind. There's the rustle of some animal, as it moves through the undergrowth dividing Rose's garden from the fields that stretch to the Wolds escarpment. In her mind she sees a fox trotting, his tail brushing the grass.

The whisper of movement is inside too. She peeks through her eyelids. Ben, now with a magnificent black cape – decorated with suns and moons – around his shoulders, joins the circle. He takes Rose's hand to his left and Maya's to his right. How Hannah wishes she'd thought more about where she was to stand, she is between Rose and Aurora. This unleashes a little ripple of hand-taking until everyone is connected. Ben begins to speak.

Hannah has never heard him raise his voice before, now the rich tones vibrate through her and on round the loop: 'Welcome friends to our rite when we welcome in the spring and Brede, the goddess of poetry and healing. We are linked in our sacred circle to which we now invite the spirits of earth, fire, air and water. Friends, as I now light the beacon which will bring our spiritual guests to us, I encourage you to consider the power and the meaning each element holds for you.'

Hannah shuts her eyes again, she can sense him walk round behind her and hears the hiss of the candle hanging in the northern corner being lit. After a moment, he speaks, 'Welcome you spirits of the earth who accompany your mother, from whom all nourishment flows to our sacred space. She provides our home, our food; we mine her for resources. We abuse her at our peril, for she has the power of great upheaval, the power to shatter all we humans presume to create. We wound her, we wound ourselves.' A silence and then he continues on to the next corner, 'Welcome you spirits of air who accompany the Lady Moon, whose hand drives all the currents and tides, we who live on the edge of this island nation know your rule. Come you spirits of the air, buoy us up into flights of the imagination, aid our reflexive powers as we seek the mirror held up to us by your Lady.'

Whether it is the heavy scents in the room or the sonorous sound of Ben's voice or something other, Hannah begins to lose the thread of the words. She sees images of winged sparks descending and then, as Ben continues on his round, feels the intense heat of fires and then hears the waves drawing back the gravel on a beach. Her hands are taken again and she moves in a circle with the others requesting the spirits to enter the sacred space they are creating and into her.

The circle comes to a halt and Rose says gently, 'I invite you, our first parents, to join us now. Lady mother we saw your full face last night, bright in the night sky, beautiful, kind and commanding. We do not forget your other aspects, the maiden moon – carefree, spirited – and the old crone – thoughtful, knowledgeable. Male or female, we can find your powers within us. Lady mother, you come with your lord the sun, a young weakling at this time of year in our hemisphere. But he will return to us strong and warm. He brings with him the promise that even at our most vulnerable we hold the key to our vibrancy. We possess all potentialities. We all have our seasons. Lady, we only have ourselves to offer you and that we do in thanks for your care.'

Rose picks up a plate and goblet, 'Lady bless this bread made from wheat from the earth, may it bring us all sufficiency in our lives. Lady bless this salt, brought forth from our brother oceans, may it bring us health and compassion. Lady bless this wine, may it strengthen our spirits.' She slowly begins to pass from person to person offering each a bit of the bread, a pinch of salt and the drinking vessel, 'Friends, as you take of this bread, salt and wine, speak to the Lady and she will listen. May she bring each one of us sufficiency, health and fortify our spirits.'

Hannah takes her salty morsel and a sip of the sweet homemade elderflower wine from Rose's sturdy fingers. Rose holds her gaze as she repeats more softly, 'Hannah speak to the

Lady and she will listen. May she bring you sufficiency, health and fortify your spirits.' Then she moves on. Hannah feels something she has rarely felt before. It takes her some time to identify it, she hardly recognises it; it is a deep sense of contentment.

After Rose has completed her round, she says they should all help light the candles and with each flame think of someone who could benefit from some healing, as well as think of those whose lives were devastated in the earthquake in Haiti. As she puts taper to wick, Hannah's thoughts skid through her clients and fix on Julia, then her own mother comes into her mind, and herself. *Am I allowed to ask for myself?* The barrack is transfigured by the undulating flames casting dancing shadows across the hangings on the walls, which have become the hue of forests and the texture of mosses. They all sit on floor cushions. Ben speaks about Brede, Brigit, Bride, the harbinger of the spring, poet, healer, her powers of transformation and healing and to awaken imaginations. 'Friends, let us pause for a moment, let us see Brede at her fire, her bright tresses catching the taint of the flames. Each one of us holds a copper pot, take it to Brede, she will ladle out our future, watch it flow from her hearth.'

Hannah has her legs pulled up to her chest and her chin resting on her knees, her eyes closed. In her mind she sees herself giving over her bowl and the tall red-haired goddess pouring the future from her cauldron. What Hannah hopes is for some image of her and Ben together, but she has to coerce it to appear and then feels she is cheating. She sneaks a look at him. He has stopped speaking and is resting back against the wall. *Are you thinking of me? Wanting me to be in your future?* Then she tells herself off for acting like a teenager.

They stand and Aurora reads, 'I bind myself today to the light of sun, to the brightness of the moon, the splendour of fire, the flashing lightning, to the swiftness of the winds, the depth of the sea, to the stability of the earth, the compactness of the rocks.' Then they all link hands and Ben and Rose close the ceremony, finishing with blessing those present and calling for peace and reconciliation within their own lives and more widely throughout the world. Bearded man takes up his squeeze box and begins to play a song, which in turn is taken up by his wife in a strong alto: 'To Brede, Brigit, fire goddess, transform and heal us ...' Then Maya's fluting soprano begins to harmonise and the three of them lead everyone back to the house where there is a buffet waiting to be eaten.

As Hannah watches they all mutate into their human selves: the couple loud and rather boorish listened to by Ben. *Why doesn't he pay me any attention?* Aurora wanting to leave to get back to Oli. Rose fussing that everyone, especially Hannah, is eating. Maya unnaturally dutiful and docile. Hannah begins to fear there's not enough oxygen for her in the room, a sense of panic pushes at the peace which her core has absorbed. *I have to get out.*

In the back garden the icy air slaps into her face. *Maybe I should go back in?* But bearded man's guffaw keeps her rooted to the spot. She hugs her arms around her in a vain hope of holding onto some warmth. *If only I could be transported magically to my bed. I don't want to have to meet, let alone speak, to anybody.* She feels everything slipping away from her.

A hand grips at her elbow and spins her around. Maya's face, contorted by anger, floats in front of her out of the dark. 'I'm warning you, Hannah, one more time, leave Ben alone. He doesn't want you, get it? And he's mine.' With that the younger woman turns on her heel to go back indoors.

Hannah's desire to get away is even greater, she runs to the end of the garden and into the shed. The candles have been put out. Their heat remains and she is glad of it. Something of the vigour she's felt during the ceremony returns, *How dare Maya? How dare she speak for Ben? I know he cares for me, I've felt it. And more than that?* Hannah shrugs to herself. *Maybe. Yes. More than maybe.* A flutter works its way through her as she straightens herself up. She notices the snowdrops in the cauldron have bloomed.

Aurora is shouting for her, Hannah hurries out and joins her friend who says she really must go now. Goodbyes are brief as Aurora rushes them both out. Ben catches them up as they are exiting the front door, he pecks them both on their cheeks and then asks Hannah if she wants to go for a meal on Friday. 'Is this a date?' She needs to be sure this time.

'If you like.'

'What do you want?' She feels a force at her centre pushing her on. The dark clouds above her head are suddenly chrome edged.

'Yes, a date.'

As she turns to go, she sees Maya's scowling face at Ben's shoulder.

CHAPTER 26

Date: 01/02/2010 23:03

This message will be sent via Nicolespringer@NSjournalist.co.uk
To: LawrenceFielding@LawrenceFielding.co.uk
Subject: Stan Poole

Lawrence
I know another apology is in order, darling, I was hideously rude to you on Friday at Miles's party. No excuse, but I was somewhat tanked and your enquiry hit me broadside. Do I have some memories of Stan Poole? Do I ever. Should I be sharing them with you, or anyone else? That's another question entirely. You know me as a forthright old soak, but, believe me darling, there's things I keep well and truly tucked away from sight (don't we all) and what happened with Stan Poole is one of those. It's taken me a good bottle of Sauvignon to get this far, I'm not sure how far it will take me, maybe I'll delete this at the end, but now I've started I want to get it down somehow.

You assure me that all this can be 'off the record', for background only. I believe – I hope – I can trust you. Yes we've had our differences in the past, but I know you to be an honourable man. Which is more than can be said of Stan Poole. You rightly identify me as the rather gorgeous blonde in the photo you found. I was less ravaged then. And a whole lot more innocent. Before Stan Poole got his hands on me – literally.

The picture is of a bunch of us who were doing a NUJ-sponsored course – one of the first I think, though they are everywhere now – at the local tech. It had been arranged for us to spend a few days in a real newsroom and Stan, to give him his due, personally involved himself in giving us a good experience, showing us all aspects of newspaper production and even giving us group assignments which got printed. My first by-line!

And he was charming, engaging, charismatic – you know all that – already a bit of a legend. So when he suggested a drink at close of business on our final day, we all jumped at the chance. Drinking – as you're well aware – probably the second most important skill for journalists (after bare-faced lying) – especially in those days and, most crucially, if you were a woman in those days. I was a novice at it – yes, you might not believe it, there was a time when two glasses of mediocre wine (on top of the g&t Stan had insisted on initially, I should add) had me slurring my speech and feeling decidedly queasy. Stan, ever solicitous, decided I should not be allowed to travel home alone and took me in a taxi which he paid for. All I remember of the occasion is doing my utmost not to throw up over this icon of the world I so desperately wanted to enter and be accepted by. I did manage to hold my stomach in check – a talent I've been blessed with and found very useful in the ensuing years – until after I'd said a relatively polite goodnight and got inside at a measured pace, and then rushed to the kitchen sink. I do have the impression, however, that Stan Poole did insinuate his rather hoary hand up between my silk blouse (saved up for over many a week of waitressing) and my sweating back.

Perhaps not, maybe it all came later. For now Stan Poole knew where I lived and he pursued me with a deftness which still surprises me. Flowers 'for his best pupil', then offers of what we might call today 'mentoring'. Followed by trips to the theatre with 'review' tickets or dinners at restaurants which he was apparently going to cover in some article or another at some stage. All very plausible to one as naive as me. Even the suggestion I come on a 'research' trip to a country hotel was accepted without trepidation, until, of course, we arrived and he signed us in as Mr & Mrs and we were given only one room key. I still held onto the thought there might be twin beds (a cost-saving initiative) right up to the moment he gave me a little push towards our four poster.

I lost my virginity to Stan Poole that night. I can't cry rape now. I could have left. Perhaps insisted he give me enough money for a taxi back home (rural public transport having already ceased until the following day). Asked for help from the hotel staff. Shouted and screamed until I got a room to myself. All these options went through my mind as I had a bath, dressed for dinner and then allowed myself to be treated to the best on the menu. I don't think I actually decided to go through with what I knew was going to happen, I just chose not to make use of any of the alternative choices. I didn't want to make a fuss. I didn't want to look stupid. I didn't want to make an enemy of this big man of the industry. I was scared, I was ashamed and, yes, I was even intrigued. Intrigued to find out what it would be like. What it would be like with him. And you know, it wasn't awful. Not how I remember it, though wine had probably dulled my senses and has dimmed the memory. It hurt a bit, it was over pretty quick, Stan made a lot of strange grunting sounds and I fell asleep pretty damn soon after.

I said I wanted to go home the next day and he replied I could not, as he had organised all these treats for me. A visit around the local town in a horse and carriage, a theatre trip and a leisurely and sumptuous lunch and dinner. He hardly let me out of his sight, hardly let go of my hand, I almost had to plead to be able to go to the loo. The second night he wanted me to suck him off, I tried to refuse, he slapped me and I did it, crying all the time. I cried all through the sex which was rougher and he seemed to get off on that. He woke me up later in the night to go through the whole routine as before with some spanking thrown in for good measure.

The next morning we left. I felt sick and dirty, I couldn't speak. To him (as he kept up a conversation of sorts all the way back) and certainly not to my friends and fellow trainees when they questioned me on my weekend away. I made something up for them which sounded vaguely plausible and folded the facts away.

I was becoming a true journalist, Lawrence darling. And the truth has remained out of sight ever since. Until now. And I saw the photo and you asked me for my memories of Stan Poole. I considered writing the bunkum I've been giving everyone else since I started to spin my tale that Monday morning. I even began to compose an email to this effect. Then I realised I couldn't do it. Not anymore.

Stan Poole didn't contact me again following those two days – though I have since understood he did facilitate me getting my first job – and I didn't see him for years. When we did meet, at some do, he was charming and erudite as ever. He even said, hadn't we once met when I was a student? He was sure we had, as he had a good memory for faces. I felt the shame, even the fear, the disgust once more. But I was more hardened by then, I kept my smile lit up as I said I didn't think so, and would surely have remembered an encounter with him, while all the time my brain was shouting bastard, bastard. And he just grinned and moved on.

We've come across each other at times since then, he's never tried to make an allusion to our first meeting again. I've sometimes tried to read his face for guilt, understanding, anything, and I've never found it there. Perhaps you noticed I didn't take up the invitation to his funeral. I was afraid I would have clapped and cheered at inappropriate moments.
Well, Lawrence, dear, do I press send or delete? A couple of whiskies will tell.

Caio, Nicole

CHAPTER 27

Hannah's supervisor, Orwell Winters, is waiting for her. His room at the SC4Tea is a peaceful cave which this morning smells of fresh coffee and spicy candles. On the bland walls hang blocks of abstract colours which sometimes remind Hannah of the sea or of a summer landscape, but today give her the impression of a volcanic abyss into which she might slip. Orwell sits on a chair and Hannah on the sofa.

They start with her last session with Darren Frost. One of her first clients who had initially repelled her, especially given his ghoulish interest in the murder Hannah had been implicated in some twelve months ago. She has grown fond of him, however. She also has him tagged as her first 'success': a client who has stayed the course until perceptible changes in their approach to life can be listed. In Darren's case, there's something less frenetic, less hard edged about him, and he is happy in a relationship which he anticipates will be long-term and has all the signs that it will indeed endure.

Orwell cautions her about thinking in terms of success and failure, 'we never know what we do' is one of his oft-repeated phrases. 'We create the safe space and people do what they need to do within it, what's important to them, whether we appreciate what that is or not.' Still, he lets her celebrate today. Doesn't contradict her belief that she has had some (small) part in the alterations Darren has made in his way of being.

Hannah is also excited to relate how she'd brought writing into the last couple of sessions. Darren hadn't been keen, said it reminded him of school, but had gone along with it. *Probably to please me, which is troubling.* She'd got him to choose three postcards from a selection she'd brought in to represent where he'd been when he first started therapy, where he was now and where he'd like to be and then write a postcard-type message from each place. It had brought some levity into the sessions, as well as helping him say something about what he thought was happening for him. The future postcard was from a holiday in the sun where Darren would have taken his (as yet non-existent) wife and children. 'Maybe I'll send you this postcard, Hannah,' he said with a smile. Then quickly, 'No, I know, it's not allowed, you've explained that. Still it would be nice.' He looked sad.

Hannah stopped herself from going into another long explanation of why there would be no deliberate contact after the sessions were finished and said, 'I won't forget you Darren.'

'No?' His look of pleasure was swiftly replaced by one of his wolf grins, 'I'm unforgettable ain't I?' It was a glimpse of the old Darren who she disliked and she banishes the image, telling Orwell only half the story.

That's all they ever are, incomplete stories, moth-eaten tales. Orwell is waiting, he can tell by now when I am holding back. She doesn't oblige him, he doesn't push her, not today. She realises this is an impulse born of his compassion for her and she is grateful. She moves on to Craig, one of her 'failures', a youngster who has come, gone and returned again, always without warning, over the last year. They discuss whether she should take him back for a fourth time. Hannah wants to but Orwell is more cautious, she had told Craig on the previous occasion he had to commit or they couldn't continue together. 'He's not ready to do the work, Hannah,' Winters says. 'Not with you.'

She's stung by the suggestion that Craig might do the work with someone else, *Aren't I good enough then?* 'He's got no one else to turn to.'

'Nonsense. He's surrounded by concerned people, maybe that's part of the problem. Refer him on.' He suggests some names and adds that two of them are trained in working with teenagers.

I am not good enough. Hannah sulks, 'If you say so.'

Orwell looks like he is weighing up some possible responses, then he says simply, 'I do.'

Might as well pack up and go home then. 'OK.'

There's a pause, then he says, 'Hannah, what have you heard me say?'

She tussles with herself, doesn't want to admit how put out she feels. She doesn't reply.

He says, 'I'm guessing you heard me as saying something critical about your capabilities. You're a good counsellor, Hannah, you're caring, you're intuitive, you're reflexive, on the whole you're boundaried. And we can't be all things to all people. Some clients will choose to work with therapists other than ourselves and it's not a negative reflection on us. Plus it's an ethical imperative we work within our competences. Hannah are you listening to me?'

'Yes!' *Angry, angry, ANGRY. RAGING INSIDE. I listen to you, do you ever listen to me?*

He smiles, 'I don't suppose you are, but maybe something is going in, like the bit about you being a good counsellor?' He sighs. 'You're still training, Hannah, go easy with yourself.'

Listen to ME. Where did that come from? Julia enters her thoughts and the story she'd told over the last session. She begins to piece it back together for Orwell and she feels his attention intensifying.

Julia had talked about coming to Scarborough with Meech, driven over by a bloke from their estate, an older man who remained nameless. 'We were stupid, kids,' said Julia. 'Thought it would be a laugh, the estate could be bleak, even more bleak in the summer when any flowers which did dare to bloom looked shabby, mucky. There wasn't a breath that summer, we were frying in all the concrete. So we thought, great, a drive to see the sea, some fish and chips, maybe some lager shandy. All on 'im.' She'd lost her aitches as she talked and her tone became distinctly more West Yorkshire.

'Why not? We thought he was flash, had this big gold watch, we thought it'd be fun.' Only it didn't turn out like that. He wanted something back, that became clear, attempted kisses on the beach, aborted fumbles in the sand, especially with Julia, and the shandy was stronger than it ought to be. "Course we didn't know. How could we? We were only fourteen.' And him? Thirty-ish. 'By the third round Meech was feeling ill, and 'e was getting insistent, I had to get us out of there. We didn't have money for the train, so I had to make 'im take us.' Julia smiled, triumphant, she looked teenaged. 'And I did. Told 'im if he didn't I'd go straight to the police.' And? And, nothing, he took them home. "Course we had to stop for Meech to be sick, silly mare. But we got home.'

Another half-regurgitated story. Hannah didn't immediately react, her breathing had become shallow and there was tension in her belly. Fear. She was afraid. She asked how Julia was feeling. The other woman shrugged. Hannah waited. Then Julia said slowly, her voice like a scared child's, 'I didn't want 'im on me, do you see? I 'ad to get 'im off me. I screamed. No one heard. No one could. It was me and 'im and I 'ad to get 'im off me.'

'What happened to you Julia?'

Still the breathy tones of a terrified little girl, 'It wasn't me it was her, 'e got to her and I had to help her, get her away. You do see, don't you?'

Hannah was struggling not to cry out, not to say shut up, I don't want to hear anymore, this is too much for me. With an effort, she said evenly, 'Did he hurt you Julia?'

Julia curled up in a ball and turned away from Hannah, she didn't make a sound. After a moment, Hannah leaned forward, 'Julia, tell me what's happening for you.' There was no reply, panic began to grow inside Hannah. *I don't know if I can control what's going on, in my client or in me.* A shaking was taking hold. Furthermore, the clock's hands were moving inexorably towards the hour being up. She forced a calmness into her veins, repeated Julia's name a few times, reassured her that she, Hannah, was here. Finally, she reached forward, her hand hovered in the air, not touching, not being withdrawn. She said more loudly, 'Julia. I need you to tell me what's happening.'

Julia's head jerked round, she saw Hannah's hand, flinched and then slammed her feet to the floor. 'I'm fine, I'm fine,' she muttered, not looking up.

Hannah pulled her arm back and her hands cradled each other in her lap. 'Looks like you went to a really tough place,' she said to break the silence. Julia nodded, her gaze still firmly on the floor. 'Can you tell me about it?' Hannah had an eye to the clock, but couldn't break off now. Julia shook her head. Hannah did some more encouraging and reassuring, but nothing was forthcoming. Finally, she urged Julia to look at her. After a moment, Julia complied, Hannah made sure she was smiling. Her client straightened, took a deep breath and caught sight of the time, ten minutes over their allotted time. 'I have to go,' she said stiffly. 'I have a meeting.'

This sounded unlikely. 'You need to take care of yourself, you've been through a lot in today's session,' said Hannah. 'Is there anything you need from me?' She wanted to hug Julia, hold her, keep her safe. Julia shook her head, handed over her money and said she would see Hannah the next week, then she walked out.

During the telling, Hannah finds she is once more run through by the emotions, the fear, the panic, the extreme sadness when Julia had gone. She sits quiet, exhausted, when words have run out.

'Sounds like a difficult session for both of you,' says Orwell.

'I'm dreaming about it.'

'Dreaming what?'

'About being suffocated. But it's not her, it's me.' She is finding it difficult to hold her supervisor's gaze.

'Are you talking about this in therapy?'

She shakes her head.

'I think maybe you should. I don't think this is all about your client.'

She sits silent, wanting to deny this, not being able to.

'You need a lot of support with this kind of work, Hannah. Make sure you get it.' A pause. 'What do you want now, Hannah?'

She forces herself to be truthful and asks for and receives a big hug. 'I bet that's what Julia wanted,' she says.

'Probably, but don't go too fast with her as she's revealing this. Let her go at her own pace. You're doing fine. Remember, Hannah, she's chosen you to disclose this to and it's a tribute to the relationship you've built together.'

'Thanks.' *Can I hold onto his compliment? Possibly, for a short while.*

CHAPTER 28

Theo is feeling content. The weekend with Lawrence in London had gone well. He's relieved this shows they do, perhaps, have something worth preserving. He is reading through the report from Leeds about Lenny Sharpe for the second time. Two local constables have canvassed the residents, with instructions to steer clear of Michelle Davis and her son. They found an elderly couple who used to know the Sharpe family.

The Sharpes were mainly 'trouble' according to their one-time neighbours, apart from the mother who 'couldn't do enough for you. Would help anyone out'. She'd died in the mid-nineties, mostly of cancer but also of a 'broken 'art' with one son in prison and another never visiting. Only her daughter was doing okay, though she'd moved away and rarely came back. Lenny was the one who never visited. Though it was difficult to get verifiable details, it did appear that he drove off one day, possibly in a summer in the mid-eighties, and never came back.

'Think his car was found somewhere hereabouts, wasn't it? But he was well gone. No they didn't bother much to look for him, he was in his thirties, always up to some scheme or other,' said the old chap. His wife remembered Lenny as being 'a bit of a ladies man. Sang Country and Western in some of the pubs, had a lovely voice. What did he call 'isself now? Cowboy somethin' or somethin' cowboy. Steel Cowboy, wasn't it? Was so proud of it, he had it on the backside of that watch he always wore, great gold-coloured thing.' The constables had tracked down something of what had happened when Lenny Sharpe had been reported missing, and their informant had been right, it hadn't been much.

Theo sets in motion the process of finding and getting DNA from Lenny's sister and also asks the Leeds PCs to check out local dentists, in the vain hope their records might help finally identify the body. But he is certain in himself, he is looking into the death of Lenny Sharpe. He is also clear, Michelle Davis has something more to tell him and he will have to speak to her again.

He puts all this aside for a moment and phones a traffic officer he vaguely knows, encountered uncomfortably at a certain club in York while out with Lawrence. On Theo's way into work he'd met Aurora. Though they'd both been in a hurry they'd paused and she'd let him make a fuss of Oli. After the usual exchanges Aurora had asked tentatively whether she could talk shop, 'I know I should make an appointment, only, well I run out of days all the time.'

'Go on.' Theo was pretending his hand was an aeroplane landing on Oli's tummy and then turning into a tickling monster. The little boy was laughing. *Absolutely adorable.* In the middle of this Aurora told him about Ray's visit to her and what he'd said about Yvonne's car. 'It's probably nothing, but I thought I should pass it on. Sorry it's taken me so long,' Aurora finished as she rushed off to an appointment at the GP.

Now Theo has decided to see if he can follow it up. The officer promises to get back to him with any traffic reports involving the Vauxhall belonging to the Everidges. As Theo re-cradles the receiver, he notices Suze is standing at the door of his glass box on the edge of the CID room. She hasn't announced her presence with her usual breezy greeting. She is hunched over her crutches, her small face caving in at the cheeks, lines dragging down at her mouth. She brings news of Westedge, something is brewing. She's had a text from her niece. There are people at Kestle's house. Theo takes Harry and a uniform.

Used to more urban settings, where he could sense the fear and the festering anger as if they are firecrackers about to be lit, Theo does not immediately feel any danger on the estate. The cold has persisted for weeks now, the air is damp, ice crunches underfoot, snow endures in grey lumps on the scrubby hillside which rises behind Westedge. There are a few young people on the street, woefully under-dressed, flesh showing between low-slung jeans and cotton zip-up tops. One or two have scarves or hats obscuring their features, though this could be more to do with the temperature than any malicious intent. Theo had parked down towards the main road; he wanted to test out the atmosphere. As they walk up the street towards Kestle's house, the pavement slippy underfoot so they have to tread carefully, Harry shivers. 'What's up?' Theo asks.

'Eyes.'

And he becomes aware of people watching, from behind curtains. The WPC skids on some black ice and a hyena's laugh emanates from one of the unidentifiable muffled faces. Theo recalls Kestle's patch of front lawn behind his gate as being clean and tidy, now it is littered with dog shit and the outer wall has been inexpertly sprayed with the word 'Paedo', the 'a' added afterwards as though corrected by a passing teacher.

It's the quietness which now begins to quicken his pulse, ever so slightly. The quietness which brings back memories of hurrying (without seeming to hurry) down a city street just before the blow came accompanied by the thickly spat word, 'Poof.' He takes a moment to steady himself and then rings the bell. The minutes it takes for a response to come allows him to think – *hope* – Kestle has gone off somewhere again. He is about to press the bell-push once more, just in case, when an indistinct, 'What do you want?' comes from the interior. Theo explains who it is and there is another long wait (or that's how it feels) before the door is unchained and opened.

The WPC is left on the doorstep looking fierce, a role she fulfils rather well, and Harry and Theo go in. Kestle is looking rumpled, unironed, possibly even a little unwashed, the smell around him suggests it. His trousers have an unfortunately placed discolouring and there are egg stains on his tie. He takes them into the back room. It holds further bookshelves, an over-sized dining table and upright chairs; all currently in near darkness as the curtains are closed and the light off, the only illumination coming in weakly through the hall. Alexi does not offer them tea, he sits in the gloomiest part of the room and softly drums his fingers on the polished surface of the table.

'We were wondering how you are doing, Mr Kestle,' Theo begins. No answer. The bulky man's gaze is on his own hands. 'Has there been some trouble?' Still nothing. Only the knock of skin on hardwood. Theo tries a few more enquiries without any more success. He considers whether their very presence is making things worse and if they should go. *Our first visit was probably the start of it.* But, of course, it wasn't. The animosity was already there, it only needed an excuse. *And we gave it one. We had to come*, he reminds himself, *before and now. It's the job.* Only right now he'd rather be anywhere else than in the close atmosphere of this stuffed room with this taciturn, scared hulk. Theo is edgy. He's been assuming Kestle is harmless. Currently, he comes over as less so. There'd be a lot of power, undisciplined power, in those large hands and arms, in the cumbersome torso. Then Harry speaks, her voice unnaturally piping. *Anxiety*, her superior officer supposes. She suggests she make tea and Mr Kestle show her his most recent photos.

He slowly shakes his head, 'Can't. With. Them. Out. There.'

'Have they been threatening you?' asks Harry.

'They say I hurt kids. I don't. I don't.' He slams his fist on the table and the room shudders. 'I don't,' he shouts. 'I wouldn't. I saw her, once, she was with her mother. I took her photo. That's all.' He balls his hands up and puts them to his forehead. He begins to cry, sobbing like a told-off little boy, tears and snot beginning to mark the polished surface he is leaning on. Harry looks around and then retrieves some paper tissues from her bag, she hands them over, though Alexi's use of them is ineffective.

'Where did you see Victoria, Vicky?' asks Theo.

'Hull. But I'd seen her before, around here, with a man. It's why I took her photo.'

'Was it when you went away, just recently, before we came to see you the first time? Is that when you saw Victoria with her mum?'

He sobs. Shakes his head.

'Is that a no, Mr Kestle?'

He shakes his head again.

'Was it another time?'

Another twist of the head, difficult to tell the meaning of it.

'Have you the photo?' asks Harry.

Then a long wail, 'Noooo. They took it, they took it.'

'Your camera? It was still in the camera?'

He's collapsed onto his forearms now and is snivelling. Harry looks at Theo. He encourages her to try again. 'Mr Kestle, Alexi,' she says gently. 'Tell me what's happened to your camera.'

In response, only soggy, snot-filled weeping.

Theo's phone sounds. He answers it in the hallway, it's Pippa, she wants him to bring Kestle in, Victoria has named him. Theo protests, 'Are you sure? Why now?'

'Of course I'm sure, sergeant. We've got him. We've just had to go very slowly, that's all.'

'I'm not sure it's a good idea, detective inspector, if the residents here see him being taken in ... they're already hostile ...'

Pippa interrupts him, 'I want him in here for questioning, Sergeant Akande, now. If there's problems with his neighbours, then he'll be safer with us anyway.' She cuts the connection. Theo looks at his phone, annoyed at being stopped short. *I doubt it very much DI Wiltshire, I doubt it very much.*

CHAPTER 29

I had to get drunk to do this. It's a thought she tries to ignore. She'd had a few glasses of wine at home. She didn't want to seem too greedy during her meal out with Ben. Even so, he'd only had a couple of glasses and she'd polished off the rest. *Did he notice? Probably.* She's suddenly tired, a heavy pressure in her chest, she's ungainly on the steep cobbled street down to the sea front. *How many other drunken dates have there been? Waiting for Rickie to never turn up and accepting a compensatory fuck from an almost stranger? Oh Hannah, this one was supposed to be different. Would have been different.*

She slithers and stumbles, and Ben catches her in his arms. He kisses her on the mouth, his breath hot and garlicky. He presses her close before pulling her onwards. *Maybe it's going to be OK. This time it's going to be OK. Why not? Why shouldn't it be?* She giggles as they hurry through the rimey shadows to his house in the Old Town. He joins in raucously, disturbing some slumbering pigeons who applaud with their wings as they scramble to an ascent. *It will be OK Hannah. This time.* They scurry on, their white breath mingling with the frosty mist wreaths.

Now she isn't laughing. They have stepped directly from the street into Ben's front room. Once the dwelling of a fishing family, the house is narrow, built on a steep slope. No floor or wall is straight or at right angles to any other. The ground floor is one elongated space which incorporates a living room with crammed-full, ceiling-high bookshelves at the front and a kitchen at the back. Between the two, iron steps spiral upwards, presumably to where Ben sleeps. *This is a mistake.*

Ben's mood hasn't changed. He may have consumed less drink than her, but he is undoubtedly less used to it. He is swaying just a little as he clamps his arms around her waist and pins her body against his. He steps back, picks up one of her hands which is limp by her side, comments it is cold but he will soon warm her up.

The words run together with a snigger. He begins to lead her towards the staircase. She hangs back.

'What, Hannah, what?' Ben furrows his forehead. 'This is what we've wanted for, for, ever since ...' He takes a stumbling step as someone might on a yacht hitting an unexpected undercurrent.

He has to be drunk to do this with me. 'Have you Ben? Have you always wanted this?'

'Yes, yes,' he comes close again and wraps himself around her. 'Hannah please don't complicate things right now.'

She feels the warmth from his body coursing into hers, the knotted coil under her ribcage is loosening. She closes her eyes, pictures his velvet chocolate gaze, deep enough to swim in. She strokes down his damp hair, knowing it to be the colour of newly fallen conkers. When he presses his mouth to hers, she opens her lips, her tongue searching out his. He tastes of sweet fermented grapes, smells faintly limey. He groans quietly, says something which sounds like 'let me in'. She puts her arms around his neck. He peels back her knitted jacket, then her blouse, lets loose her breasts from her bra. He kisses a trail down from her shoulder to her nipple, which he teases with the tip of his tongue. Each touch sparks against her skin. She undoes his shirt. He is smooth, hairless, a selkie with a sonar for a heart.

She unbuttons her trousers, takes his hand and guides it down to between her legs. He is clumsy at first, rough fingered against the delicate oyster skin. Finally he finds her clit and playfully nudges it, fondles it, a curious silverfish amongst the weed. Her body is kindling. Her doubting mind, however, is not quite doused. *You slut, Hannah, you bad girl.*

She tries to turn away from the commentary. She hears her own breathing and his. Somewhere nearby is the clink of metal against metal, a yacht's rigging in the harbour. She unzips and pushes at his jeans so that she can ease his penis into her hand. She feels its weight unbend and is suddenly scared. She has done this before, in her hand, in her mouth, in her, no trouble. Yet now? *I can't, I can't do this.* She lets go. She is shot through by ice.

It takes a moment until Ben is also still, straightening so he can look at her. 'What?' he snaps. His face slackens, 'Hey, hey. It's OK.' His thumbs dab at the tears on her cheeks. The sharp sour smell of seaweed comes off his fingers. He looks tired, suggests they go upstairs to bed, to sleep. He tries to move, only with his breeches at half-mast he almost tumbles.

She has to laugh, mid-sob. She follows him up the spiral of blue fairy lights up to the first floor, doors disclose a bathroom and a small study at the front of the house and spare bedroom at the back. Ben's room is up once again, under the eaves. It is dark, the navy curtains drawn back to reveal above the rooves the slumbering castle headland, grey taffeta wrapped about its shoulders. 'It's beautiful,' she breathes.

Ben stands behind her, gently massaging her shoulders. She turns into him and begins to unclasp what he had minutes ago hastily re-fastened. He asks her if she is sure. She doesn't reply. Kisses him so hard it feels like a bruise and continues to undress him while he does the same for her. The air is cool against her igniting skin. She pushes him onto the bed and sits on top of him. 'Wait, wait, wait.' He stretches over, gets a packet out of his bedside cabinet. 'Don't need it,' she says.

He puts his arms round her and they kiss, supping from the inner shell of the other. They turn over. He's heavy on top of her. She parts her legs. Feels his penis enter. A tidal bore – excitement, joy, an easing of sinew, of champed nerves – rolls through her. She responds to his rhythm and he to hers. They are moving together, held by furnaced limbs, mouth against ear, mouth against cheek. Inarticulate. Primeval. Sated. Done. Spent.

Slowly, slowly she becomes aware. His skull against her clavicle. Her legs aching. His weight compressing her chest. Their humid bodies rapidly cooling. They crawl under the duvet, lie on their backs, side-by-side, skin against tenderised skin from shoulder to hip. Sounds from outside begin to encroach, voices from revellers leaving a nearby pub, the rustle of a night creature finding sanctuary in fallen leaves, and behind it all the muted thrumbing of waves on a harbour wall.

    She sleeps. Some. It's dark when she wakes. Ben is snoring boisterously. *Run, Hannah, run. Get out of here, you dirty, bad girl. You think Ben loves you? Likes you? You fool.* There's no escape from the script looping through her head. Her brain is beginning to ache. She feels slightly sick. She's cold. She wants to scream, 'Stop it, shut up, shut the fuck up.' Only there's no stopping the words dripping on and on, grinding into her neck, into the tender points in her body. She gives up. *OK, have it your way.* She inches herself out of the bed and into her clothes, all the while watching Ben for any sign he might surface. She need not have worried, he snores on luxuriously. She creeps noiselessly away and into the damp night. Outside she takes a deep breath, *No glancing back, Hannah, keep going, it's what you're good at after all.*

Chapter 30

For a man who could take a post-grad qualification in looking awkward and being obtuse, Lawrence is out-doing himself, has been since he arrived at Theo's late last night. *I don't have time for this. And I don't want another intense discussion about whether he can face being 'out' to his world. Not now, on a Monday morning. It's rubbish timing, with the on-going investigations.* Then Lawrence announces his intention to spend much of his time 'checking up on' Hannah. *Do I look like a B&B owner?* Theo douses his retort with the sumptuous breakfast Lawrence has created. The out-of-season raspberries melt into the Greek yoghurt with honey. Theo takes a sip of the filter coffee, normally a rare weekend treat. It is smooth with the merest intimation of bitter. There are freshly baked croissants. He had woken to the smells of yeast, butter and coffee. He had felt treated by them, then cheated by the lack of warm body beside him.

Now he's getting to the point of irritation. He has to be in work soon and he knows Lawrence has got something to say, has had something to say since his unannounced appearance. He's standing with his back against the sink in the kitchen, in Theo's petite rented terrace house which doesn't really accommodate his bulk. He is clutching his mug and he is moving almost imperceptibly from one foot to the other. Theo sits back, he reminds himself of the good times they've had, of the laughs, of Lawrence's dry wit, of those large hands holding and comforting him when he's felt worn down. He glances at the clock, he'll be late, but he can manage it. 'What is it Lawrence? I've got ten minutes, then I have to go.'

Still Lawrence doesn't get to the point, saying something about needing advice and Stan Poole's computers being unlocked and things being not as they should be.

'You've found porn,' says Theo flatly.

Quick nod.

'Child porn?'

Blue eyes, abruptly wet, search the ceiling. 'It can't have been his,' the voice is husky, desperate.

'What, the computer? The folder? Or the porn?'

'He wasn't like that.'

'How many images? One? Two? Ten? Twenty? Fifty? A hundred? Hundreds?' He gets a slight nod at the last one. Theo keeps his voice dispassionate, underneath he is broiling at Lawrence's loyalty, at what Stan Poole has done. *Every image is a child being abused.* 'You don't get hundreds of image of child porn on your computer by mistake. You'll have to hand it over. I'll tell you who to contact.'

'Must I? Stan's dead.'

'Yeah, and his computer might lead us to paedophiles who are very much alive.' Theo gets up, begins to stack his pots, Lawrence is still guarding the sink.

'He was not a paedophile!' Lawrence sounds angry. 'He tried to delete it.'

And that makes it better? Then, for a moment, Theo is stayed, he looks at the man he loves and sees his distress. He goes up to him, he is smaller and slighter than Lawrence, he has to reach up to put his arms around the rigid shoulders, 'I'm sorry, I know what he meant to you, and you have to do what's right. Think of Hannah.'

'I am thinking of Hannah. Imagine how hurt she is going to be hearing this about her father.'

Theo straightens a little and looks up into his lover's stern face, his square chin is clean shaven, he's had his greying hair cut short and severe. 'There's every chance Stan's proclivities didn't stop at looking at pictures. Hannah may already have been hurt by her father in very real ways, and if that's true she needs support.'

'No.' Lawrence jerks away and starts to noisily clear the table, the clattering over-laying his words, 'Hannah's a bit fragile, but nothing like that has happened to her. I'd know.'

Theo leaves him to it and goes to get ready for work. When he returns to say goodbye Lawrence is cleaning, unnecessarily, Rose is coming in during the afternoon. 'I'm off then,' Theo says. 'This is who you need to contact,' he puts down the piece of paper where he's written the details. 'Will I see you later?' He gets a grunt as a reply. He shouts goodbye from the door and gets no response.

DI Wiltshire doesn't look like she's had much sleep. She is triumphant. After being questioned to the early hours and then left in a cell, Kestle will break. *You're running on adrenalin.* Theo watches her drain her cup too fast, it's coffee rather than her usual herbal brew. *You're going to make a mistake.*

He retires to his cubbyhole. There are two messages, one from Suze, the other from the traffic officer, both wanting to talk to him. He goes to find Suze first. He has to wait while she fields some phone calls and then an irate civilian worker who's unhappy about the way one of the police sergeants has treated her. Once this is dealt with Suze tells her assistant she's taking a break and Theo accompanies her down in the lift and out of the building. It's grey and the air freezes their breath as they make their way slowly through the snicket, into the graveyard and to Suze's hideaway, the renovated Victorian mortuary. They perch on the tile-covered benches around the walls, Theo can feel the chill coming through and worries about damp patches on his trousers. Only Suze has something to tell him and he needs her information. She takes out her baccy tin, then puts it away again, says her daughter had asked her to stop, 'Thinks it'll be the death of me.' She snorts a half laugh. 'It won't be the ciggies that get me, other bits'll start falling apart before then.' Her navy eyes are solid in the gloom.

'Must be difficult,' offers Theo.

She glares at him, 'They said I should never have kids. Not with this.' She knocks over a crutch with some violence. 'But nobody can say when they'll die. I'm a good mother. They mean the world to me.'

Theo makes a noise which he hopes is both soothing and agreeing as he settles the crutch back within her reach. His gaze wanders over the pastel posies which decorate the ceramic-lined walls. In places the glaze is run though by fine lines, cracked, perhaps on firing, though the damage didn't become obvious until they were exposed to the elements. He wishes she would get to the point.

'Family, it's the most important thing in the world, don't you agree DS Akande? You'd do anything for your family to save them from danger, wouldn't you?'

His response is non-committal. *What have you done?* He tries to divine it from those blocks of navy in her pinched face.

'Can't save 'em from death, though, can I?' Silence. She sighs, her tone becomes less steely, not that it could ever be described as a gentle voice, 'Sorry, Theo, you didn't come here to get an earful of my bellyaching. It hasn't been a great morning so far.'

'It's OK. What's on your mind?'

'Apart from dying and leaving my kids without a mum?' She looks over at him and then half smiles. 'You're looking for a camera? Yvonne Everidge's uncle has got it. He found it taking his dog for a walk, on the hill above Westedge. Wants to give it over. You go there, don't ask too many questions, and you'll get what you're after.'

Ask too many and I won't? That's the bargain? He doesn't like it, on the other hand he realises it is the only one he's being offered and Kestle's face, his frightened expression on being led away by Pippa yesterday, comes to him. *Perhaps an investigation into petty thieving and harassment can wait, can be handed over to the uniforms?*

'Sometimes you can't keep your family safe,' Suze is continuing as she readies herself to stand up, collecting around her shoulders her thick woollen shawl patterned with narrow colourful stripes. 'Can't save 'em, from themselves at least.'

* * *

'I hate it when he cries. Why do babies cry like that? It goes right through me, like I'm naked in a typhoon.'

'Hannah,' Izzie's voice is unusually firm. Hannah looks up at her, the familiar face is serious, her hair is tautly pulled back into a bunch, a flousy fringe threaded with grey frames her pale forehead. Her expression is determined, 'Hannah, we can spend another session talking about Aurora and her baby. Or you can tell me what you've really got to say.'

And it starts, the unravelling of the story from the muddled heap of wool. It is messy, incoherent and it isn't about Hannah. It is about another girl and her father. Not about Hannah and the renowned journalist and editor, Stan Poole. Hannah weeps for this other little girl, the lost one, the scared one. *It's my fault, it's my fault. I'm bad to the core. Open my arms with a blade and see the poison run.* Hannah feels the shame creep up over, a dense, overpowering cloak fitted with a muzzle. She cannot meet Izzie's eye for a very long time.

* * *

Later in the day, Theo has occasion to recall Suze's statement, 'Can't save 'em from themselves.' Before going to Westedge he put in a call to the traffic officer, then he set off with Harry. Yvonne's uncle was reluctant to let them in, had the camera behind his front door, ready for their arrival. Even when Theo and Harry did get into the hall, and no further, all they could prise out of him was the story of discovering the camera in some bushes up on the hill. He could take them there if they wished. He fixed them with dull eyes in folded skin, ever so slightly rheumy and bloodshot in one corner. He didn't look fit enough to do much walking on the hill, but the dog certainly existed and his wife backed him up.

Theo left it. He tells Harry to handle the camera with gloves, in case there are useful fingerprints. He doubts there will be. Pulled up in the road around the corner from the Everidges' house, they inspect the photographs, then they go on to call on Yvonne. At the door, Theo has a momentary hesitation, *Maybe I should hand this all over to DI Wiltshire?* She will undoubtedly remonstrate at him questioning someone involved in her case without her say-so. *But it had been my case first. Yvonne my witness, my victim first. And this is only a friendly chat.* He rings the doorbell.

Paul opens the door. Theo hasn't seen him since their dash to Hull. Today the lad is dishevelled, in tracky bottoms and a sweatshirt, his hair uncombed. His face is pouched by tiredness and has lost some of its bloom. *Lost its innocence.* Paul does not return Theo's smile, Yvonne is out. 'For long?' Paul shrugs, he's still not learnt to lie well. 'We'll come in and wait,' says Theo decisively, and nor is the young man capable of contradicting an adult.   He leads them into the sitting room, offering them, with poor grace, some tea. They accept and while Paul is in the kitchen, Theo surveys the room. It hasn't changed since his initial visit, except for the removal of the Christmas decorations and it is perhaps a little more untidy. His gaze travels across the many photos, of Victoria, of Paul, of the two of them together, of them with Ian or Yvonne or both, in different landscapes belonging to various countries. *A tale of a happy family. A tale I'd never quite believed.* Paul returns with a tray and serves them, he then appears unsure whether to stay or to go. Harry invites him to sit, asks him what he's doing at home, and receives the answer, 'Revising.' She asks him a bit about his coming exams and he responds with as little information as possible. His face is tense. He sits on his hands. Is intent on the carpet.

'Must be good to have Victoria home,' says Theo, taking a biscuit, *Breakfast was a long time ago.* Paul nods. Theo continues, 'Guess there's been a few difficult times too, though, after all you've been through?' Another nod, an unhappy nod. 'When did you find out Paul?' Theo keeps his voice steady. 'About what your stepmum had done?'

Paul glances up through his fringe, he bites at his lip. Shakes his head.

'You can tell us, Paul, you're not in any trouble, nor is Victoria, we just want to know what happened.'

Another nibble at the lips, maybe he is gathering himself to say something, only he doesn't get the chance as at that moment Yvonne bangs into the house. She yells up the stairs and then turns into the living room, coming to a halt as she realises who is there. She looks from person to person. Paul sinks further into his seat. 'What's going on?' his stepmother says sharply.

Theo stands, 'Hello Yvonne, we've come round for a chat.'

'Mrs Everidge to you. And you shouldn't be talking to my son without one of his parents present.' She thumps down her shopping bags, they spill over with food.

'He's seventeen, Mrs Everidge,' Theo says evenly.

'He's still a child and he has no right to invite you into my house. Please leave.' Yvonne's voice is getting close to a screech.

'If we did leave, Mrs Everidge, we would have to ask you to come with us.'

'I would not.'

'Then we would have to arrest you.'

'What the hell for?' the words come out at top volume and top octave.

Now that is a question, for kidnapping your own daughter? 'We have evidence, a photo of you and Victoria. Plus that little scrape you had on Cottingham Road was recorded. I wonder who we might find living near there? A cousin of yours perhaps?' A guess based on a photo on her uncle's hall of him and his wife flanking a bride, the legend saying: 'Holy Trinity, Hull.' Yvonne's face is chalk.

'Come on Mum, please,' Paul sounds desperate. 'Tell them.'

Her voice remains strident, 'I had to, don't you see? Ray was going to take her away from me. I had to stop him, make everyone see how dangerous he is. There's no harm done. Vicky didn't mind. It was like a little holiday for her.'

'And what about Alexi Kestle?'

'He's a paedo, everyone knows it. If it wasn't Victoria, it'd be some other little girl.'

'But it wasn't Victoria, was it?'

She slumps onto the arm of the nearest armchair. Shakes her head. Says quietly, 'I had to stop you lot asking questions. Victoria was getting tired, she might have said something. When you wouldn't arrest Ray, I had to come up with someone else, just to shut you up.' Then she brightens. 'There's no harm done though is there?'

Theo doesn't reply. He's on his way past Yvonne to call Pippa when he is halted by Paul shouting, 'No harm done? You stupid, ignorant woman. You've made Vicky into a liar. Made me into a liar. She hated it down there. She wanted to be with us for Christmas, not with some fucking second cousin. She told me. She didn't dare tell you. Was too scared she'd upset you, that you wouldn't let her see her dad anymore. She was scared, so scared. You selfish fucking cow.' And with this he pushes past Theo to go upstairs. He is weeping.

Yvonne calls after him from her perch, 'Now, Pauly, don't get upset.' She turns back to Theo and Harry, giggles, 'Teenagers eh?'

* * *

Izzie comforts her, sitting beside her, holding one of her hands, 'Thank you Hannah for telling me. You've done tremendously well today.' Hannah feels the comfort and is grateful, *I don't deserve it. I shouldn't have said anything.* Bringing those wispy, hard-to-pin-down memories into a narrative which can be spoken, which has some consistency, is very wrong indeed. For they make no sense, it is their quality, lack of unity. She's not even certain what she has been saying is the truth, hers or anybody else's. *Liar, Hannah, you're a liar, you should be punished for that.*

'No, no, we don't do that here, Hannah,' Izzie contains the punishing hand. 'Be gentle with yourself.'

Why? I don't deserve it.

'Tell me what's going on for you.'

'I shouldn't have said all the stuff, about Dad. It's not true.'

'Funny, I believe every word of it.'

'Then you're a gullible fool.'

'I don't think so.'

Now it's worse, I've insulted Izzie. Hannah wants to grab the words back, 'I'm sorry, I shouldn't have said that.'

'It's OK. You're just telling me how hard it is for you to believe yourself, believe in yourself. Who called you a liar?'

Dad. 'No one. Me.'

'Now that I don't believe. We've got about five minutes left. No, no need to jump up, let's sit here for a little longer like this. You've had a tough session, you need to take care of yourself. Is there anyone you can go to after this, who could be with you this evening? I'd rather you weren't alone.'

She's had a text from Lawrence saying he is in town. *I don't want to see him. How can I face him after what I've just said? Ben? If only I could.* They've exchanged restrained and polite texts since, since, she struggles to find the right word, *Their date?* Each reassuring the other that it had been a good evening, one to be repeated. *But he's lying. He doesn't want to see me. No point in hoping he does. Anyway, think he said he is away at a conference until tomorrow.* 'Aurora,' she says. *No, can't bother her with this. She doesn't want me around Oli, not in this state, I know she doesn't. And I don't blame her.* She feels herself oozing poison.

'Sounds like a good idea.' Izzie turns to pick up her diary to check the time of their next session. It is unnecessary, they both know what they've got booked in, she is closing the session down.

Come on, Hannah tells herself, *don't grizzle, don't be pathetic, you've got to leave now.* 'I don't want to go,' she says, the words come from a child's mouth, not from her own. *Hold me, Izzie, keep me safe.*

'I know. And I'll be here for you, next week.'

Which is all you can say. That's the deal, you know it, I know it. You can't heal the chasm, it's too big even for you.

* * *

In some ways Yvonne Everidge is magnificent in her delusion, Theo has to concede. She is sat in the armchair, still in her pink puffer jacket, refusing to go with them. The police are to blame for all this. 'If you'd only arrested Ray, it would have been enough, you could have let him go after. Then we'd have had no more nonsense about access weekends, or longer. I have nothing more to say.' And she takes out her phone to play what looks like some kind of online bingo, oblivious to Harry's reasoned argument.

Theo is seriously considering whether he and DC Shilling will have to manhandle her out of the house when Ian arrives, summoned by Paul, who reappears and settles on the top step of the stairs. Mr Everidge says he knew nothing until his son's call today and Theo accepts his word. The man looks tormented, worried, by turns, about Vicky, Paul and what is going to happen to Yvonne. Theo reassures him neither of the children will have to answer to anything, but he must persuade Yvonne to come to the station. Initially Ian balks at this, surely this could all be cleared up here and now. He echoes his wife, 'No harm done.'

Anger shudders through Theo, he thunders, 'Mr Everidge, an innocent man has been questioned and held in a cell because of what Yvonne did. Not to mention the money spent, the hours spent. People were worried. Scared.' Harry's eyes widen and eyebrows lift. Paul folds over on himself, resting his forehead on his knees. He begins to whimper. Ian glances up at his son, makes a move in his direction and then turns back to his wife.

'Yvonne, love, you need to go with DS Akande and DC Shilling. You need to go now.'

'No dear, I have to pick up Victoria soon.'

'Paul and I will do that. Please Yvonne, just go, I'll phone Arnold, he'll know of a good solicitor.'

Her thumbs are still working on the keypad, more erratically now, 'I don't need a solicitor, dear.'

'Yes you do.' His voice is loud. He stands up straight and is suddenly taller than Theo, there's some muscle outline under his shirt sleeves now he's taken off his jacket. 'Yvonne, get up and go.'

She drops her phone into her lap and lifts her face to him, pale, bony, panicked, 'I can come back, here, can't I?'

Ian crosses his arms. 'I don't know,' he says sadly. 'I don't know anything anymore, only you need to go. Now.' He emphasises the last words and this jolts his wife out of her apparent reverie. She gets up, there's an awkward embrace between her and Ian, she calls a goodbye to 'Pauly' who doesn't lift his head and follows Harry out meekly to the car. Theo stands for a moment with the two devastated men. *Ray would have understood Yvonne better, accepted her need to take matters into her own hands.* He wants to say something reassuring, can't think of anything, so mutters, 'Thanks, you've done the right thing,' before hurrying out.

Pippa, however, has not done the right thing, not in Theo's opinion. She has sent Kestle home, 'He'll be alright. We'll keep an eye on him.' The anger which has been whooshing around Theo's body since the morning, since hearing about Stan from Lawrence, almost explodes. He grits his teeth, forces himself to say nothing. 'And don't think of going to Westedge yourself, DS Akande,' DI Wiltshire says to his back as he turns. 'I've still got to decide what to do about your recent insubordination in withholding vital information in my case and interviewing a suspect without my permission. Besides,' she softens her tone slightly, 'I've got plenty to keep you busy.'

Which is what she does, all afternoon, requiring reports to be made up and the camera to be sent to the appropriate crime lab, phone calls to be made to chase down where on Cottingham Road Yvonne's cousin lives and an initial interview over the phone with her to be made. By the end of it, Theo is flagging, he wants a large drink, he wants to put his feet up, he wants to forget about mothers who stow away their daughters for reasons understood only by their miserable selves. Even so, he is planning on passing by Kestle's house. Pippa reads his mind, 'I've got officers down there, if I hear of you oh so accidentally driving by, there'll be trouble. Understand? This is my case.'

Then you're responsible when Alexi gets roasted to death, oh so accidentally, in a house fire. Theo tastes the sourness in his mouth. He turns and goes, not responding to Pippa's cheerful adieu.

His house is inhabited when he returns to it after driving erratically through the darkening streets and swearing at any driver who dared to get in his way. He stands on the threshold, wishing the building would be empty, or that he had somewhere else to go. He doesn't, however, and so he drags himself into the front room. It is warm, lights are low, candles flicker around the small mantelpiece, Nora Jones croons through the loudspeakers and a good (very good) bottle of red wine stands open on the coffee table. Lawrence comes in from the kitchen bringing with him the smell of onions sautéed in butter and spice. 'Shit day?' he asks. Theo nods, feeling like his spine might crack with the effort of staying upright.

Lawrence comes up and plants a kiss on his forehead, then on his mouth, holds him for a moment around the shoulders, allowing Theo to let go of his effort to stand. 'Sit. Have a drink,' Lawrence whispers. 'I'll draw you a bubbly bath.' Theo sits, sips some wine, before nodding off in the corner of the sofa. He allows himself to be taken care of for the rest of the evening. He talks about the frustrations of the day. Lawrence listens, doesn't interrupt, doesn't try to solve anything, he just listens. It is only later that Theo asks Lawrence about his day. 'I got in touch with your contact and he'll pick up Stan's computer tomorrow from my home. My neighbour will let them in. I'll have to make a statement.' Lawrence sounds unhappy. Theo strokes his arm as they sit side-by-side on the sofa, the bottle of (very good) red wine is now empty.

'And Hannah?'

'I texted her and went round, but she wasn't there. I'll try again tomorrow.'

CHAPTER 31

Earlier in the afternoon, Hannah watched Lawrence from the long narrow window at the turn of the staircase. She knew he could not see her even when he scanned the house. He rang the doorbell, several times, clattering the letterbox cover and calling out. He went round the back, knocking on doors and windows, finally leaving after ten minutes, glancing back as he did so.

She had returned to sitting on the floor of the landing by her father's office where she is now. She's been there since coming back from Izzie's, an hour ago, maybe more. She's tired, thirsty, still she cannot move. Her arm throbs from the razor cut. She had to blood let, *Get the poison out.* She did ring Aurora, left a message, asked her to come round. Next door is dark and quiet, no one home. *No one to care. Ah well.*

She reaches up and twists then pushes the door knob, she crawls into the room. She lies down by the desk, her knees tucked up to her chest, her arms wrapped around her knees, her temple and ear against the harsh texture of the carpet. She closes her eyes. *I won't cry. I'm too empty to cry.* Time passes, there's the over-wound clock with its erratic ticking informing her minutes are being frittered away. *Time to get up, get up Hannah, don't make a fuss.*

With an effort, she does open her eyes and begin to uncurl herself. As she does so, she sees a book propping up a corner of the bookcase which would otherwise be slumping over. As she's already sorted, removed and given away much of its contents, she can slowly ease out the volume secreted below it. It is a battered, leather-covered address book. In his time, her father knew some important, famous even, people. She notices that against some of the entries, the entries for men, Stan Poole has recorded the name of a car, presumably the one they owned.

The folder her father had hidden or lost is on the desk. She stretches up and pulls it down to her – ground – level. The sheets spill out every which way, releasing the smell of ink and rotting paper. She feels the chill of the room, she's not turned up the heating and has been sitting without moving for too long, a stiffness infuses her joints. Ink and paper. Newspaper ink and newspaper. The scent on the hands which held her. The odour of the room where she was being held by those hands. She looks at the sheets tumbled around her. 'Maybe it's a code,' Ben had said. She touches the photo of the white lily, then the one of the wildcat. *Who had I been?* It occurs to her what the cars represent, or rather who. The memory is there when she lets it in.

Not just my dad then. How like him, methodically making sure all his friends had a share, got a turn. 'Generous to a fault, Stan Poole,' how often had I heard that? She turns her head to where her father's computer had once been. He'd have moved onto the new technology. *He loved gadgets, it's why this folder stops.* Then it occurs to her, *Lawrence has Stan's computer.* She imagines it's why he came round, to tell her what a despicable whore she is. *Your fault Hannah. My fault.* She feels sick.

I have to get out. Out of this room. Out of this house. She recalls the plump bedraggled Loretta Lynn, her carved-up arms, dancing with the waves. But Loretta Lynn didn't want to die that day, it was plain to see. *You do, though, don't you Hannah?*

CHAPTER 32

Aurora rings Theo at 9 p.m. 'I'm worried about Hannah. She left a message for me, said she wanted to see me, only she's not been home since I got back and isn't answering her mobile. She sounded odd.' Theo, mellowed by the wine and the comfort of being close to Lawrence, suggests Hannah had gone out somewhere with someone. 'Ben's away,' replies Aurora. 'I suppose Maya might have dragged her out. I don't know her number. I'll try Rose or Ben.'

She rings back after she's tried both; plus she'd got a number from Rose for Maya, tried it, no response. Ben's already on his way back to Scarborough from York, he'd agreed with Hannah to speak to her earlier in the evening and hadn't been able to get hold of her. He's worried enough to forego his conference dinner and head over.

'Perhaps we should go, to Hannah's house,' Lawrence sounds strained, his expression is somewhere between worry and pleading. 'Aurora's got a key, we could have a look round.'

Theo would have preferred to stay befuddled with the drink and take his lover to bed. However, he can see any romantic possibilities are now off the agenda, so with an effort he pulls himself together. He gets dressed again for the outside, in jeans and jumper and duffle while alternating coffee with water to try and clear his head. As both have drunk too much to risk driving, they walk the fifteen minutes to Sea View Lane. The cold sobers them. They find Aurora striding the floors of her living room. Max, who is drinking a lager in front of the football, is telling her to calm down, while she is retorting to her husband that he should get off his arse and do something useful. A row is brewing. Theo suggests Aurora takes him and Lawrence next door and Max send Ben over when he arrives.

The house is unlit and chilled, the curtains undrawn, there is one mug and one small plate on the draining board in the kitchen.

The *Marie Celeste* comes to Theo's mind. The other two stand in the hallway, silent, all Aurora's fire drained away, they look to him for an answer. He doesn't have one. Someone knocks on the half open front door, they all jump. It is Ben. 'Hannah, is she ...?' he begins. They all shake their heads.

They troop upstairs. The two bedrooms and the bathroom on the middle floor appear unlived in. Theo and Lawrence check the office, notice the papers on the floor. 'A break-in? A scuffle?' asks Lawrence tentatively.

'I doubt it.' Theo does begin to wonder whether they should be touching quite so many things without gloves.

Finally, in the attic, they find signs of a life being got through. Hannah's bed has been slept in, there's a slew of clothes falling from a chair to the floor, and a clutter of files and books to do with her course on the desk. Her bathroom, though not untidy, is obviously in use, a hand towel is damp.

'Oh,' Lawrence is by the sink. He picks up a razor blade, there is a stain of blood on the porcelain. He turns to Theo, his blue eyes begging for reassurance.

'It's not enough blood for ...' Theo pauses, '... for anything serious.'

Lawrence goes back into the bedroom carrying the blade before him as if it were a slightly distasteful religious relic. Theo follows.

'She cuts herself,' Ben says.

'What d'ya mean?' Lawrence blusters.

'It's a way of coping with the pain, the mental pain, letting it out through cutting her arm with a razor blade.'

'And you didn't stop her?'

'Don't you think I tried?' Ben retorts.

Lawrence is shouting at Ben, 'You fucking therapists, you're supposed to be helping people, what were you doing letting her go on with this ...?'

'I did my best to support her,' Ben's voice is stiff, its volume held down.

'Support her? Support her ...? What if she's injured herself, is bleeding ...?'

'She always did it safely,' interrupts Ben, still talking staccato.

'Safely cutting herself? What are you saying man?'

Ben replies, 'She knows where to cut, how deep, to keep the blade clean, treat the cut. She made sure she did it safely, as safely as cutting can ever be.'

'But this time, maybe this time ...'

Theo puts his hand on Lawrence's shoulder, feels him shaking. 'There's not enough blood,' he repeats.

There's a silence. Then Aurora says, 'Where the hell is she?' Another moment of quiet into which a bar of Mozart begins to play. Aurora dives into the pile of clothes and comes up with a mobile, it stops ringing, she checks the screen. 'It's Hannah's. That was her sister-in-law.'

'She never goes out without her phone,' says Lawrence.

'Did you call her brother?' Theo asks Aurora.

She shakes her head. 'Didn't think of it, you know they don't really get on.' They listen to the message, Veronica is demanding Hannah respond to her phone calls and emails. 'It's your mother, she should go in a home,' she finishes desperately.

'Not there then,' Aurora says.

They all look from one to the other, the worry and the question 'What now?' are palpable in the room. Through Theo's sluggish mind comes the thought, *I should take charge, I'm the one with experience here.* The idea that this might be a crime scene batting at the back of his mind, he suggests they go back to Aurora's. Once in her bright kitchen, coffee and some homemade biscuits sustaining them, all things are more possible.

Lawrence starts to contact the hospitals, Aurora the people on Hannah's phone list and Theo the station. Nothing's been reported in. When he disconnects he hears the tail end of Ben's call to his neighbour. It's clear Hannah hasn't been seen; however, Maya has been. Ben dials again, he snaps, 'Maya, pick up, I know you're there.' Theo has never heard him sound so brusque, so annoyed. Ben breaks the connection and punches in the numbers a further time. On his third attempt, Maya responds. Ben briefly explains Hannah has gone missing. There's a pause, then, 'So what? So what? Maya, if you know anything you'd better tell me right now.' Another short moment, then, 'Stop bullshitting me and tell me what's been going on.' This time he gets a reply to which he listens intently. 'You idiot Maya,' he says, before stabbing at the 'end call' button. There's quiet in the room, they have all stopped what they are doing and are staring at Ben. He explains, 'Maya met someone last night in a bar who was searching for Hannah, she told him where to find her.' His voice is laced with disgust.

'I don't suppose she got a name?' Theo asks.

'Steel Cowboy.'

Lawrence begins to say what use is that, Aurora halts him, 'You know him, Theo?'

Theo remembers as she says this, sees again the jacket with the name in the design on the back. He nods, 'I don't get the connection.'

'For god's sake man, who is he?' asks Lawrence, beginning to bluster once more.

Theo hesitates, wary of the consequences of discussing police business. Ben mutters something about confidentiality.

'Blow confidentiality,' says Lawrence.

'Telling us his name,' Aurora starts slowly, 'could help find the connection. Wouldn't it override any confidentiality imperative?'

She's right, and Hannah is maybe turning from a misper to a victim of a different sort. 'I talked to him to do with the remains found by the A64 a few weeks back. His name is possibly Davis, his mother is Michelle and he lives on the Millstream Estate in Leeds.' He glances round at blank faces. 'I'll phone Leeds, get a PC to see if Steel Cowboy is at home.'

'And meanwhile Hannah might be out there with this murderer,' says Lawrence.

'I didn't say he was a murderer, he wasn't even born when my body died.'

'Still, we should be looking for them,' says Ben. 'We can't risk not doing anything.' His tone is determined, he's already reaching for his coat.

'But where?' asks Theo. 'Where do we look?'

Chapter 33

The grey day slips seamlessly into a clouded night. Hannah is sitting curled up at the foot of the South Cliff gardens, leaning against a wall which the constructors may have intended to replicate a cliff face. Sharp rocks held in by cement poke into her back, she's shuffled herself around to find a little niche where this won't happen. The wall builders (some hundred years ago) also created a sweeping path linking the old South Bay pool and the Victorian Gothic Spa. It would once have been a busy promenade, the series of alcoves created by the curving wall, a place to rest and chat. Not on a dark February night. Hannah has seen a few runners slogging past, and dog walkers mostly intent on their mobile phones, a few pausing for a moment to contemplate the sea and the horizon. None have noticed her. She is secreted away.

The sea has crept in while she has been there, quietly easing up to the edge of the promenade, now it is slopping over the edges, sending out fingers of foam to pull itself onto land. The breeze is warmer than it has been. Hannah is cosy in her layers. She watches the flop of dark water slide ever closer. Not for the first time, she imagines slipping into its grasp, being cradled to the deep. It is mesmerising. It is enticing. The first touch of a wave on her toes, however, brings her to her feet. An autonomic response to the icy fingernail nudging at her. It is pushing her away, not inviting her in. She glares at it. *You're right not to have me. I'd contaminate even you.* She shifts her gaze to the undulating body, its sleek skin stretched to where it becomes sewn into the sky by the horizon. It is beginning to take back the earth, soon there won't be a path for her to follow. Perhaps it is this which prompts another part of her to goad herself into action. *Come on Hannah,* she tells herself sternly, *stop feeling sorry for yourself, there are people much worse off than you. Children, families, blown up, blown apart, in Iraq, in Palestine. I am lucky, have much to be grateful for. Move Hannah.*

Slowly she does. Carefully she makes her way towards the Spa, judging the inundation from the sea so she just about manages to get away with no more than a dampening spray to her ankles. Then she hears a voice, calling her name. It is coming from the beach huts situated a little way above and back from the walkway. She looks up. The figure is stringy, in low-slung jeans and a top, the hood pulled up, the voice a low tenor. *Do I recognise him? Maybe. Think I saw him earlier, walking through the gardens? Could it be Craig, my young client? Whoever he is, he is definitely shouting to me.* She climbs the steps, is within paces of him, stops. His face is shrouded. However, she's sure it's not Craig. Some weird sense of politeness holds her from turning away immediately.

That's a mistake. He's grabbed her, his arm locked around her throat. She recalls some self-defence for women class she did once and stamps on his foot, kicks back at his shin, neither actions are particularly well aimed or forceful. She feels weak, stupid. She feels the scrape of a metal blade against the underside of her chin, 'I wouldn't try that if I were you, Hannah Poole.'

* * *

Aurora suggests they start with where Hannah is fond of walking, the South Cliff gardens, 'Maybe she's stumbled, hurt herself, isn't able to get home.' She says she'll get changed into something warmer and she and Ben can begin.

Theo's phone rings, there's a brief silence after he answers it, then a torrent of jittery words. He picks through them as they land. He gathers this is someone called Loretta Lynn, a Michelle Scraggs' daughter, from the Millstream Estate, worried about her brother, 'You left your card with Mam, said we could ring.'

He tries to get some clarification, 'Is Michelle Scraggs, Michelle Davis?'

'Yes, Davis was the name of the bastard who fathered our Jade.'

'Is your brother, Steel Cowboy?'

'Yes, it's the stupid name he gives 'isself.'

'Do you know where he's gone?'

'He's here in Scarborough, left me a text, said he was going to sort out the mare who's going to shop Mam.'

'Shop her for what?' Theo knows this is not a priority question, but worries he may not get another chance.

Loretta Lynn doesn't reply, only reiterates they have to find her brother. 'He's high, he's not 'isself when he's high.'

'Where would he go?'

'To the beach huts, South Bay. That's where we'd alus go.' And Theo suddenly has an image of the woman he is talking to, Loretta Lynn, the rotund lass, shivering, soaked through, eyes red with the salt, arms like old ripped carpet. She'd gone there too, to do herself harm. She shuts down her phone. When he tries calling back, she doesn't respond. He calls the station, who can he drag out for back-up? *Not Chesters, please.* Only that's who is on-call. He tells him to bring a uniform, PC Trevor Trench will do fine.

* * *

The beach hut smells of old socks which have never dried properly. It didn't take much for her captor to dismantle the padlock and gain entry. He's reclosed the door and used a rope he's found to hold it firm, she's studied the knots and reckons she wouldn't manage a quick exit. Apart from anything else, he's pushed her into a deck chair and secured her to it and a nail in the wall with her scarf wrapped around her neck. The square room is almost bare, there's a sink with a cupboard under it. *There might be utensils in there which could help me, only I can't reach it.* There's a few more beach chairs stacked up against the back and a bare illuminated bulb hanging down on a flex from the roof.

The young man, her jailor, is walking the floor. She can see the regular tremors which wrack his slender frame. He sniffs constantly, rubbing at his nose with the back of a shaking hand. When he'd said his name was Steel Cowboy she almost laughed out loud. She doesn't feel much like laughing now. She's afraid and he's sloughing terror like it's dead skin. She's tried the 'You don't want to do this', 'My friends will be looking for me' and 'I've a friend who's a policeman' tactics, none of which have had any effect. Now he's got her here, he doesn't appear to know what to do, he just paces and fingers his knife.

Think, Hannah, think. And there is something knocking at the back of her mind if only she could retrieve it. *If only I didn't feel so tired, so hungry, so thirsty.* She's tried asking for some water to no avail. *If only I wasn't so desperate for the loo, I could get my head straight and something would come.*

* * *

Theo wants them to stay behind, but Aurora is determined not to be left at home. She points out Theo hasn't anything to drive, and once she's designated herself driver, the others all pile in. For the first time in ages, she is feeling energetic: *My brain is working, I am close to how I remember myself to be 'BM'. A warrior. An Amazon.* She drives them all down to the Spa; Theo and Lawrence quiet in the back, Ben fidgeting in the front. She wants to tell them it will all work out.

They are met by a police car and DC Chesters and PC Trench are introduced. Chesters is an excitable whippet, his short dark gelled hair standing on end adding to the impression. Trench is a silent bulldog, his uniform dripping with every kind of police device imaginable. Aurora watches Theo in discussion with them, she can tell he's taking control, notices how sexy this makes him. Lawrence is standing beside her, she suspects he's noticed too.

Ben has turned away from them, is leaning against the sandstone sea wall looking out across the waves. She goes up to him, slips her arm through his, feels the tenseness in them, his hands shoved, balled, into his pocket. 'She'll be OK,' says Aurora. 'Hannah has more resources than we think.'

'I've been a blind idiot.' His voice grates out of his throat. 'I didn't see how jealous Maya was. I didn't realise how much Hannah means to me. And I thought I had some insight. Didn't see what was in front of me.'

Aurora hugs his arm with hers. She senses he doesn't want to be comforted.

Theo says he, Chesters and Trench are going for a recce and for the others to stay put. She watches them disappear into the shadows of the undercliff, suddenly subdued by the import and the seriousness of what is happening. She sends out a message to Hannah, *Hold on, we're coming.*

* * *

Inexplicably, she must have closed her eyes and dozed. When she comes to wakefulness, she is sore, unsure of where she is, until she opens her lids and sees Steel Cowboy squatting close to her, inspecting her. Her desire to pee is even greater. *I will not wet myself.* She tenses every muscle she is able. Then she remembers, 'Poker, it's your poker name.'

'She has been talking then? Julie? Or Juliaaaa, making her sound like the fucking stuck up bitch she is. I didn't believe Mam when she told me. Julie had been blabbing to some psycho, it didn't make any sense, but I asked around, worked it out, not a psycho, a counsellor, you're easy to find on the web. You look better in your photo than you do now.'

Hannah wonders whether the situation liberates her from not being able to speak about her clients. Then Orwell comes to her and his comment about her being only 'relatively boundaried'. She keeps her mouth shut.

Steel Cowboy is talking for them both now anyway, the words becoming slurred as they trip over themselves and his tongue. 'Julie is a bitch, keeps the screws on Mam, makes her take all the blame for what Julie did. And now the body's been found, Mam's going to prison. Not if I have anything to do with it. Julie can go to hell, I'll deal with her too, when the time comes. But you, Hannah, mustn't be allowed to say nothing.' Here his voice turns mocking, high-pitched, a parody of her middle-class accent, 'Not to your friend the policeman.' His tone turns meaner again, 'Not to anyone. Get it? Without you to back her up, Julie won't be able to do nowt.'

'I'm not going to say anything, I'm not allowed to,' Hannah tries to keep the words steady as she lies. 'What happens in a therapy session can't be talked about elsewhere. Not even a judge can make me reveal anything. It's like being a priest.'

The lad's eyes flick from side to side, his tongue licks his cracked lips. 'Mam's always speaking to the priest, I tell her not to, she says he can't go blabbing.'

'And nor can I. Let me go now and I'll say nothing about this either. We can go our separate ways and it'll be our little secret.'

'What about your friends, looking for you.'

'I was joking, to scare you. My boyfriend's out of town.' 'Boyfriend' settles uneasily in the mouth. 'No one's expecting me home.' *That much at least is true. I hope someone is missing me.*

The trembling starts up again and he is sweating, 'Christ, I need a drink.'

'Then let me go and you can have one. I'll give you the money.' *Where is this calm coming from?* She didn't know she had it in her. Surface only, underneath she's shaking too.

He moves towards her, puts the knife down on the concrete and leans over to untie the scarf. She can smell the sourness of his underarms, she closes her eyes and tries to do the same with her nose. There's a sound from outside, a footstep maybe. Steel Cowboy freezes. She reassures him, it's a gull landing awkwardly, a dog walker who has merely passed by. He sits back on his heels. He's watching her. She notices the colour of his eyes, a soft blue-grey, among the acne scars. They are focused on her now. The scarf is loose but she isn't sure it's completely untied. The knife is by her feet. *If I dive down would I get it before he does?*

* * *

Aurora hasn't thought about Oli for the last hour, not consciously. *Why should I? Max is there and he's a good dad. Why should I spend every waking minute worrying about our son?* She realises it's what she's been doing since she finally accepted he was hers. Forever. She wonders if she should phone home. A woman approaches along the road from town. She's shapeless in her dark coat. She circles the police car. Aurora goes forward, 'Can I help you?' *Do I look enough like a police detective?* Obviously, as the woman asks her for Detective Akande, pronouncing carefully the unfamiliar name. 'He's busy. Can I help?'

'I'm Loretta Lynn, I need to talk to my brother, stop him from doing something stupid.' As she steps under the harsh light of the one street light, the youngster's face is exposed as a leathery skull, her synthetic textured hair dyed a lurid green and pulled up into a top knot. Aurora says she will take Loretta Lynn to her brother.

Both Ben and Lawrence raise objections. 'I don't think it's safe,' says Ben.

'Is that wise?' chimes in Lawrence.

She ignores them, tells Loretta Lynn she must be very quiet and steers her along the shadowy path to the beach huts. They meet Chesters first, an unhappy outpost, he asks them what they are doing in a harsh whisper. Aurora explains, holding tight to Loretta Lynn's podgy arm, worrying she might run off, either towards the huts or the other way. Chesters lets them go on, the lap-lap of the water beside them covering any noise their feet might be making. They reach Theo and Trench huddled just below the lip of the steps leading up to the level of the huts. Aurora pushes the other woman in front of her, 'Loretta Lynn,' she says quietly.

At that moment there's a scream. A woman's, from behind the thin wooden door in front of them. It's Hannah screaming.

Aurora lunges forward, then is roughly pulled back. 'Not you!' Theo spits into her ear. 'You go get Chesters. There's back-up coming, get him to get it here quickly. Trench, let's go.'

* * *

Hannah flings herself forward. She is hampered by the scarf caught somewhere and the chair collapsing over on top of her. Still, she has the knife. Her hand is on the knife. 'No!' Her captor's voice growls up from his chest into a vicious shout. She is tossed aside, sent spinning across the floor. Her head smashes into the robust base of the cupboard. A shriek breaks from her, she did not know she could make so much noise.

'Shut up, shut up you bitch,' shouts rain down with kicks, into her back, her neck. Dizziness overwhelms her. *Let me die, let me die now.* Wood splinters. Heavy boots. Yelling. Men's voices. A woman's screeching, 'Kev, Kev, don't do it, don't be stupid. Think what it would do to Mam.' Metal falling to concrete, jangling painfully into her ear. Sirens in the distance. Paddington Bear, she can smell the duffle, leaning over her, 'It's OK Hannah, I've got you, it'll be alright.'

Only it won't be alright, folded over on herself she can smell her own urine. It won't ever be alright again. *Bad Hannah, bad girl, look what a mess you've made. Look what you've made me do.* She closes her eyes shut. Tight. Block it all out. The voices recede. She is floating. Floating away.

CHAPTER 34

Theo is exhausted. The previous night, after watching Hannah being taken away in an ambulance with Ben and Aurora following in her car, Theo had arrested Kevin Scraggs, ensured the beach hut was cordoned off for the CSIs the next day and left Trench on guard. That was the easy part. He then had to decide what to do with Loretta Lynn. In the end she made the decision for him, she tried to run away and, when Chesters prevented her, she drooped and started to whine. He couldn't arrest her for anything and yet he still wanted to be able to find her, 'Where do you want to go love?' His accent growing stronger in answer to hers. 'Where's safe for you?' She said she wanted to go to Four Lanes, the psychiatric hospital on the edge of town, where he had taken her the last time they'd met. He turned to Lawrence, explained he would have to go with Loretta Lynn, *He's stayed for me, not gone to Hannah.*

Lawrence had smiled, 'No problem, I'll get a taxi.'

It would have been good to hug, briefly, companionably, only Theo was aware of Chesters gaping at them, he managed a brief squeeze of the hand before turning away. 'Chesters,' he reprimanded, 'get your chin up off the floor. You're driving us to Four Lanes.' Theo had hoped to pump Loretta Lynn for some information, only she'd clammed up and he knew by the morning she'd be drugged up. He filled in the paperwork and an hour after leaving him returned home to a slumbering Lawrence.

Theo's sleep was fitful. He had risen early, managing not to wake his lover, grabbed a scant breakfast, *Lawrence would be horrified,* and got into the interview room by 7 a.m. Sobered up and with a bacon buttie inside him, Kevin Scraggs was no more forthcoming than his sister. He admitted to the offences which could not be denied, didn't appear bothered about the prospect of prison. When asked, he said his assault on Hannah had been to get money for drugs. Beyond this he would not be budged.

Then came the futile trip to Leeds where Michelle had been brought into the station. She was clothed in a sack of a dress and clumpy platforms, which only emphasised her chubbiness. She smelt of cheap cider and her eyes were pink and puffy. She claimed she'd been mithering over her son all night. 'What have you done with 'im?' Theo explained he was being held and the charges. She scowled, 'You have no right taking him.'

'I think you'll find we have every right, a woman's in hospital badly injured because of his actions.' He had a sudden vision of Hannah, blood seeping from the ugly gash on her head and into her hair. 'We took your daughter to Four Lanes. I'm sure she'll be allowed visitors.'

She shrugged, scowled more deeply, 'She won't want to see me.'

'Now, Ms Scraggs ...'

'Mrs Davis.'

'Mrs Davis I want to talk about Lenny Sharpe.'

'Any chance of getting a drink round here?'

'Water?'

'Coffee, strong, your colour.'

Theo sent the WPC who is sitting in with him out and waited for her to come back with coffee for all of them. He was beginning to flag. Once Michelle had taken a swig from her cup, he reiterated, 'Lenny Sharpe, Mrs Davis?'

'What about him?'

'You know him?'

'Knew him. The Sharpes were a family in the estate, everyone knew them.'

'And what about Lenny? How well did you know him?'

She gulped down some more liquid, Theo could feel her gaze on him. He could sense some of the anxiety which had been around her when he'd visited her. Only today she managed to maintain her belligerence, the Dutch courage no doubt, 'I knew him, he was a neighbour, I'll say no more about 'im.'

'Tell me about going to Scarborough with him. We know you did. Your son told us.' It was a guess. Theo didn't like using this kind of method, but sometimes the ends did justify the means.

'He what?' She slammed her cup down and coffee slopped over. Then she grinned, showing off a couple of chipped front teeth, 'Oh I get it, inspector, you're having me on, right? I'm not as stupid as I look.' She tapped the side of her head. She sat back, 'I'm here voluntary, ain't I? So I can go now? Or you arrest me and I'll get a lawyer. I've got a card here see?' Theo saw, it was a well-known swanky firm. How could she afford one of them?

He softened his tone, 'I'm guessing Lenny Sharpe hurt you, Mrs Davis, was that what happened? He must have been twice your age, you were only a kid, it would have been self-defence.'

Michelle flushed behind the ears, looked down. 'He was a bastard. Couldn't keep his 'ands to 'isself. But I didn't do nowt to 'im and you can't prove I did.' It was her last word on it or anything else, no matter how Theo cajoled or commanded or inveigled. Theo had to let her go.

He started to drive back to Scarborough, *Still don't think of it as home,* and panicked himself by narrowly missing a cyclist. He pulled into a café in a lay-by, he ordered eggs on toast and wanted water, all they had were fizzy drinks, he took a luminous orange one. He sat down. He texted Lawrence, 'On my way.' 'Should I wait to eat?' came back almost immediately. He replied, 'Best not.' He looked out at the gathering dusk and commuter traffic slicing along the road which he still had to travel. *What a wasted day. I badly need to speak to Hannah.*

* * *

Hannah has been on a long sea voyage tied to some kind of raft. At times it's been peaceful, the water as soft and welcoming as a mattress of down, at others there were waves tipping her this way, then that, so she felt obliged to grasp tight the edges of the vessel.

Mostly it was dark, the sky crouching over her, the belly of an arching cat. Once the black was split open by rays – orange, red, violet – and she felt certain she was seeing the sun rise, only the light was slipping away instead of getting brighter.

For a short time Ben joined her, sitting cross-legged, his back against the flimsy mast. She wanted to tell him to be careful he might snap it. He explained she had been mistaken about him, he hadn't meant anything, only to be friendly, to help her, he knew she would understand and there would be no hard feelings. She nodded and turned her face away. When she next looked he had gone.

Why then is he sitting by my bed? She asks him, though she can't hear her words, only someone else moaning like an idiot.

'Better not to try and sit up, you had a nasty thump to the head. Can I get you anything?'

The idiot continues to whimper, he leans in closer. Finally she manages to say, 'Thirsty.' She is pleased to hear her clear articulation.

'I'll have to check with the nurse before I give you anything.' He doesn't move and smiles, 'Hannah, you'll have to let go of my hand so I can go find a nurse.' He smooths some hair away from her eyes, 'I won't be a moment, I promise.'

Maybe he is a second or a minute or an hour, she can hardly tell, she's adrift again for a while, she has to cling tightly to the lifeline outstretched towards her to bring her back to shore.

'Hello Ben,' a nurse comes in. 'I didn't know that she was one of yours.'

'Hannah's not my client, she's a friend.'

Yes, only a friend.

'Right, well, we'll have to make sure she gets the best treatment then.'

Hannah is conscious of various activities going on around her and being done to her and the nurse's chatter going over her. She becomes aware there are other beds in the room with people in them. The nurse leaves having said Ben can give Hannah some water. He puts his arm around her shoulders, lifting her up slightly, the whole room sways and she knots her fingers into his clothing. 'It's OK, sweetheart, I'm not going anywhere.'

Why are you saying that? The water dribbles from her mouth, though enough enters to give some relief. He mops her chin. She tries to flinch away, *Don't touch me if you don't want me.* Dizziness sets in. She closes her eyes as she lays back down, the ocean closes over her.

* * *

Theo is exhausted and the egg and sugary drink have settled uneasily on his stomach. He relaxes a little as he reaches the familiar sequence of roundabouts which brings him into Scarborough from the A64. His bed is not too far away. Then he notices the pall of smoke. It's coming from Westedge. He's driving right by it, the smell is insinuating itself into his car. He slows, turns left, there's a crowd up ahead, in front of Kestle's house. He stops. He searches for evidence of Pippa's posse. *No one.*

He calls it in and gets out of the car. The odour is more intense, acrid as synthetic materials have caught. He imagines Alexi's photos curling in the heat, melting, their colours melding, the man cowering in his upstairs room, the smoke would clog his lungs before the fire burns his flesh. Theo forces himself forward even faster, his legs awkward, leaden. At the back edge of the crowd, youngsters, some as young as six or seven, shout, 'Pee-doh, pee-doh, out, out, out.' They lob stones so they just miss each other. *It's a game to them.*

He pushes on through past mainly men in their twenties and thirties, hoods pulled down or scarves pulled up. They are silent, staring, brutal. They hardly move even as they let him past, a human forest. 'What are you doing? There's a man in there,' Theo's words come out hoarsely, are easily ignored. He thrusts on and almost ends on his knees, his legs practically folding under him. He's at the front of the crowd now, a few yards from Kestle's front wall. There's another barricade facing him, between the wall and front door. In the dark, with the billowing smoke, *Is that Ray Marchant?* Theo slams through the gate. Hands grasp him and try to repel him. Fury propels him, 'Let me go, fuck you, there's a man dying in there.' His arms are pinned behind him. He snaps his face back and is nose to nose with Ray. Theo shouts again, 'Let me go. I'll arrest you all for murder.'

Ray spits, 'Leave it detective. Go. You're not needed here. We're dealing with it.'

Theo lets rip another tirade. *Where's my back-up? Where the bloody hell are they?* Over Ray's shoulder he sees the front door open, dense grey smoke swirls out and in the middle are two men he recognises as Ray's cousins, with Kestle doubled-up, choking, between them. The barricade forms a protective circle around them and manoeuvres into the street and away from the jeering crowd towards Ray's mother's house. There's mutterings of dismay coming from the watching forest of young men. Someone throws a rock which would have hit Theo if Ray hadn't shoved him to one side. Ray faces the increasingly unruly throng, 'Shut up you Neanderthals and go home. Can't you hear the sirens?'

There's shuffling and some insults tossed into the glowing night, another rock which falls wide of the mark. However, the sirens are getting nearer, and the forest begins to dissipate. Theo turns to see for the first time orange glowing in amongst the thick smog, glass in an upstairs window shatters, splinters fall around him, graze his cheek.

Ray roughly pulls Theo down the rapidly emptying street until they reach his car, a fire engine followed by a police car scream past in the opposite direction. 'Go home,' Ray says. 'It was a simple house fire, Mr Kestle had to take refuge in me mam's house. He'll be safe there, don't you worry, Mr detective. Don't you see? We handle things in our own way here, so go home.'

Theo doesn't resist, he'll make a full report tomorrow. Right now he can't cope with explanations. He wants to be away from all this, away from all this suffocating and muddle-headed vigilantism. *I want to be somewhere I belong, I want to be home.*

* * *

Hannah sleeps and wakes and sleeps again, it feels like for a thousand days. For a moment her father is there, 'You're a liar Hannah, never could tell the difference between reality and fantasy, a dreamer. No one will ever believe you. It didn't happen, no one noticed, they would have noticed.' She wakes. Ben isn't there, he has gone, gone forever. *I told him to go.* The thought makes her cry. 'Good lord what's this noise about?' a passing sailor asks, his skin as pale as a gutted fish.

'Ben?'

'He's gone honey. Don't fret, he'll be back, he's attentive that one. You sleep now, he'll be here when you wake.' His words are a spell, it sends her to the depths for a century.

When she opens her eyes, she sees things with more clarity. She is in a small ward of about eight beds, the one opposite is occupied by an elderly woman who is sitting up in a pink bed jacket, knitting. She smiles, 'That's better, you had a bit of a night didn't you pet?'

Hannah smiles back, 'I'm sorry, did I keep you awake?'

'It's alright, I don't sleep much anyway, that's why I've got these to keep me company,' she indicates some headphones by her bed. The movement causes her pain and she tenses up her face. 'I like listening to audio books. Do you like listening to audio books?'

'Probably.' Hannah's not sure. She gets caught up in the routine, a nurse, then a doctor comes, pronounces she'll be able to go home soon if she can demonstrate she can eat some breakfast and go to the loo. She tries both. It's all very slow and painful, however she apparently passes the test because they start to talk about discharge. Is there someone who can look after her?

Lawrence visits. She can tell he's not slept much either, though he is upbeat, she'll soon be home, soon be a hundred times better. He is avoiding eye contact with her. She isn't well enough to challenge him. Aurora and Ben are there too. In between she rests and drifts, unwilling to think about anything very much. Not what happened to her, not about her father, not about what needs to happen next. The nurse suggests they contact her next of kin, given as Stephen when she was admitted, to come and take care of her. She is appalled. Ben returns at that moment with some tea. 'Stop her, stop her,' Hannah says frantically.

'I only suggested we call her brother,' the nurse says crossly. 'We need someone to discharge her to, especially given she was concussed.'

'Don't worry, you can discharge her to me. I'll take care of her.'

The nurse is satisfied with this and goes off to ready the paperwork.

Ben sits, offers Hannah her drink. She shakes her head, 'Why did you say that?' She is angry.

He is taken aback, slowly puts his paper cup on the bedside table, 'I thought, well I assumed ... Is there someone else you'd rather ...?'

'Stop assuming stuff about me. You don't know me,' the rage roars up from her foundations, she is speaking too fast, too loudly. Pink bed jacket turns up the volume on her headphones and closes her eyes, others peek their way, curiosity taking them away from magazines or TV. 'Get away from me, don't touch me, don't ever touch me again.'

'Hannah, please,' his voice is soothing, he tries to catch hold of one of her flailing hands. 'I'm not going to hurt you, you're safe with me.'

She hardly hears the words and tells him to go several times, with more expletives added with each repetition.

He's managed to grab her hands, he holds them down between them, gazes into her eyes, says firmly, 'If I leave, you stay in here. Is that what you want?'

'Aurora will ... Lawrence ...'

'No, Hannah, they are discharging you to me, do you understand?'

She sees him, then. Ben, his face reddening, his hair the colour of treacle, his dark eyes, wells of kindness. *Can I trust you? I don't know. I wish I could know. Do you understand?*

'Hannah, you can stop fighting now. Let me take care of you, please.'

Really she has no choice, she is drained of everything: words, thoughts, fear, anger. She lets herself be parcelled and processed out of the hospital: transferred from there to Ben's car, driven (feeling increasingly nauseous), helped into her parents' house and then (finally, finally) tucked into bed where sleep overwhelms her.

CHAPTER 35

Lawrence tries to persuade Theo to have a lie-in, 'Surely they can't expect you in, you were up half the night.' He fusses over the scratch on Theo's cheek.

Theo bats him away, a tad roughly, 'I don't have to go in, I want to go in, it's my work.' He wants Lawrence to finally get this about him. *My work isn't just something I do.*

Lawrence sighs, 'I guess I'd say the same if you tried to keep me from writing. Off you go then, I'll sort out these trousers and shoes from last night, they're covered in mud. I hope it is only mud.'

Theo pulls on his coat, 'Will you go and see Hannah?'

Lawrence shrugs. 'I'll have to get back to London soon. I can only do so much remotely.' As if this was any kind of answer.

At the station, Theo is aware of sideway glances. Suze confirms that Chesters has been a blabbermouth. 'They'll get over it,' she says, patting his sleeve. 'Find something else to gossip about. They know you're a good officer.' She gives him a firm look. 'A good man.' Hoyle is less sure about Theo's calibre as an officer, is cross with him for leaving Westedge without briefing his colleagues. He doesn't bother to defend himself, merely apologises, says he will prepare a detailed report. Hoyle dismisses him saying actions may still be taken against him, the DI likes to keep his sword of Damocles sharpened.

Theo buries himself in his report writing and only surfaces when he gets a call from reception. There's a Maya Short to see him. *What could she want?* He goes down to collect her and notices the eyes following them as he leads her through the squad room back to his desk. Chesters, making no pretence of hiding his interest, is like a dog catching a scent on the breeze.

Theo has never met Maya before, though has heard enough about her. Today she doesn't look particularly outlandish, wearing figure-hugging jeans and a jacket with large orange flowers on it which she has opened to reveal a black jersey cut with a low scoop neck. Her dark hair is pulled back in a ponytail and her face is discreetly made up, emphasising her oval green eyes with curled lashes.

She takes off her jacket and sits, legs primly crossed, bending ever so slightly forward. She smiles widely. 'I thought I'd better come in when you didn't come to find me,' she says sweetly, as if he'd missed out on a date with her. 'Thought you might want to know about Steel Cowboy or whatever his stupid name is.' He nods in encouragement and she goes on, 'It was terrible what he did to poor Hannah, I really didn't think he'd do anything like that, of course, I didn't. I wouldn't put Hannah in danger. He said he knew her and had lost her contact details.' Theo doesn't believe anything he is being told. At that moment, Chesters comes up and offers to get them drinks. Maya accepts without taking her attention away from Theo. He can see Chesters salivating as he goes away to fulfil his errand.

'What did Kevin Scraggs say to you, Maya, exactly?' Theo asks.

'Is that what he's really called? If I'd known that, I'd have left him well alone. Now let me think,' she puts a beautifully manicured fingernail painted with rubies to her glossy lips. 'Oh thank you dear,' she accepts a cup from the returned Chesters and takes a sip.

'You can go, Chesters,' Theo says. The young man reluctantly backs away.

'He wasn't very coherent most of the time, but I do remember him saying something about his dad. How his dad had died, or been killed, before he was born and it was some Julie Carter's fault, only she was trying to put the blame on his mum. Though I had the impression they'd both been involved, his mum and this Julie, his mum defending his dad?'

'And did you get his dad's name?'

'Sharpe, I think, Lenny maybe?' She looks through her lashes at him.

She's flirting with me, Theo is surprised. *She must know I'd not be interested, even if I weren't spoken for.* 'And the connection with Hannah?'

'This Julie was telling her everything in their counselling sessions. He thought Hannah would go to the police with the information or some-such. Wanted to protect his mother, which is quite sweet when you think about it. Only awful for Hannah, of course. Have I been helpful? I do hope so.'

Theo agrees she has. He calls Chesters over to see her out, *Why not give the lad a treat. I wonder whether he'll be led astray?* Then he focuses on the question, *Do I have enough to go back to Michelle Scraggs? And how do I find Julie Carter? Hannah would know.* However, it has been decided a DC she doesn't know will take her statement about her assault and it will be left for a day or so. Kevin Scraggs isn't going anywhere. But Theo is impatient to get his answers.

Chapter 36

'I don't know why you give him such a hard time, he's obviously besotted with you and you like him, don't you?' Aurora is babysitting Hannah while Ben is working. It's not necessary as Hannah is out of the concussion danger zone, even so Aurora has taken a day off to be with her and she is grateful. When she's on her own her thoughts gather around her, a coven of malevolent witches, inside her head, not haunting the house as she'd previously imagined.

Aurora hasn't asked many questions, has said she'll listen if Hannah wants to talk, but in a tone which suggests she'd rather not hear. Instead they've been chatting about various things. Max, why Aurora loves him despite being irritated by him, and his business, which might be picking up. Veronica and her obsession with putting Val Poole in a home. And, of course, Oli's development from a baby into a little boy. He's been playing the game of bringing a different coloured brick over to Hannah for her to exclaim over and hand back for about the last thirty minutes. Aurora has got into a tangle with trying to knit him a cardigan once again. Hannah has straightened her out a couple of times already. It now sits on her lap while she watches her son with a fascination Hannah wonders if she could ever have for anything or anyone. She is suddenly tired. She lies back on the sofa. They are in the snug, cluttered by the dark heavy furniture beloved of her mother.

'You OK?' asks Aurora. 'You look flaked out.'

'Think I could do with a nap.' She rouses herself a little, 'Thanks ever so for coming, I wouldn't have wanted to be on my own.'

Aurora gets up and reaches down for Oli, picking him up and almost throwing him into the air while he squeals with delight. 'Come on then boy, let's go and see about some tea for us and Daddy. Shall we? Yes, shall we?' It takes a while for her to pack up and actually leave, Hannah is practically asleep when Aurora gives her a quick peck before letting herself out the house.

As usual, her rest doesn't last long. The panic seizes her body, she finds it difficult to get oxygen, something is being stuffed into her mouth, there's a shadowy figure leaning over her. She hears the clatter of metal on concrete. Smells sweat. Sometimes the person materialises, and it's Steel Cowboy, though not as he'd been, far larger and stronger and dominating. Or it's her father. Or there's both of them. Sometimes the stinking shadow remains – *too close*.
    She wants to scream. Chokes on whatever noise she might have made. Lifts herself up to defend herself. *Can't make them go away. Can't make the cry for help come out.* She wakes, thrashing at the blanket as if it were the attacker. She sits up. The sudden movement jars at her bruises, makes her head swim. It takes a moment for the room to settle about her, for her to realise she is alone, for her breathing to calm. She whimpers a little, for once alone feels lonely. She squints at her watch, *Ben will be here soon.* She props herself up more comfortably, it's gloomy, it's chilly, she cocoons herself into the blanket and waits.
    Maybe Aurora has a point, I am too hard on Ben. She vaguely recalls screeching at him this morning because of something, *I can't even remember for what, some imagined slight. And yet it felt real at the time.* She can bring back to mind the rage surging up through her until it was an ocean in her ears. Her voice high pitched, nagging, irrational. Even as she spurted it all out, she knew it wasn't Ben she wanted to yell at: *It's not fair. Love me, love me. I hate you.* He'd not hurt her so much it felt as if she was being split apart. *And where is Lawrence? Talking of people who have let me down. Ben hasn't, Ben hasn't. Why hasn't Lawrence called round or texted? He knows, he knows now how bad I am, how evil, he knows about the poison in my veins.* She sees him with her father, laughing at some shared joke or memory. *He probably*

knows what Stan Poole did and thinks it's OK, cos that's what little girls are born to and for.

Why am I hard on Ben? Cos I can. Cos I know he'll be back. Cos I need to be hard on someone. She buries herself further under the soft wool. *Stop thinking, stop thinking.* She squeezes her eyes shut. In a moment of lucidity she wonders if she should call Theo about Julia. She knows her supervisor would say she must, as he had done with Dr Greene's murder investigation last year. *Murder trumps therapist confidentiality.* Still she doesn't move. Her joints ache with holding her limbs on. Her skull pinches at her brain.

She must have dozed as she is woken by the sound of the front door being softly closed. She knows Ben's tread. She wills him to come in. Even tries to call out to him, though her hoarse greeting is lost in the folds of the blanket around her. The hall light is turned on and seeps round the edge of the snug's door. She hears Ben move through the house, use the bathroom, probably look in her bedroom for her. Finally he returns downstairs, tries the kitchen, the living room and, at last, the room where she is ensconced. He pauses in the doorway, quietly seeking her out in the near dark and gauging whether she is awake. He is back-lit, she can appreciate his trim figure, his hair the hue of conkers. She cannot see his eyes properly, she knows them to be kind. Aurora's words come back to her, *Why am I so hard on him?* She shifts to leaning on her elbow, 'I'm sorry.'

He comes into the room, turns on the side light, closes the curtain, 'What for?' He perches on the edge of the sofa.

She can see his eyes now, their tender quality, 'I've been mean to you. I've been taking everything out on you and it's not fair.'

He pushes back the damp hair from her forehead where the hospital dressing has still to be removed. He smiles, then kisses her on the lips. She wraps her arms around his shoulders and he embraces her. She breathes him in, his scent of cotton and almond overlaid by the odour of the world outside, of the drizzle and the car fumes from the street, of the dust and furnishings of the room where he's been working. Maybe even a hint of an aftershave or a perfume lingering from a client who is overdoing it in a wrong-headed attempt to entice their therapist. *Do you love me more than them?* She quickly scotches the thought. *Don't spoil it Hannah, don't spoil this moment.* He draws back, maybe sensing a withdrawal from her. Offers to make her some food, get her a drink. 'I need a bath,' she says. 'Will you wash my hair?' As he begins to help her up, she worries he's misinterpreted what she wants, 'I'm sorry I can't, we can't … it's too soon.' *Will you, can you, wait, until I'm ready?*

He kisses her again, grins, 'I worked as a hairdresser in Adelaide. No really, it's true.'

'You're a terrible liar Mr Cartwright.' The tensions in her back and neck eases. She laughs. It is centuries since she's laughed like that, out loud, without restraint.

CHAPTER 37

Theo has his two confessions. He could join his colleagues for a Friday after-work drink. Only the confessions don't conclude the case.

Ben had phoned yesterday morning to say Hannah wanted to see both Theo and Lawrence. Lawrence went reluctantly, 'How can I face her?'

'You're her friend, she needs you,' Theo said firmly.

Hannah had been in the living room, seated on the settee in a patch of sun. She was ashen, except for the livid discolouring around her temple, however her grin was genuinely warm and she hugged both of them. Her business with Theo was quickly despatched, she gave him Julia (or Julie) Carter's contact details. Then there was a pause before she turned to Lawrence, 'I know you've been avoiding me.'

Lawrence shifted uneasily in his chair. He'd made Theo promise not to leave him whatever happened. Theo suspected the same guarantee had been exhorted from Ben who didn't move either. 'I thought you needed time to rest, to recover,' Lawrence said.

She shook her head, 'No, I know why you've not been here, it's because of Dad isn't it?'

She already knows, thought Theo. *I knew it.*

'You've got to believe me, Lawrence, it wasn't my fault.' She pauses, swallows, continues very quietly, 'Dad hurt me, I mean really hurt me, when I was little. I didn't want for any of it to happen.'

Lawrence had become a granite block. Theo wanted to shake him, *Say something, she's your friend.*

'Do you understand me, Lawrence, when I say he hurt me? It was ...' again the pause, the swallowing, the (what looked like) huge effort to go on, '... I'm talking about sexual abuse.'

Silence. Ben put his hand on Hannah's arm. She looked down, a rag doll which had lost its wadding.

Theo said quietly, 'I'm sorry Hannah, I really am.'

Her head jerked up, 'But not surprised?' Her gaze went from Theo to Lawrence and back again, 'What do you know? Tell me.'

'Lawrence, you have to say something,' Theo snapped. 'You're not being fair.'

And Lawrence spoke, slowly, deliberately, flatly, he was catching nobody's eye, 'I took Stan's computer, it had photos on it, I had to hand it over to the police.'

'Photos? What do you mean? What do you mean Lawrence?'

He too had difficulty spelling it out, 'Child porn.'

'And you never told me, you never fucking told me? How long have you known?'

'I didn't want to upset you.'

'Upset me? Upset you more like, you always were an emotional coward.' There was a quiet after this outburst, a stretched quiet. Theo searched for something adequate to say, before he could open his mouth, Hannah asked, 'Were there a lot of photos?' Her tone was strong, she was sitting straighter.

Lawrence nodded.

'Were there photos of me?'

He looked unhappily at his hands and shrugged. 'As soon as I realised what I'd found, I handed it all over.'

'He had to, Hannah,' Theo said, feeling the need to defend the collapsed man in the chair beside him.

She nodded, then turned her attention to Theo. 'Will they want to speak to me? To Mum and Stephen?'

'I expect so.'

She was back raising her voice at Lawrence, 'So when were you going to tell me?'

'I tried to Hannah, just couldn't find the right time. Couldn't find the right words.'

'Hah, and you a writer.'

'I love words but words fail me.'

'Don't hide behind quotes, you cold sod.'

He stood up in a sudden movement, went to the wide windows and stared out at the garden where the green Aspen tongues were just beginning to show. 'Sometimes things are wordless and finding out someone you liked and respected and looked up to, was a father figure of a sorts, could do that sort of thing, there aren't words for it.' Theo could hear the anger underlying what Lawrence was saying.

'Oh Lawrence,' Hannah said quietly, sounding deflated.

For a moment, no one moved, then Lawrence turned back into the room. His voice belied the pinkened corners of his eyes when he said he had to be going. Normally, he and Hannah would have given each other a bear-hug, not yesterday, they hardly looked at each other as they said goodbye. Theo felt awkward as he embraced Hannah, torn in his loyalties. Once they'd left, he tried to initiate a conversation about what had just happened. Lawrence would only respond that he'd done his best, before changing the subject. It soon became clear he wasn't merely running away from Hannah, he was exiting Scarborough. He said abruptly he intended to get the next train to London which was leaving in twenty minutes. His parting from Theo, therefore, was also perfunctory, the distance already gathering between them.

Once at the police station Theo allowed his work to consume him, even though a part of his mind followed Lawrence on his solitary journey. He had arranged for Michelle Scraggs to be brought over from Leeds, hoping an unfamiliar setting might make her more jittery and prone to talk. After checking she was safely on her way, he was about to call the number Hannah had given him, when reception told him there was a Julia Carter come in for him. When he met her, he remembered her from his visit to Michelle's house. She was still as elegant, in a burgundy tailored trouser suit and discreet (but expensive) jewellery. However, he could see under her careful make-up her face was drawn. Sleep had been eluding her. He called DC Harry Shilling down and they went into one of the interview rooms.

Julia began with, 'I understand you're interested in Lenny Sharpe?'

Evidently, the problem with Lenny Sharpe was that he liked young girls (not as young as Stan Poole liked them, but too young to be exactly legal). 'Though we saw ourselves as older than fourteen, dressed ourselves up, but we were kids.' He'd taken them for a day out in Scarborough, he had a car, money, he gave them change for the slots, they played ball on the beach. 'He fancied himself, took his shirt off – we just saw a hairy-chested old man. I remember, we laughed, me and Meech. Laughed at him.' Then there were the fish and chips and the lager, the strong type. 'We wanted to go home, only he was digging in for the night, ordering another beer. He began pawing at me,' Julia shuddered. 'I'd had the odd fumble with the boys on the estate, but this felt, well, different. I insisted he drive us home, started to make such a fuss people were turning to stare, so he grabbed his denim jacket and said, alright then.

'We could tell he was angry, walking fast in front of us. He'd been too mean to pay for parking so his car was right the other end of the Esplanade and he tramped us up through the gardens. It was getting dark, it wasn't night by any means, but there were shadows and the undergrowth was thick.'

She stopped. She asked for a drink of water and didn't continue until she had drained her cup.

'Meech needed a pee and scrambled off the path. He went after her, said he'd keep watch. I let 'em go. I was so narked with the both of them. She'd been moaning, her feet hurt in them stupid shoes she'd insisted on wearing and the lager was making her feel funny. And Lenny, I was furious with him. Then I heard her screaming, shouting and I scrambled after them. They were in this bit which was flatter, curtained off by these shrubs gone wild. And there were buttercups everywhere. I hate bloody buttercups. He was on top of Meech, his jeans halfway down his bum. I ran up and started to drag him off. She was kicking him by then and I suppose with his pants down he was at a bit of a disadvantage. We were going to run off, only he grabbed my hair, swung me round, I lost my footing, was in amongst all this yellow, the smell was foul, and he had his hands pushing up my skirt, pulling down my knickers, he had this heavy watch thing, gold, engraved, it was scratching me, my thighs and, you know, under my knickers. Then bang, he went limp.' She was silent.

'What happened Ms Carter?' asked Theo gently.

Her gaze travelled up to his face, her features were pinched, puzzled almost, 'Meech had hit him, with a rock.'

'He was dead?'

'I don't know. I struggled out from under him. And then I ...' she stopped again, contorted her nose as if there was a bad smell.

'Then you?'

'Hit him again, with the rock. I was so angry, Sergeant Akande, I'd never been so angry. It was a blur. There was all this yellow and then all this red.' Another pause. She'd lost her vigour.

'And then what happened?'

'We ran, ran like hell. One of us, I don't know was it me or Meech, must have got his car keys, maybe they'd dropped out of his pocket. My brother had shown me how to drive on the streets of the estate, round and round. We didn't have enough money for the train, we had to take his car.' She gave a beseeching glance, as if this was the crime she was being questioned about, she could have been fourteen again, not a CEO of a globally successful company. 'I didn't mean to kill him. I've tried to bury it, deny it almost. Only I had to tell you, detective, because of what happened to Hannah. She oughtn't to have got hurt.'

It didn't take much to persuade Michelle Scraggs to corroborate Carter's story, though she claimed to have launched the final decisive blow. 'He raped me, the bastard, he deserved it,' she finished more defensive than Julia. Then she crumpled over, agitated, whining for a cigarette and a drink. Her histrionics were beginning to grate on Theo, especially given the day he'd had. He forced himself to hold onto his equanimity, to imagine her as the defenceless young lass she once was. He saw her back into the police car which would take her home and agreed to one stop at a service station for one tinny.

He'd known it as soon as he'd spoken to Julia and Michelle, but had given himself the night to think it all through. Firstly, from the date both women had agreed on, Kevin Scraggs was certainly mistaken about his parentage, his conception came a while after Lenny Sharpe was left for dead. Secondly, Theo may have his confessions but neither of them reveals the whole story. They tell of Lenny Sharpe being killed in the wrong place. His body was found along the A64, a good ten miles out of Scarborough. It was unlikely he could have walked that far, especially with at least two blows to the head. The two women could be giving him the wrong location. *But why would they do that? They were already admitting to murder? Or rather, manslaughter.* No, Lenny Sharpe had somehow moved (or been moved) from the South Cliff gardens to the spot where he was found.

    Theo goes back to the statements and notices something. The heavy gold watch. Sharpe's former neighbour had said it was inscribed: 'Steel Cowboy'. Julia and Michelle had talked about Lenny showing it off and the damage it had done during the assault. It had split Michelle's lip open as well as grating across Julia's thighs. Theo searches through the other reports he has on the Sharpe case. No watch was found with the body. What had happened to it?

Chapter 38

'The coldest February in twenty-four years' and 'more snow chaos on the way' had been the morning headlines for Saturday the 13th. Hannah wraps up in her padded jacket and woollen scarf and hat. She gingerly begins the descent on the steep path from the end of Sea View Lane to the old South Bay lido. She doesn't need to be told, she can smell the snow on the wind whipping up from the coal-coloured water.

She still finds walking tiring and painful at times. She picks her way down, the chalky pebbles clacking against each other like so many white snooker balls. This is the first time since Steel Cowboy's attack that she's given her muscles a good stretch, and they are protesting. She's been taking taxis or the bus or, more often, Ben has ferried her around. He wasn't keen on her going off on her own today, 'What if you fall? Or are too tired to come back up?' He'd paused in the middle of putting on his socks seated on the edge of her bed.

'I'm not ninety-four,' she'd said, kissing him on the top of his head, his hair was fly-away, smelt of her coconut shampoo. 'I need to begin to get back to my routine, to my life, to what brings me pleasure.' *I don't want to be afraid of going there alone.*

Walking a pleasure? It would not have been something she'd have said before coming to Scarborough. But there's something revitalising about it. She pauses to draw breath. *Normally, in this amount of time, I'd be down there.* She looks to where the sea is launching itself against the wall of the lido, its snowy spume presaging what's fulminating in the sky. *Weak, Hannah, pathetic.* Then she hears a gentler voice, *Take it easy, Hannah, you're doing fine.* She recognises it as Izzie's tone. She tries it on herself again, *Come on Hannah, one foot in front another, that's the way.*

She'd seen Izzie the previous evening. She'd spent most of the hour crying. Every time she began to recount something, the tears came. Izzie sat next to her, held her, passed her tissues. Hannah submerged herself in the comfort of it all. She spoke about Lawrence, gone with hardly a word and barely a communication since. 'He'll never forgive me, he hates me. For what I did.'

'For what your father did. It's more about whether he can forgive your father, and whether he can forgive himself for not being there for you.'

Hannah sniffed, tried to regulate her breath and her voice, 'He's always been there for me, supported me, I guess this is just too hard for him.'

'I imagine it *is* hard for him. And it's even worse for you. You're the one who's been hurt here, Hannah.'

'He doesn't understand how I didn't know, how I could have buried it all those years. False memory syndrome, I hear someone putting it forward as fact every time I turn the radio on it seems like.' She blew her nose, took another tissue, sat straighter. 'Then I read in an article in *The Psychologist*, did you see it? A professor arguing the opposite, saying we need to hold onto the notion that memory is largely accurate.'

'This isn't about arguments between researchers, Hannah, this is about you. I believe you, I believe what you say.'

This had set off another bout of sobbing. *It's too hard, it's too hard to be believed after all this time of being silenced.*

She reaches the base of the incline. The waves chase each other around the curve of the old lido's basin before throwing themselves over the path in front of her: shoo-shoosh-woa-wumph. The final declaration of existence resounds through her body. Overhead, the seagulls are keening, the wailing of lost little girls.

She'd put a proposition to Izzie. 'OK, maybe I didn't make Dad do it.' *Maybe.* 'And it's not my fault Lawrence is upset. But I know I'm bad. When I'm around little children I feel so angry.' She whispered the last part, dropping her gaze. *Don't look at me, don't judge me.*

'Who is angry Hannah?'

'Me. It's in me, I try to keep it hidden, but it doesn't always work. It's mine.'

'Let's think about this another way,' Izzie said gently. 'You were very young when all this started, little children can't easily make the distinction between what's going on internally and what's happening externally. What happened was violent. Violence equals anger. It was coming from the outside, but it didn't feel that way to you. Whose anger is it Hannah?'

She didn't reply, only wept some more. 'I feel so guilty, so ashamed.'

A hefty gull lands nearby, fixes her with his yellow eye. 'Not yours, not yours,' it putters.

There is a squat wall some way back from the one being battered by the sea. Gratefully Hannah perches on it. *Perhaps Ben was right, I won't make it back. And there's no one around.* Where she's sat delineates the sides of the old pool. She's seen railway posters from the 1930s showing this pool when it was in action on a splendid summer day. There are crowds of people, women in colourful low-backed dresses and hats tied with brightly striped ribbons. They are watching a diving display. It's all very different today, bleak, cold and washed over with a palette of grey. Yet she has to rest.

Yesterday had been something of a marathon all in all. Maybe that explains all those tears?

In the morning she'd seen Julia for what was probably the last time. She had agreed with Orwell she couldn't work with Julia after all that had happened and, anyway, she needed a break from taking clients. Julia was the only one she decided to see face-to-face. The others had been short-term and were already moving on from her, given her absence since her assault. Winters had stressed she wasn't obliged to have a final session with Julia either, but it had felt important. Julia had been solicitous, apologetic,

Hannah had to repeat a number of times she didn't hold her culpable for anything. Julia was grateful, which Hannah forced herself to sit and hear without minimising. Then Julia had become subdued, 'For all those years I thought I'd killed him, I mean I tried to blank it from my mind, but deep down I thought I was a murderer, I should be pleased ...'

'Only?'

She sighed heavily, leant on her knees, her head lolling forward, too weighty to lift up. 'All those wasted years, all those lost years, thinking I'd done this terrible thing. It's been worse for Meech, of course. She's gone on a bender, I haven't been able to get a sensible syllable out of her. I was lucky to have got out when I did, otherwise I could have been her.'

'Lucky? You worked hard.'

Julia shrugged, 'I could have been her. Maybe I should have stayed. Maybe I could have stopped it all sliding away from her.'

With every gain, there's a loss, Hannah reflected. *Every day something to grieve. If Julia had known she'd not killed anyone, if I'd sought help earlier, would we have lived our lives differently? Guilt is a terrible thing.* She was glad Julia agreed to see another therapist, someone Hannah recommended.

'I'll miss you,' Julia said. She said it simply, without any qualifier. Hannah felt the truth of it. They parted shortly after.

It was a relief to have found out that Julia had gone to see Theo voluntarily. When Hannah had given her statement to the DC about the assault on her, she'd not mentioned Julia. It was easy not to, the officer didn't ask many searching questions, after all Steel Cowboy was pleading guilty. When she did finally tell Theo, she felt treacherous.

But I don't need to, she exhales deeply. Slowly, slowly she begins to walk up the circuitous and rickety path through the cliff gardens. The black skeletal trees are hunched over under the glowering sky.

DI Pippa Wiltshire, her afternoon visitor yesterday, had been more pressing than the DC. She'd been given the task, as she explained, of having a 'first conversation' with Hannah about Stan Poole. Hannah had written down her statement, piecing together the fragments to make a coherent narrative. She had handed it over, hoping it would satisfy the DI. It did not. Wiltshire firmly, if not uncompassionately, insisted Hannah say what had happened. She did as she was bid, repeating robotically what she knew she had put on paper. *It was like I wasn't saying it, I was watching someone else telling a story, a horrible story, but one I couldn't be touched by. No wonder there were the floods with Izzie later.*

She pauses for breath as she enters the arch into the Italian garden. She leans against the chilled stone. The statue of Mercury, the winged messenger, has a precarious stance on tiptoe in the centre of the frozen pond. Fronds break through the ice, their pale green frosted and brittle.

She hadn't intended to tell DI Wiltshire about the folder of images and the address book, her notion of her father's 'system' had all seemed too fantastic when she'd considered it again. But it had worked as a diversionary tactic. Pippa had not immediately said, 'What nonsense.' And she had departed with a satisfied smile.

It takes all Hannah's energy to get home and she sleeps until Ben returns to make her dinner. Later, as they both are settling down in front of the TV in the snug, they hear the front door open and slam shut. Hannah is trying to figure out what Aurora or Rose might be doing, coming round unannounced at this time of day, when the room door is pushed open revealing a glowering Stephen. She knows her brother has been ringing and Ben has been politely blocking his calls. She also guesses Stephen's been contacted by the police too, about their father.

Ben begins to get up, greet Stephen, then is on his way to usher him out into the hall when Stephen starts to rant, 'How dare you Hannah? How dare you spread your lies about Dad, your dirty little fantasies? Think what it is doing to our mother. My wife. My children. Why are you determined to ruin our family? Isn't losing Dad difficult enough without you besmirching his name?'

Ben tries to interrupt, takes Stephen's arm to propel him out of the room. Stephen is having none of it. His face is pricked out in vermilion. He struts over to stand in front of Hannah and continues to shout, repeating his accusations: she is deceitful, letting her imagination run away with her; she is destroying their family.

Hannah thinks she may buckle, her head thumps, the force of his allegations pounds down, caving in her shoulders. Finally, from somewhere, she finds the capacity to drag herself to her feet and put some distance between her and his masticating mouth. *I won't cry, I won't crumble, I won't let him get to me.* 'Stephen, just shut the fuck up.' She tries it out under her breath first, then quietly and then more loudly, until finally she is able to cut through his monologue.

To her amazement he does stop. They look at each other across the constricted floor space, the gulf between them growing in significance. She remembers him supporting her on her bike when she first tried to pedal without stabilisers. She remembers him pulling her along on her most favourite toy, for a few weeks anyway, her roller skates. She remembers him treating her to her first proper pop concert, staying with her all through, as he'd promised their parents, despite the ragging from his friends. She wonders if he recalls any of this. His jowly chin is quivering. He might be about to speak again. 'Please leave, Stephen. We can discuss this at another time, when you're less angry and I'm recovered.'

'There is nothing to discuss,' says Stephen the professional, his voice is moderated at least. 'If I hear you've been repeating your lies again, I shall bring an injunction, I shall bring an action for slander. Understand?'

'Just go.' And to her further astonishment he does. Ben comes over and hugs her. She can feel the tautness in his body even as he tries to reassure her. 'I'm OK,' she says and it's the truth.

'What a bastard, a fucking bastard,' his words punch their way into her neck.

See? See, I'm not making it up. She strokes his back, her turn to soothe.

'Come away with me. Come and stay with me, Hannah,' his voice is hesitant.

She releases her grip and looks him in the face, his jaw is clenched, his pale skin ruddying around his nose. *You don't want me to move in with you.* She shakes her head.

'I mean it Hannah, come away from here.'

'To *stay* with you?' she stresses the second word, thus bringing emphasis to the impermanence of what he is suggesting. 'I don't think so. I like it here. I've made friends with the ghosts. Nothing terrible ever happened to me here.' She turns back towards the sofa, 'Now didn't we have something to watch, a quiz show with Ant and Dec?' She smiles, knowing the expression of horror he'd be trying to hide. 'Only teasing, we've got the documentary about scientists discovering which particular synapse in the brain makes us mad. All I can say is thank god for scientists. How would we know we were insane without them?'

CHAPTER 39

DI Wiltshire cuts off any discussion, 'Alexi Kestle is being offered housing in Hull. It's what he wants. I would say no more about it, DS Akande, then I don't need to bring up your interference into my case.'

Which brought us to what really happened. Yvonne is being charged with wasting police time and perverting the course of justice. It is expected her punishment will be lenient. The situation surrounding the Everidge family is being reclassified from criminal to child protection, but before she hands it over completely to social services, Pippa wants the full story from Victoria. And Victoria is insisting she will only speak to Theo.

The DI can modify her tone within minutes from attack to coaxing. Even so, Theo imagines she's not best pleased to have to bring him back in.

The meeting is held in the same room as before at SC4Tea. This time Ian and Paul have accompanied Victoria. She's looking perkier, her cheeks fuller and pinker, she's pleased when Theo notices her new trainers which light up when she walks. *Yet, there's something in your eyes, isn't there little one? You've lost trust in this world of adults.* Theo feels sad, *What a mess we adults make sometimes.* He is opposite the girl, while DI Wiltshire is to one side.

Victoria sits between her stepdad and stepbrother, holding a hand of each, she speaks clearly and concisely: 'Mum had said it would be like a little holiday, a bit of fun, going to stay with her cousin. But I mustn't mention it to anyone.' She hesitates before saying more quietly, 'I didn't really know why. She said it was our secret, it would be like when I was younger, just the two of us. But I thought she'd tell everyone, where I was, I mean, so no one would worry. When I was there I couldn't go out much and wasn't allowed to speak to anyone or call my friends or Paul or Dad.' She looks quickly at Ian, 'I mean Ray.' Ian gives her an encouraging smile and squeeze of the hand. She goes on, 'I kept saying, Mum I want to go home and she'd get upset like I was being ungrateful and this was all for me, a treat for me. But it wasn't. I had my pressies ready to give to everyone too, for Christmas, I'd saved up and everything. And I knew Paul had got me new Playmobile stuff, like I'd asked. Mum came down in the afternoon on Christmas Day and we had dinner, but it wasn't the same. She gave me a new swimsuit and said I'd get my proper stuff later. But you have to have Christmas at Christmas, else what's the point?' She runs out of breath, drops her head, whispers, 'I wanted to go home. But I didn't want Mum upset.'

Can't save 'em, from themselves. Suze's words come back to him. *You poor kid.* Even so his anger at Yvonne is tinged with a modicum of pity. *She must have been desperate.* 'You're doing really well, Victoria. Can you tell us a bit about what it was like with your Mum's cousin? What was she like with you?' *Would there be grounds for false imprisonment?*

Victoria shrugs. 'She was fine. We made cakes together. She showed me how to make clothes for my doll. Mum's rubbish at sewing. I think,' she pauses, 'I think she said to Mum I should go home, a couple of times. I don't know.' Her head stays bowed.

'But she wouldn't let you out?'

'It was Mum saying it, don't go out unless I'm with you.'

'Tell me what happened on the 12th of January, when you called Paul.'

Victoria straightens, levels her eyes with Theo, they are dark like her father's, becoming flintier like her mother's. 'I thought I could do it on my own. When I was out with Mum I saw a bus with railway station on it going by, so I thought if I got it I could get a train home. I'd sit upstairs at the window and when the bus went past, I'd look at the clock. That way I knew what time to sneak out, just as the bus was coming. I had enough money for the bus, but when I got to the station I saw I didn't have enough for the train. I got scared then,' and her voice echoes this panic. This time Paul gives her a reassuring pat and grin. 'I don't have a mobile. It was this nice lady, she was cleaning with this big mop thing and she asked me if I was OK, I don't think she was English. I said I was waiting for my brother only he hadn't arrived and I didn't know what to do. I lied.' Her gaze challenges Theo to reprimand her.

'You did fine. You needed help.'

She nods, 'She let me phone Paul on her mobile and he said sit tight he'd sort everything. So I did, the nice lady stayed nearby, I think she was worried about me. And, I don't know, it was a bit later, DC Shilling turned up, only I didn't know it was her then, but she said who she was and showed me her card and everything and she said Paul was on his way and would I like a milkshake?' She stops. Finally adding, 'I felt so happy. The milkshake was the best ever. Then Paul came running up and it was even better.'

'You've done a brilliant job Victoria, you really have. We only need to know one thing now. What made you say it was Mr Kestle who took you?'

Her eyes widen. She shakes her head. 'I don't want to talk about it. I don't have to do I?'

She's scared. 'I'd prefer it if you would. You're not going to get into trouble if you tell us what happened.'

'And Mum?'

You're a clever mite. 'You know, Victoria, it's not very nice being accused of something you didn't do. Has it ever happened to you or one of your friends?'

She gives a noncommittal movement of the head.

'I'm sure you can imagine how upsetting it is.'

'I didn't want to say it,' the words rush out, perhaps there's some relief at articulating them. 'I didn't want to upset anyone. I don't know Mr Kestle, why would I want to upset him?'

'So what happened? Did someone suggest you say it?'

Slowly she nods, says quietly, 'Mum did. She said it would mean you'd stop asking questions and nobody would get into trouble.' Her voice practically fades away as she once again hunches over, 'I suppose she meant she wouldn't get into trouble. But now she is. And it's my fault.'

'None of this is your fault,' Ian says, a tad too loudly.

She turns her face towards him, her eyes are too shiny, 'If I hadn't said I was happy to see more of Dad, none of this would have happened.'

Ian pulls her close, 'None of this is your fault Victoria, none of it, believe me.'

Theo adds his reassurances to Ian's. *You must believe us, Victoria.* For a moment, he thinks of Hannah, her distress, the razor-cuts up her arms. *You must believe us, Victoria.* He brings the interview to a close shortly after, they have what they need. He's rewarded afterwards with some moderate praise from Pippa, even a brief smile.

Afterwards he goes back to the piles of non-computerised reports he's been trawling for the last few days to find a trace of Lenny Sharpe's watch. He'd started with people arrested for handling stolen goods in the Leeds area in the weeks following Lenny Sharpe's trip to Scarborough. Today he unearths what he is looking for, the watch appears in one list of recovered goods. *Bingo. Two results in one day.*

This leads him to a serial offender, a novice crim all those years ago, who is currently incarcerated for more recent burglaries with much richer pickings than what he stole from his first victim. Chesters has worked with him, diligently and uncharacteristically quietly. Two days later they go together to visit their suspect. He looks older than his years, a persistent cough wracking his withered body. He is quick to admit what he'd done twenty-odd years ago, robbing from his dishevelled and disoriented hitchhiker and dispatching him with a blow from a metal wrench when he fought back. 'He was high or something.' *Concussed.* 'He shouldn't have struggled.' The prisoner is dying of lung cancer. He is looking for some kind of absolution. Still, he isn't prepared to take full responsibility for Lenny Sharpe's death.

Released from the confines of the prison, Theo wants to breathe fresh air. Murder is never pretty or neat, but Lenny Sharpe's final demise appears to be particularly senseless. *Killed for the pawn value of his watch.* Theo doesn't want to return directly to the busy-ness of the police station. He takes Chesters to a quiet country pub he's discovered with Ben and Lawrence, buys them both ham sandwiches, made with substantial slabs of homemade bread, and a half each of the locally brewed Peg Fyfe. They settle onto a bench seat by the side of the open fire in the corner of the small bar area, wood panelled and hung with arbitrary objects such as a pair of old skis and a battered copper coal scuttle. Theo is beginning to miss his companion's usual chatter, he asks him what's up. Chesters looks unhappy, his normally spiked hair droops.

'Is there a problem?' Theo queries. *I don't fancy you if that's what you're worried about,* he thinks sourly.

'My brother,' Chesters begins nervously. 'He's, you know, like you.'

What? A police officer? Smart? Black? Theo holds back his exasperation and waits.

Chesters has the attitude of a boy who knows he is failing an exam. He takes a gulp of his drink and says very quickly, 'He left home when he was eighteen, Dad told him to get out. I miss him.'

'Why don't you contact him?'

Chesters shrugs, 'I was only twelve. Dad said we must never talk about him in the house. I didn't know how to stay in touch.'

'You could find him now?' Theo is working at being gentle.

Chesters nods.

Theo guesses he already has. 'So why don't you phone him?'

His discomfort oozes from his every pore. 'Dad, he said Chris is a pervert.'

In some ways Theo admires his companion's bravery for spitting this out and he can see the struggle going on in the lad's confused face. This trumps, for the moment, anyway, his rising desire to shout back something obscene. Even so, his tone is strained, 'Your dad's wrong if he was basing his judgement solely on your brother's sexuality. Give Chris a call, if you miss him.'

Chesters' voice is eager, he gives his whippet impression again as he says, 'I do, we used to have such a good laugh and he always looked after me, even when I was being a right pain ...' He doesn't add the last three words of the phrase, blushing again. He drains his glass, asks if they are having another one.

Theo says they should be getting on, he doesn't think he can remain polite for much longer. He reminds himself how lucky he was with his own family's reaction to his own homosexuality. *Lucky? Why should I feel lucky?* He tries to feel a bit sorry for his DC.

'Thanks sarge,' Chesters mumbles as they get into the car. 'I will ring Chris, I'd like to talk to him again.'

Theo is driving; he hates Chesters' caution on the roads which rise and dip across the Wolds. There is some satisfaction, he supposes, in his subordinate giving such weight to his opinion, despite him being unclear on whether he's a pervert.

CHAPTER 40

It is the first weekend in March and Aurora and Max are having their first dinner party since the birth of their son. Aurora says it's to celebrate the missed birthdays, including her own at midwinter which had got subsumed by death and funerals and making Oli's first Christmas extra special. Under her instructions, Max has reinstated the dining table. He's set it with the silverware, the orange lawn napkins and table mats and the candles in their crystal holders, all of which had been put away or left unused since 'BM'. While Oli is spending the day and his first overnight with his paternal grandmother, his mother has spent most of the day in the kitchen. She's had two conversations with her father and another with a cousin in west London to create the Indian feast now spread before her guests.

Aurora has dressed in her favourite gold-coloured salwar kameez made of stiff silk, she glitters with amber jewellery and has piled her black hair on the top of her head. She has also persuaded Max into one of the kurtas they'd bought him on a visit to her family in India. It is dark green and the long shirt flatters his girth. She smiles at him, loving the way he is playing the genial host.

Hannah's hair is glowing auburn in the candle-light; her pallor has been tempered by some recent sun, her hazel eyes are bright, her hands animated. She is wearing a red velvet dress which hugs her figure and has lace at the V-neck and the cuffs. Theo sits next to her, Ben opposite and Lawrence next to him. All three of them have dressed up for the occasion, Lawrence adding a dicky-bow and Ben a patterned waistcoat to smart shirts and trousers. Everyone is talking at once, arguing about whether Brown should be given a chance to be PM or whether his moment has passed. 'It's inevitable anyway,' Lawrence says. 'He'll make a mess of it and then we'll have an election.'

'And the Tories back in?' asks Ben. He and Lawrence generally sit on opposite sides of the political fence. 'Can't say I've been over-joyed with this government, but Cameron would be worse.'

'We'll have him, like him or not. Not on his own, though – in some kind of coalition, with the Lib Dems most likely.'

'You think so?' says Hannah. 'Don't we need wars for coalitions?'

Lawrence is adamant and Hannah has to concede he is normally correct in his political forecasts. There's a coolness between them, a tautness. *They're being too polite. Not looking at each other properly.*

Max refills everyone's glasses. The conversation moves on. Lawrence complements Aurora on the food, which is fast disappearing from the multicoloured earthenware serving bowls and plates. He asks her in detail about her cooking methods. Theo talks with pleasure about the DI position opening up with Hoyle retiring.

'I'll never get him to Scotland Yard at this rate,' Lawrence moans. 'They don't want rid of him anymore – despite him being a poof, he keeps solving cases.'

Aurora knows through Ray Marchant that Vicky is spending more time with him, 'while things get straightened out'. Ray had spoken almost sympathetically about his ex-wife, whose second marriage is now 'very dodgy. I don't think Ian gets it, gets her anymore, if he ever did.' 'Do you then?' Aurora had asked, not at all sure she did. Ray had nodded, 'Yeah, in a way, we're used to sorting things our way at Westedge.' He'd also told Aurora that Kestle had moved to Hull, 'In with a woman, can you believe it? Met her on the internet. Seems he didn't want to admit it to anyone, didn't think his mother would approve.' 'I thought she was dead?' 'To us, maybe, not to Alexi, not entirely.'

Lawrence has brought dessert and he and Theo go to the kitchen to make the coffee and put the final touches on his creation. Ben and Max have something to discuss for their five-aside club, so Hannah and Aurora move into the peace of the sitting room. Aurora still feels hesitant about asking Hannah how she is, worried about what might come out. However, they are both in a mellow mood, so she risks the question. Hannah turns those glinting eyes on her, 'Do you really want to know?' Then she glances away before she receives an answer, 'I'm aware it's not easy for people to hear.' The room is lit by candles which send out wavering shadows onto the earthy browns and wicker in the decor. The curtains remain open. Warmth has finally returned to the land. The grass to the privet hedge is pricked by purple and white crocus crowns and by tiny yellow narcissi trumpets.

'You can tell me what you want to tell me,' says Aurora, wishing it were true.

'OK. I'm doing OK, mostly, I'm working a lot on my case study, nearly finished it, then I'll be accredited and I'll have to decide what to do.'

'You'll stay here though?' *I want you to.*

'I don't know. I think I want to work as a counsellor, but I'm worried I'm not ...' She pauses, is maybe searching for the word, '*Fit* enough. If I don't do that, I could go back to editing and proofreading. In which case my contacts are in London. Though I don't know if Lawrence will have me back ...'

'Surely he will ...'

'... or I want to be there.'

Aurora hears the sadness. She can't imagine the rift between Lawrence and Hannah can be permanent. *Me and Max are always falling out, it doesn't last.* She's not even sure what it's been about, except it's wrapped up in the news coming out about Stan. 'Anything from Val?'

'We spoke. She's not angry, or at least she's not expressing it. She's more in denial, I think, pretending nothing has changed. She's drinking too much. Veronica says dementia is setting in. I'd guess it's the drink. Veronica wants rid of her, only she's in a bit of bind, cos if I'm the devil incarnate she can't dump her mother-in-law on me.'

'I don't know how they can go on like they are. There's evidence, proof.' She's beginning to regret opening up the conversation, it's threatening to turn her lovely food, her lovely evening, acrid. She forces herself to carry on listening, not to say anything which could bring the conversation to a premature end.

Hannah's gaze turns back into the room, she runs teeth along her lower lip. 'Sorry, don't want to spoil the atmosphere.'

'No, no, I asked.'

Then the others burst in, Ben laughing at a joke Max has made, Theo and Lawrence bearing trays of glass dishes, a jug of coffee and cups. Hannah immediately pulls her mouth into a smile, is exclaiming over the mound of meringue, fruits and cream being offered her. Aurora knows it's an act and tries not to be too glad of it.

They eat the sweet, drink shots of liqueurs, play cards, sing along to CDs of hits from the eighties, even dance a bit. They reminisce about being young and irresponsible. Surprisingly, in Aurora's view, Ben manages the best stories of a disreputable past culled from his trip to Australia. It's after 1 a.m. by the time they grow less riotous, more reflective. 'This has been great,' Theo says, he's seated on a floor cushion, supported by the arm of the easy chair where Lawrence is sitting, he leans back and Lawrence bends down to kiss him. Hannah is more asleep than awake on one of the settees, nestled into Ben's side, his arm draped around her. Her intake of alcohol has been the least moderate amongst them. She mumbles her agreement.

'We should do it more often,' Ben says.

'We could have lunch Saturdays, after the five-a-side. What do you think dearest?' Max hugs Aurora to him where they are sitting on the other sofa.

His boyish excitement infects her, the drink – *More than I'm used to these days* – and good company have already made her reckless, 'Sounds great.' The others add their enthusiastic encouragement to the plan before making their moves to go. She watches them walk, or in the case of Hannah stumble, down the path and thinks, *Why not? It would be fun, wouldn't it?*

The night air is spiked with the nip of the waves which lie unseen and unheard not so far away. She breathes in its briny cocktail. The moon is a gauze-covered pendant hanging in the sky, its light silvering the white flowers in the hawthorn hedge opposite. *Spring is finally on its way.* Max winds his arm around her waist and whispers into her ear, 'Come on my beauty, while we've the house to ourselves.' She laughs and allows herself to be drawn inside.

Thank you

Thank you to you the reader for spending time with my story. If you have any comments, please send them to AvenuePressScarb@talktalk.net.

Thank you to all those who supported me in this endeavour, gave me advice and encouragement; especially Sue, Jane, Ruth, Ros and my many writing friends. Thank you to those who represent the very best in therapy and helped me know myself better, especially Annie. Thank you to my husband, Mark, for his unstinting love, sustenance and backing, which has got me through the hard times and much, much more.

Thank you to my copyeditor extraordinaire, Charlotte Cole, http://charlottecoleeditorial.com, and my equally wonderful proofreader, David Powning, www.inkwrapped.com. Any mistakes which remain are entirely my own.

The Art of Survival is part of the Hannah Poole psychological crime series based in Scarborough. If you have enjoyed it you may like to turn the page to find out more about the others in the series: *The Art of the Imperfect* (long-listed for the Crime Writers Association Debut Dagger Award 2015); and *The Art of Breathing*. Both from Avenue Press Scarborough.

The Art of the Imperfect by Kate Evans
Long-listed for the Crime Writers Association Debut Dagger Award 2015

The death of the renowned psychotherapist Dr Themis Greene in Scarborough sends storm waves through the intertwining lives of three of the small seaside town's residents. The murder in the town perched on the edge of land and sea pushes Hannah Poole, Aurora Harris and DS Theo Akande to the borderlands. They are forced to explore the edges of reason, understanding, justice and love. What they discover gets them through but is far from perfect.

This isn't gritty crime, this isn't cosy crime, this isn't police procedural. This is poetic storytelling which peels back the psychological layers to reveal the raw centre.

Due in 2016 ...
The Art of Breathing by Kate Evans

The past is in front of us, it's always there waiting for us. So believes Hannah Poole as she and her family struggle to come to terms with the full impact of her father's abusive behaviour. The past won't leave others alone either: a retired DCI; an academic; the elderly widowed wife of a former coal miner. And where does the brood of a local building firm fit in? DS Theo Akande has a puzzle on his hands, further complicated by a suspected death where the body can't be found. A puzzle Dorothy L Sayers might well have been proud of.